LEOPARD

D1743274

Published by Boson Books

An imprint of Bitingduck Press
Formerly an imprint of C&M Online Media, Inc.
ISBN 978-1-938463-30-3
eISBN 978-1-938463-31-0

For information contact
Bitingduck Press, LLC
Altadena, CA
notifications@bitingduckpress.com
http://www.bitingduckpress.com
Cover art by Johannes Ewers
www.zazzle.com/seawolf

Author's note

This book is a work of fiction with a historical backdrop. I have taken liberties with historical figures, ships, and time frames to blend in with my story. Therefore, this book is not a reflection of actual historical events.

LEOPARD

THE FIGHTING ANTHONYS
BOOK SEVEN

MICHAEL AYE

Books by Michael Aye

Fiction

Non-Fiction

To:

My Comrades, our Viet Nam vets
All gave some!
Some gave all!

CHARACTERS IN THE FIGHTING ANTHONY SERIES

British Officers and Seamen:

Vice Admiral Lord Gilbert "Gil" Anthony – Commands the British fleet in the Caribbean. First son of Retired Admiral Lord James Anthony (deceased) and Lady Anthony.

Captain Sir Gabriel "Gabe" Anthony – Second son of Retired Admiral Lord James Anthony (deceased) and his mistress Maria Dupree.

Bart – Long time cox'n and friend to Admiral Lord Anthony.

Dagan Dupree – Supernumerary on *Trident*; Gabe's uncle and self-appointed guardian.

Jacob (Jake) Hex – Gabe's cox'n and friend.

Rear Admiral Rupert Buck – Recently promoted to flag.

Rear Admiral Dutch Moffett – Commander of Antigua.

Admiral Peter Parker – Commander of Jamaica squadron.

Admiral Sir Winston Kirkstatter – Replaces Admiral Buck.

Lord Ragland – British Governor of Barbados.

Lord Skalla – British Foreign Office agent who replaces Sir Victor.

Captain Stephen Earl –Lord Anthony's new flag captain.

Captain Austin Albright – Captain of merchant ship *Georgetown*, Grand Cayman.

Captain Robert Schoggins – Captain of marines on *Trident/Leopard*.

Lieutenant John Jenkins – Captain of *Zebra*.

Lieutenant George Jepson – Captain of *Revenant*.

Lieutenant David Davy –Captain of *Tomahawk*. Gabe's friend.

Lieutenant Justin Holton – Lieutenant on *Trident*.

Lieutenant Greg Kirk – Captain of *Bulldog*.

Lieutenant Leonard Montgomery – Captain of *Lynx*.

Lieutenant Mahan – Lord Anthony's flag lieutenant.

Lieutenant Con Vallin – First lieutenant on *Trident*, then *Leopard*.

Lieutenant Daniel Bufford – Second lieutenant on *Leopard*.

Lieutenant Tolbert – Third Lieutenant on *Leopard*.

Midshipman Jarvis Jackson – Midshipman on *Leopard.*

Midshipman Daniel Glen – Midshipman on *Leopard.*

Midshipman Hunter – Midshipman on *Leopard.*

Robert Cornish – Physician and surgeon.

Mister Pittman– Master on *Leopard.*

Ronald Laqua – Fourth lieutenant on *Trident* and *Leopard.*

John Waters – Master on SeaHorse.

LeMatt – Lord Anthony's secretary.

Josiah Nesbit – Gabe's chef and gentleman's gentleman.

Silas – Lord Anthony's steward.

Chen Lee – Rear Admiral Buck's servant.

Crowe – Rear Admiral Buck's cox'n.

Fleming – Rear Admiral Buck's secretary.

William Eden – Chief Resident Grand Cayman.

The Ladies:

Lady Deborah – Lord Anthony's wife. They met after pirates had attacked the ship Lady Deborah and her first husband were aboard. Her first husband was killed by the pirates before Lord Anthony's ship came to the rescue. The marriage between Lady Deborah and her first husband had been one of convenience; when she and Lord Anthony met it was love at first sight. They later married and had a daughter, Macayla.

Faith – Gabe's wife. They met in *HMS SeaWolf* where Gabe had survived an explosion but was wounded. Faith and Nanny were walking on the beach and came upon him. They hid Gabe and nursed him back to health. Gabe and Faith fell in love, but with her being an American and with Gabe being a British sea officer it was difficult. New son, James Gilbert Anthony.

Betsy – Dagan's love. She is the sister of American General Manning's deceased wife. She is a young widow who lives with the general. Dagan met Betsy during the time General Manning was being held in Saint Augustine as a paroled prisoner of war.

Lady Linda Ragland – Wife of Lord Ragland, Governor of Barbados.

Rebecca/Becky – Lord Anthony's sister. She lives in England with her husband, Hugh, and daughter, Gretchen.

Maria Dupree – Gabe's mother and Dagan's sister. She was Admiral Lord James Anthony's mistress of many years.

Olivia Cunningham – Admiral's Buck fiancée.

Ariel – Dagan's ward, and Lieutenant David Davy's wife.

Hannah Bodden – William Eden's niece, Lieutenant Vallin's girlfriend.

The Americans:

Lum – Slave on Faith's family plantation. He kills a man attempting to rape Faith. He spends time with Gabe on board ship as his servant, and then when Faith and Gabe reunite, he leaves the sea to be with her and Nanny.

Nanny – Like Lum, she was a slave on Faith's family plantation. She was a personal servant to Faith's mother and has been Faith's nanny since birth. She loves Lum.

.

A Sailor's Lot

Got on a ship in Portsmouth
Headed for the Caribee
My life forever changed
Since the press gang caught me

The fury of battle
Is like thunder in my head
I hear the wounded crying
And I see the silent dead

And when I hear a bosun's pipe
I want to run and hide
But damned if I know where to go
I just want to stay alive

Now it's been five long years
Since this war has begun
The politicians sit at home
While I sit behind this gun

-Michael Aye

PROLOGUE

"DAMME, SIR, A PRISONER, I was made a prisoner! The audacity of the man, the black-hearted scoundrel. He sailed his ship, Rattlesnake, with two prizes right into our harbour, Lord Anthony. The damnable man sailed right into Georgetown Harbour, just like it was a holiday. Hellish bold...hellish bold, that's what the whoreson was. Pulled his pistol and made Captain Neill and I prisoners when we stepped through his entry port. Imagine that. We had ourselves rowed out to inquire if we could be of service and the thanks we get are to be made prisoners. Impertinent rogue. Two loyal British subjects deprived of our freedom in our own harbour. It's not safe, your Lordship. If the rascal can take us with no respect or concern for the Royal Navy, what will they do next? Sack the town, take our women, or just take the whole damned island." The man speaking was Captain Austin Albright, of Georgetown, Grand Cayman.

He sat in the great cabin of Lord Gilbert Anthony, Vice Admiral and Commander in Chief of his Majesty's naval forces in the West Indies. Others in the cabin, besides Lord Anthony, included his flag captain, Stephen Earl; his flag lieutenant, Patrick Mahan; and his cox'n, Bart.

A time or two when Albright was on the verge of what Bart considered stepping over the line of proper etiquette, he made to rise and intervene, but a slight wave of his Lordship's hand made him return to his seat. Lord Anthony could see Albright was a desperate man, and allowed his ranting.

"We don't have a fort or even a company of soldiers to protect us from these hellish rogues, My Lord." Albright stopped talking and picking up a glass, he drained the last bit of sweetened lime juice from it. His mouth was dry and he'd become hoarse as he spoke. Setting the glass down on the admiral's mahogany table, he paused.

Silas, the admiral's servant, had been standing at the pantry. Seeing Albright's action inflamed him. He rushed to the table with a rag, wiping away any water circles and made a show of moving the coaster Albright had ignored or missed.

Clearing his throat, Albright said, "Hmm, I thought you Navy men drank a bit more hearty beverage than lime juice."

Captain Earl had been a bit put out with the man's ranting, as had Bart. He rose suddenly, and while trying to remain civil, said, "Sir, the sun is hardly over the yardarm."

The admiral smiled inwardly at how quickly his captain had risen to defend the Navy's honor and reputation. Ignoring what might have been a request for something stronger, Lord Anthony asked, "Would you care for some more lime juice, Captain?"

A subdued Albright nodded, "If you please, Sir."

Silas filled the glass from a silver pitcher, and then sat the glass down on the coaster, emphasizing the coaster as he did with a hard look. Lieutenant Mahan was quick to note, Silas had appeared without being called. The cabin servant had found it to be rewarding on more than one occasion when the crew wanted to know what was in the making, so he tended to remain close unless instructed otherwise. Beads of condensation covered the outside of the metal pitcher as the ice inside cooled the beverage. Silas touched the pitcher to his face when he returned to the pantry. The cooling sensation felt good in the Caribbean heat.

Looking inside the pitcher and seeing that there wasn't enough of the juice to fill a glass, Silas turned the pitcher up and drank from it. No use in it going to waste, he thought.

Once Silas had left the cabin, Lord Anthony spoke, "You say you were detained?"

"Not detained, Admiral, made a prisoner. Captain Neill and I were placed inside the pirate captain's cabin and made to stay there overnight. I tried to leave but a rogue stood guard at the door."

"Were you harmed in anyway?" Anthony asked.

"No, not physically," Albright admitted. Saying

this, he took a chair and sat down. Leaning forward, he placed his head in his hands. From this position, he muttered, "I've been ruined financially."

Lord Anthony and his officers looked at what they now knew was a broken man; a man who had nothing and nowhere to turn. No wonder he ranted so.

Raising his head, Albright said, "I do not have the financial backing or contracts that some enjoy. No sir, my Lord," he continued, "I've been ruined." Rising suddenly and striking his fist in the other hand Albright swore, "Damnation, Admiral, you've got to do something. We're not safe."

Hearing the unmistakable sound of a blade being pulled, Albright realized his mistake. He'd overstepped his bounds. What he didn't realize was how close to death he'd actually come. Looking at the fierceness of Bart and the naked blades of Earl and Mahan, Albright sat back down and grabbed the lime juice. Gulping down half the glass of juice, he managed, "My apologies, Admiral."

Letting the man calm himself, Anthony spoke in an almost fatherly way, "Tell me about your losses."

Setting his glass down and making sure it was on the coaster, Albright cleared his throat. "McCollough, Captain David McCollough is the blackheart who commanded the Rattlesnake. He is a man of daring with little concern for a fellow seaman. He took our ships, Captain Neill's and mine, along with all our cargo."

"What were you carrying?" Lieutenant Mahan asked.

"Cotton, sugar, molasses, and lumber, some of it was mahogany, and sixteen slaves. He took it all. My entire cargo," Albright repeated in anguish. "But that's not the end of it. He said he'd ransom our ships back to us. The following morning, after a sleepless night on Rattlesnake, we were given parole to go raise the ransom. When we returned and paid the ransom, the contemptible lout gave us a certificate, as we were being released, that would exempt us from being taken again for a period of forty-two days. I had lost my cargo and was in debt for twenty thousand pounds, but I had my ship, or so I thought I did. When I returned to my ship, I found the bastard had left me a hull only. During the night, while I was locked away, he stripped my ship of everything they could. Every line, cable and rope; her running riggings, spars, sails, ship's provisions, my desk, wine cabinet, even the spare anchor."

Albright was almost in tears as he placed his head in his hands again. "I'm ruined. You've got to do something," he shouted in desperation. "We are not safe and not a Navy ship around."

"Why did you come to Barbados?" Anthony asked. "Admiral Parker is in charge of the Jamaica squadron and it's a lot closer."

"I did go there, but there's been word of a French fleet being sighted and Admiral Parker has sent his fleet out looking for the Frogs."

"I see," Lord Anthony said. "Were you able to learn anything of McCollough's plans while you were being held?"

"Humph!" Albright snorted. "They talked openly and made no secret of their plans, my Lord. They figure that they have naught to fear from our navy."

Bart not liking the barb made a point of clearing his throat. He was given a disapproving look from Anthony.

"Cuba and Puerto Rico was to be used as their main rendezvous but they also talked about Cat Island as well. They talked of several ships, privateer ships that routinely meet there."

"Well, the Dons are not lifting a finger to object," Mahan interjected.

"I heard one rogue saying that they'd make a good profit taking my cargo and their other two prizes to Martinique. There was more but I can't remember," Albright admitted. "I do remember them saying a thirty-eight gun French frigate was patrolling Trinity Bay while they were anchored at Fort Royal."

Lord Anthony thanked Albright for bringing the privateer's activities to his attention. He promised that he'd send some vessels to patrol around Grand Cayman when he had them to spare. He surprised everyone when he promised Albright that he'd see that a few Navy contracts would be sent his way once he was able to outfit a ship.

After the destitute captain had taken his leave, Lord Anthony asked his flag captain, "What do you think, Stephen?"

"He's right about not having any protection. I just don't see how we can do much with the few ships we have. We are stretched to the limit now. I recall Lord

Skalla mentioning a report from Lord Howe, that stated after a battle where the Colonials were defeated, the captured guns and ammunitions were the finest England had to offer." This brought a chuckle from the group. "The Admiralty has failed to realize the significance of the privateers. Were it not for the American privateers raiding our ships, Washington's armies would have long ago surrendered due to a lack of supplies."

"Aye," Anthony agreed. "It's damnable that it took Lloyd's refusing to insure our merchant ships for Parliament to order the Navy to provide escorts to protect our convoys. Even with our escorts, Americans continue to raid with more daring and success than I care to admit." Standing, Anthony set his empty glass down. "Albright was right about one thing, gentlemen. They, our loyal subjects on islands like Grand Cayman, are perfect targets for the Americans. Captains like McCollough, in fast, well-equipped, and well-manned ships can strike our people at pleasure. That has to be brought in check. When Markham returns in Dasher, we will set sail with a squadron to instill a little fear and make life less pleasant for these raiders."

"They'll just move to less troublesome waters, my Lord," Lieutenant Mahan volunteered.

"You are right, Patrick, my concern is not where they go as long as it's out of the Caribbean. The Caribbean is my responsibility, not the entire ocean."

Hmm, Bart thought, I better dust off 'is blades and oil up 'is pistols. Lord Anthony is ready to fight.

Faith to Gabe

Baby, I see shadows – on your mind
It's a faraway place – that's calling you tonight
I see the mist – that fills up your eyes
After all these years – don't look so surprised
It's that damned old ocean – I want it to go
But listen closely – I want you to know
If you're going – I'm going too
Cause baby I'm wrapped up in you.
Yes baby I'm wrapped up in you.

—From the song "Shadows on Your Mind,"
by Mike Fowler

CHAPTER ONE

THEY STOOD BEFORE GOD, their family, fellow officers, and friends. They vowed they'd never love anyone but each other until death. Ariel wore a gown of white, while Lieutenant David Davy wore his navy dress blue uniform. In fact, the church fairly bulged with officers wearing their Royal Navy uniforms, hot as it was. Dagan wore civilian attire as he proudly walked his ward, the beautiful Ariel, down the aisle. Her life with Davy would be happy, this Dagan knew. Compared with the hell she had known as a sex slave to the renegade Witzenfeld.

Dagan had entered the Rathskeller, and seeing Ariel, he had taken her, killing her bodyguard in the process. The act had been done to draw out Witzenfeld. However, the renegade had been at sea. Dagan did kill his lieutenant, though. Looking at her, hardly more than a child, he knew he could never return her to such a life where she'd be used up, addicted to opium and probably dead by the time she reached her mid twenties. That was all behind her now...that life of hell and degradation. Davy met her at Gabe and Faith's house and had instantly fallen in love.

Dagan had watched the boy grow up from the first day he boarded *Drakkar* as a snot nosed midshipman to now, captain of his own ship. A small ten gun sloop, in truth, but it was a start. He was a good man, a seasoned officer and he loved Ariel. Above all, he loved her and she loved him. What Ariel didn't know was that her young naval officer husband was a very wealthy man. Prize money had done that. Prize money made during an unnecessary war. Would the war come between them as it had Gabe and Faith? Dagan hoped not, prayed even that it wouldn't.

The ceremony was now over. The bride and groom were walking down the aisle of the church. Stepping outside, Davy's band of brothers held their swords high in an arch as they passed and climbed into Lord Anthony's carriage to be swept away to a private cottage for their honeymoon. Only Lady Deborah and Faith knew exactly where the couple was headed. Of course, the carriage driver and the servant sent to take care of their needs also knew the destination.

While Dagan had taken Ariel, it had been Lady Deborah and Faith, along with Livi, Admiral Buck's lady, and of course, Lady Ragland, who had transformed Ariel into the lady she now was. She had been educated as a lady and comfortably interacted with the upper crust of Barbados' society. Not that that mattered to Dagan. He was just happy she'd been given the opportunity to see what life offered. A real life, free of the deprivation by black-hearted rogues.

Lord Ragland walked up and shook Dagan's hand. "A fine day, Dagan, I congratulate you." Dagan was polite and smiled, as he shook the governor's hand.

The ladies came over then. They were all dressed in gowns of various colors and the latest style. Some of the ladies were showing more wares than a gypsy peddler. All of them were fanning themselves. One lady was bold enough to say, "Well, there goes one of the islands most eligible bachelors." Dagan smiled at this comment. A young naval officer would indeed be considered quite a catch for some planters' daughters; as Ariel would be for their sons.

As the carriage pulled away, amid all the flower throwing, rice tossing, and good wishes, Dagan saw a sign had been attached to the back of the carriage...She got him today, he'll get her tonight.

"Don't let it bother you," Gabe said. He'd seen the sign as well. After a moment, the two looked at each other and smiled.

"Aye, young love," Dagan said. *Still, the sod who did it better hope it never got out*, he thought.

As the crowd dispersed, Gabe watched Faith taking their son from Nanny as she seated herself in their carriage. Davy was a lucky man. However, he was also a realist and knew first hand the hardships that the war, the Navy, and one's duty put on a man's marriage. He and Faith were just now building a bridge to repair the strain on their relationship caused by the war. *Did Ariel know Davy's ship, Tomahawk, was set to sail with Lord Anthony in a few weeks? Could she handle the separation?* At least, Faith, Deborah, and Livi would be there for her.

***

IT WAS THE LATTER part of March, 1780. Almost four months since he'd brought in the captured French 74 *Le' Comete*, two frigates, a corvette, and a sloop; plus they had retaken *HMS Foxfire*. They had destroyed a French eighty gun ship of the line and sunk or destroyed a dozen ships and craft belonging to American privateers at Isle St. Marie, thereby ending the threat to England's merchant ships in the Indian Ocean. "A complete victory," Lord Skalla had declared. So had Lord Ragland and even Gil, his brother, Vice Admiral Lord Gilbert Anthony.

Dagan had been wounded, but survived and had promised better days for Faith and him. However, returning did not turn out as expected. Faith was there with open arms. But so was Admiral Buck's replacement, Sir Winston Kirkstatter. He was quick to damn Gabe's actions. He cared not for what Gabe and his squadron had succeeded in doing. He'd overstepped his authority assuming command of "his" squadron and using his flagship so that she could be called a hulk and nothing more. Who had made him a commodore?

When Gabe tried to explain Buck had given his approval, Kirkstatter snarled, "A wounded man on the verge of death could hardly know what he was approving." When Lord Skalla was mentioned, Kirkstatter went into another tirade, "Just who the hell gave this spy the authority to interfere with Admiralty orders? By God and dammit sir, did you not know the Dons are out? They've taken British forts in Louisiana and are marching toward Mobile and Pensacola. The governor in St. Augustine is demanding more troops and ships. The Dons are sailing here with a fleet while you, by God, played admiral and headed to the Indian Ocean."

Kirkstatter wrote a scathing report to London recommending that both Gabe and Lord Skalla be broken. The report was flashed in Lord Anthony's face with both Admiral Buck and Lord Ragland protesting.

Kirkstatter snarled, "I'd expect you to cover for your brother, Lord Anthony, but he exceeded his authority. He caused my station to be undefended and harm to come to his Majesty's ships. He'll not command a bum boat when I'm through with him. I will have to take *Le' Comete* as my flagship."

Lord Anthony had remained quiet, realizing that to argue was futile. He'd write his own letters and so would Buck, Lord Skalla, and Lord Ragland. But for now, he'd had enough. Kirkstatter's last threats and comments went too far. Anthony rose quickly, knocking his table chair backwards and landing on the deck with a loud bang. His face was flushed in anger, and his knuckles were white as he pushed down on the thick mahogany table. There was menace in his voice as he spoke, "You, sir, you forget yourself. You forget you are at this moment under my command. You have no flagship, you have no command, and you have nothing unless I say you do. You'll not take *Le' Comete* unless I say so. It is I, sir, who decides if she is to be bought into the service and where she is to be sent. I may send the ship to England and let the Admiralty decide her fate."

Kirkstatter swallowed hard. Had he gone too far? It was known Anthony was in with the First Lord. "My apologies, my Lord," Kirkstatter replied, deciding it was better to sound contrite. He'd already mailed his report. In fact, it was on the same dispatch vessel that carried Lord Skalla. He had been recalled immediately. What he didn't know was that several letters praising Gabe's actions had also been sent.

In the meantime, Gabe waited. Gil had bought *Le' Comete*, now *Comete*, into the service and sent Kirkstatter away. Barbados had had its fill of the man. Gabe's relationship with Faith had indeed mended as Dagan promised. She apologized for her actions. Actions brought on by fear. Doctor Cornish said being a new mother had a lot to do with her feelings. Faith's involvement in the wedding had seemed to make her more loving.

At times, when she was away helping, he'd kept little James. It was a pleasure getting to know his son...his son; the heir to the title and the only male heir.

He'd attended several social functions with Faith. He'd dined and danced at the homes of planters, the governor, and even at his brother's. Would he ever want to go to sea again? Well, that decision might be made for him. In two weeks, Gil would sail to deal with the privateers and whatever force he came up on. It had been a while since Gil had sailed in harm's way. *How would Lady Deborah handle him being away? She had little Macayla, of course, still...still.*

CHAPTER TWO

L AZY PUFFY WHITE CLOUDS floated overhead, casting fleeting shadows below. A pelican rose up, flapped its wings a few times, and then settled back down on the piling it was perched on. Sanderlings, or as some called them, scurry birds, were out in flocks. Their little black legs were a blur as they ran back and forth on the beach picking and probing with their bills for some tiny morsel left in the sand by receding waves. Pyramids of sails could be seen as a convoy set sail to Antigua, and now Lord Anthony's squadron made its way out of Carlisle Bay.

Dagan stood next to Ariel, who stood next to Faith and Lady Deborah. They'd stand there until the last ship was out of sight, and then take Lady Deborah's carriage home. Dagan would then join up with Gabe, and after Ariel's things were packed up from their lodging at the Islander, the two would meet up with their comrades for a wet.

"She's going to miss Davy," Dagan volunteered as Gabe approached him.

"Aye, but she'll return to her room at our house and Faith will keep her busy, especially with little James starting to crawl about. Besides, Uncle, do you recall what Stephen Earl said when the subject of marriage came up?" Smiling, the two repeated the words in unison, "If the Navy wanted a man to have a wife, they'd have made room in his sea chest."

Lady Deborah's carriage rolled by with little Macayla hanging out the window waving. "Bye, Uncle Gabe." He waved back, thinking how fast the girl had grown.

"Faith seems to be in a good mood," Dagan said. He'd seen how happy she'd been at the wedding.

Gabe recalled Faith asking, "Do you not think the wedding was just grand?" He'd just grunted. He'd learned when Faith wanted an answer, and when a grunt was enough. But looking at his wife in her gown and all prettied up made him understand why men were so willing to tie the knot. He'd been smart enough to tell her that she was the most beautiful bride at the wedding. The compliment paid dividends that night when, in truth, he was again awed by her natural beauty. No wonder poor sailors didn't stand a chance when beautiful young vixens cast their spells on them.

***

THE PALMS RUSTLED ON the thatched stoop as Gabe and Dagan entered the Anchor Tavern. They paused to let their eyes get accustomed to the dark tavern after leaving the bright sun.

"Ah, Dr. Cornish, you've a tankard already,"

Gabe said in greeting. The good doctor raised his tankard in salute as Jonah Hex, Gabe's cox'n, motioned to the girl at the bar for two more tankards. It was a sassy little wench she was, swaying her body as she approached the table.

Leaning low enough to give Hex a good view of her wares, she ran her hand up and across his shoulder and face. "You be needing anything else, love, you call me." Smiling, Hex answered, "No worries."

Cornish shook his head, "You'd think we were in a brothel the way those two have been going on." This was not true, of course.

The men had been discussing the way Kirkstatter had treated Gabe. "I'm glad the man has left," Doctor Cornish had volunteered. "Seems like I've had enough of his kind to last me a lifetime." However, the subject of Kirkstatter was not broached in Gabe's presence.

"Do you think his Lordship was ready to feel a little water under his keel?" Cornish asked.

"Aye," Gabe replied, "Said it was time to get Bart to sea and give Barbados a break." This brought a chuckle as Gabe knew it would. The admiral's burly cox'n had gained a reputation at the card tables. Not that he'd really hurt anyone but he never ran out of carousing money, and he never spent his own.

"It looks like the bay is empty now that the convoy has sailed and the admiral is taking his squadron out."

"It does look suddenly deserted but there's a good force still left to make life miserable for anyone looking for a little action," Gabe responded.

"Has Barbados ever been attacked?" Cornish asked. "I know several other islands that have been attacked."

"Not to my knowledge," Gabe answered. After another round was brought to the table, Gabe said, "I've been ordered to take *Trident* to the yards at Antigua. They've done all they can for her here. We will have *Bulldog* escort us."

Cornish laughed at this, "A sloop escorting a warship, now I've heard it all."

"Would you rather we sail alone and chance sinking?" Gabe asked.

"No," Cornish replied, suddenly very somber.

"Have you told Faith?" Dagan asked.

"Yes," Gabe replied. Nothing else was mentioned on the subject; Dagan would hear the rest later. "In truth, Doctor," Gabe was saying, "you don't have to make the trip. You are still *Trident's* surgeon, but you may come or stay as you wish."

"I'll go," he replied. "I've stepped on enough toes caring for Admiral Buck."

"I saw him at the wedding and he seems almost his old self," Gabe said.

"Aye, he'll raise his flag again," Cornish replied. "He and Livi will seek passage back to England soon. They have decided to get married when they return."

Dagan suddenly nudged Gabe and nodded toward the tavern entrance. Once Laqua's eyes adjusted to the dimness and he was able to make out the patrons, he quickly found the table he was looking for, and made his way over. "You sent for me, Captain?"

"Aye, Lieutenant Laqua. Let me be the first to congratulate you." Laqua stood for a moment, and then a smile broke out on his face.

"It shouldn't be a surprise," Dagan joked, "having Gabe as one of the three captains on the board."

Smiling, Laqua said, "Can you guess who asked the most difficult questions?"

"I didn't want it to look like I was playing favorites," Gabe said.

"You didn't," Laqua admitted. "I guess I can safely return your books."

Hex ordered another tankard and told the bar wench to be nice to Laqua, as he had just been promoted. After a while, Laqua asked, "You called me lieutenant, so I'm not a passed master's mate? What ship have I been commissioned to?"

"For now, the *Trident*," Gabe replied, "but don't worry, when I get a ship you will be one of my lieutenants. And...," Gabe said, after a sigh, "Lord Anthony has promised you a spot should fate not be kind to me."

"Aye, aye," the group said in unison.

"Now, Lieutenant, I expect you'd better go see the tailor and get fitted out as a young lieutenant should be."

"Thank you, sir. I just wish Mr. Hays was here," Laqua said.

"He's got a ship," Cornish volunteered. "Though I've no doubt he'd have chosen different had he been given the opportunity. When do we sail?" Cornish asked.

"As soon as our new lieutenant can get himself a set of uniforms," Gabe replied. "Hex, you better go with Laqua and make sure the tailor doesn't scam our new officer."

***

HMS BULLDOG WAS A sixteen gun sloop of war. She was ship-rigged, sleek, and had an appearance fitting her name...a feisty vessel. Lieutenant Gregory Kirk was her commanding officer. He was considered an able mariner and a good captain, firm but fair. He had been a midshipman on one of Lord Anthony's ships. Now he was to escort *Trident* to the dockyard at Antigua. He'd heard of *Trident*'s last voyage. A proud and victorious voyage it was. He'd hate to see the ship scrapped after distinguishing herself as she had done. Would Kirkstatter, the arse or Admiral Arse as the men, officers and seaman alike had labeled him, cause her to go down in infamy because of his biased accusations? How many captains could have done what Sir Gabe had done? Was the man jealous of Sir Gabe's accomplishments?

Hopefully, Sir Gabe would overcome and rise above Kirkstatter's slander. Slander, it just dawned on Kirk. Slander was exactly what it was.

He'd been invited to Sir Gabe's house to dine that evening. He was looking forward to it. He'd heard Captain Francis Markham say that Gabe was the luckiest man around. With a wife like he had, who needed the sea? Well, he'd see for himself. He'd bring a little gift for Sir Gabe's little boy. One of his men had carved a whale out of a piece of whalebone...a white whale. He looked forward to the meeting but was nervous. After all, Gabe was Lord Anthony's brother and he, Greg Kirk, was one of the admiral's captains.

***

GABE WOKE UP IN the predawn hours. A lifetime of habits at sea was hard to break, even when one had been ashore these past few months. Lying next to him, Faith slept the sleep of contentment. When he'd went to sleep she had been nude, exhausted from their lovemaking. At some point, she had risen without waking him and put on her nightgown. It was in case she would have to get up with little James. Since Gabe had been home these past three months, he'd started sleeping the night through. "Knows his daddy is home," Nanny had said. In some ways, being beached had been a good thing; a time to get to know his son, and getting to know his wife again.

It was as Dagan had said, "Faith will be waiting with little James." She had welcomed him home as a wife, mother, and as a woman who wanted to satisfy her lover. It had been a time of healing; both physical and mental healing, for him and Dagan. Since he'd been home, they'd gone out visiting, dancing, and to dinner as a family. Something he could only vaguely remember happening in his childhood. That had partly been due to society. Admiral Lord James Anthony was hardly concerned with his reputation but he did care greatly for that of his mistress and his son. The times he did remember were fond times... most of them, including Dagan. He went to sea then and he'd been at sea most of his life since going aboard his first ship as a middy. Trying hard, Gabe could only think of a few, a very few, times he'd been ashore this long. Would things change tomorrow? Faith seemed to understand that his leaving on the morrow might mean anything. It was not a peaceful time, it was war.

When he'd tried to prepare her for the inevitable, she had put her finger across his lips and then kissed him. "We'll be here when you get back," she said. "No matter how long it takes. You just come home to me and James."

Ariel would be with her. Nanny and Lum were a big part of their lives but they did not provide the same companionship Faith got from Deborah, Ariel, and even Livi.

Admiral Buck had spoken to Gabe when they'd had a minute alone. "I will take care of your family, Gabe. You keep your mind on the sea, the ship, and the enemy. I will keep an eye on your family."

Smiling to himself, Gabe recalled Lord Ragland making similar remarks. Faith had gone further, "Who do you think is going to mess with us with Lum and Sam around?" Lum would cause a man to think twice about harming his family. But one look at Sam and a body would rather, as Lum said, "French kiss a rattlesnake." Gabe had never quite understood the term, "French kiss", but he got the overall jest. Sam, or Sampson, was a huge bull mastiff. He'd saved the dog and brought him home, but he was all Faith's dog. He went almost everywhere she did, often lounging in the carriage when she went in somewhere. More than one person had changed his direction when they'd come too close to suit Sam. He'd rise up and give a low deep growl and all of a sudden the individual would find an alternate route. Sam had never actually bitten anyone...well, only one rogue. Faith's deranged Uncle Montague. He had shot Lum and was intending to have his way with Faith when Sam tore a door down and killed the man. The dog loved Faith and little James. He tolerated Gabe. Faith would hug the big brute and let him kiss, Gabe called it "lick", her face.

Once, after Sam had given her a big lick, she held her face for Gabe to kiss. "You want me to kiss you after what he just did?" Gabe asked incredibly.

"Humph" Faith snorted. "He doesn't seem to mind after you've kissed me." Gabe leaned over and kissed the air next to her face. "Well! I see who really loves me. Come on, Sam." The big dog got up, shook, and gave Gabe a look that said,

"You see who she loves."

He could hear noises from the kitchen. Lum was probably building a fire in the stove for Nanny to make coffee. No matter how early he had to leave, Nanny would, at least, have coffee and a pastry ready for him. He suddenly wondered if Hex and Dagan were stirring yet.

"Whatcha thinkin', Cap'n?" Faith asked, mimicking one of his sailors.

"I was thinking how beautiful you are and how much I enjoy loving you."

Faith gave him a passionate kiss, and then pulling the gown over her shoulders, whispered, "Then prove it, sailor." Gabe proved it.

CHAPTER THREE

THE EARLY DAWN SEEMED to last forever. When the sun finally did rise above the horizon, low dark clouds were overhead. In the distance, the dark clouds and the sea seemed to merge. Rain started to spatter down, just a few drops to start with, and then they increased. Lieutenant Con Vallin had the watch. He had just recently arrived in Barbados. Admiral Anthony had sent him to *HMS Trident* as a temporary assignment. Not a bad assignment, a trip to Antigua and then back aboard *Bulldog. Trident* only had a crew large enough to sail the wounded ship to the dockyard. Of course, nothing had been said that they had to rush back. A night or two in Antigua would not be amiss.

Vallin liked the Caribbean. He didn't feel the looks and stares here that he felt in England or Scotland. His father had been the wayward first son of a Scottish lord. He'd traveled to the colonies, which was nothing out of the way in his father's eyes, but he then did the unthinkable and married a Creek Indian princess. It didn't end there.

When the wife died in childbirth, the father,

instead of leaving the lad with his mother's people, had brought him home with him to Glasgow. As a child, Con's life was that of any boy. It was when he was older that his life changed. His complexion was darker than his Scottish relatives and while his hair was black as a raven, his father and other male Vallins had red hair. He was faster, stronger, a better marksman, and with time, a better fighter. He had to be. There was always some bully who wanted to try him.

Once his grandfather died, his father became lord of the manor and soon took a bride. Con was sure it was the new bride who pushed his father into sending him to the navy. Con had grown up near the sea, and enjoyed it, so at the age of fourteen he was sent aboard his first ship. His first captain was surprised that the son of a Scottish lord was as dark as he was and had probably guessed why he was sent to sea. At any rate, he felt affection for the boy and while Con received no special favors, he was always assigned duties where an old hand taught him well.

That was seven years ago. Most of his time had been spent in the Caribbean and Indian Ocean. He had always hoped he'd find a way to the colonies to see his mother's people, but thus far, that hadn't happened. He'd only returned home to Scotland one time. While his father welcomed him, his wife had been cordial at best. He had two brothers, both redheaded and very white. They seemed happy being around their half Indian brother, but Con knew it would be a relief to his father's wife when he left. His father had always been generous and Con was given an allowance that afforded him more freedom than some. His life aboard ship had been good. It took a while for a new officer or captain to accept him. However, his abilities as a seaman always won them over. He'd been a lieutenant for just over three years now. His last ship was headed to England, so he asked for and received a transfer to *HMS Seahorse*. Now that he was assigned to temporary duty, he felt a sense of freedom not felt on the flagship.

After reporting on board, he'd met Lieutenant Laqua with his shiny new uniform and the two became friends. Of course, Laqua told him about Sir Gabe's exploits and how he now was under a cloud. He'd met the captain two days ago and, while he was friendly and receptive, Vallin could tell his mind was elsewhere. At quarters that morning, he'd come on deck, made sure *HMS Bulldog* was on station and that the horizon was clear, and then he went back below.

The deck pumps were still rigged and had to be manned, one hour out of four. Not bad, but certainly not good.

The cry from the lookout startled Vallin as he'd been deep in his own thoughts. "Looks like flotsam in the water, two points to larboard," he called down. Vallin walked over to the larboard side and looked over the rail. The clouds and rain made it hard to see but sure enough there was debris floating on the ocean.

At first, just a piece of bulwark, and then the stump of a yardarm, a large chuck of grating, a section of a longboat, some rope, and half-submerged barrels. Vallin was about to send for the captain when he realized Sir Gabe was on deck.

"Have somebody see if they can hook a piece of the debris and see if we can get an idea of what ship it might be from," Gabe said.

"It's probably from one of the ships in the convoy that sailed earlier in the week," Hex volunteered.

"Might be," Gabe grunted. "Signal *Bulldog* to close," Gabe ordered.

When the ship was within hailing distance, Gabe picked up the speaking trumpet and ordered Captain Kirk to sail back and forth, looking for more flotsam or maybe even a body. After an hour of searching, a body was found clinging to a partially submerged hatch cover, and then there were more bodies. Sharks were also spotted.

"Deck thar! Ship just off the larboard bow, just off the horizon," the lookout advised.

"Signal *Bulldog* to investigate," Gabe ordered. Vallin curiously climbed up the shrouds a few feet trying for a better view. After a moment or so, Gabe asked, "Can you tell anything of her?"

"Not much, Captain," Vallin replied. "She appears jury-rigged, not under full sail."

As soon as Vallin was back on deck, Gabe ordered, "Alter course, Mr. Vallin, so that we may close with this ship."

"Aye, Captain."

A few minutes later, the lookout called again, "She's jury-rigged right enough, sir. Only a stump of a mast standing with sail."

Within the hour, *Trident* had closed with the wounded ship. She was the *Leopard...HMS Leopard* of fifty guns. A new two decker who had been the main escort for the convoy who'd anchored in Carlisle Bay, not a week before. The convoy must have been attacked, and one of the enemies' ships must have carried some weight for *Leopard* to look so beaten. Gabe could see but one officer on deck as *Trident* closed.

"We will cross, I think," Gabe advised Laqua. "Roust out the surgeon, Jake," Gabe said to his cox'n.

Soon they were on board the battered ship. The only standing officer was a young lieutenant. He had been the third lieutenant on the ship. "It was a surprise attack, Sir Gabe," Lieutenant Tolbert explained. "We didn't know the Dons had joined in the war as allies with the colonials. There were three ships in a line, and as they closed they opened up their gunports and cut loose. The captain was struck down, the first and second lieutenant, and a helmsman were all killed with the first broadside. The next two Dons passed in succession with guns blazing, blasting us to hell. We were dead in the water. The convoy and the other escorts scattered as the captain had ordered, with instructions to rendezvous in English Harbour."

Doctor Cornish returned on deck to report on the captain's condition. "He has a splinter in his face and may lose an eye. His left arm will have to be removed as it has been shattered in several places. How soon will we be in Antigua?" Cornish asked.

"Two, maybe three, days sailing, slow as we are," Gabe answered.

"I will remove the arm now, then. To wait much longer will only result in gangrene," Cornish said.

"Alright," Gabe said. "We will try to lie hove to while you do what you can for the captain. We will also effect what repairs we can. Lieutenant Vallin, cross over to *Trident* and have the bosun and the carpenter return with their mates." Seeing an overturned gun carriage, he added, "Have the gunner come over as well."

With the combination of *Leopard's* and *Trident's* surviving professional men, repairs could be done more effectively and hopefully before anymore enemy ships showed up.

Damn, we are near helpless, Gabe thought.

CHAPTER FOUR

THE ECHO OF THE salute had not cleared the harbor when the signal for 'captain, repair on board' was hoisted. Anticipating this, Gabe had made provisions and had Lieutenant Tolbert aboard *Trident* prior to land fall. Rear Admiral Dutch Moffett was in command of British Naval Forces in Antigua. He had been Lord Anthony's flag captain some years before, so Gabe didn't feel the apprehension he usually felt when reporting to an admiral.

Moffett's flag lieutenant was waiting at the entrance when Gabe crossed through the flagship's entry ports. "The admiral will see you below, Sir Gabe," the lieutenant announced, letting Captain Kirk and Lieutenant Tolbert know they'd have to wait. The flag captain must have been ashore as it was the first lieutenant who invited them down to the wardroom for a quick glass.

Once announced, Admiral Moffett called Gabe in using his first name. He'd known Gabe since he was little more than a boy, so titles and rank were not used. Moffett asked about the family and inquired about Lord Anthony, Lady Deborah, and Macayla. He then surprised Gabe. "I congratulate you on your recent victories." Lifting a glass in a toast, he said, "It's bad business, this thing with Kirkstatter, bad business. Has influence, I'm told. Otherwise, war or not, he'd be on the beach. Not sure what the Admiralty was thinking."

Gabe reported their finding the *Leopard*, barely making way under jury-rig. After he finished his narrative, Moffet leaned back. "I'd just gotten word our ground troops were finally making a show of it with the tide turning in our favor. Now the Dons are out. Spain doesn't care what the colonies do. This is just a chance to get a knife in us. Maybe win some leverage that will pry us out of Florida or somewhere similar." Sitting forward in his chair, Moffett asked about Captain Price, *Leopard's* captain.

"Doctor Cornish feels he should be able to fully recover, given time. Of course, he's lost his arm but that should not prevent him from returning to sea."

"And *Leopard*?" Moffett inquired. "You said you'd been able to repair her so that she's serviceable."

"Aye, sir. Paint and provisions and she'd be ready to sail," Gabe replied. "Of course, she is in need of officers and men."

Moffett nodded, his hands together making a steeple under his chin. He leaned back and then as if making decision, he said, "The men you have on *Trident*, if you added those to *Leopard*, would that give you a full complement?"

"Close, sir," Gabe replied.

"And you have two lieutenants with you?" Moffett asked.

"Aye, sir, one of them was just promoted from a master's mate."

"Do you trust him, Gabe?"

"I do, sir. I made him an acting lieutenant while in the Indian Ocean. He was in temporary command of *Trident* and brought her home."

"Hmm, young but an officer you trust. Of course, I'd have to loan you an officer so that you'd have someone to help stand watch," Moffett said.

"I'm not sure I understand, Admiral," Gabe replied.

"Gil has to be made aware the Dons are out. I got his dispatch about the privateers. He will be close in to Spanish waters. I don't want him surprised by some fleet out of Havana or San Juan. I'm going to put you in temporary command of *Leopard*. Your orders are simple. Find Lord Anthony and make him aware that Spain has joined the war. You will then be under his orders. *Bulldog* will sail along with you." Moffett then paused again as if in thought. "Have you ever met a black British naval officer, Gabe?"

"No sir. I have heard of John Perkins though. He is, or was, one of Admiral Rodney's officers."

As if not hearing Gabe's reply, the admiral spoke again, "I have the addition of a new sloop, the *Lynx* of fourteen guns." Moffett continued,

"Her commander is Lieutenant Leonard Mont-gomery. He is a pleasant man, a fine seaman; well spoken and he is black. I'm thinking his *Lynx* would be just the type of shallow draft vessel Lord Anthony could use in his search for priva-teers."

Gabe let his mind absorb this. "May I speak openly, sir?"

"Of course, Gabe, there's just the two of us here."

"You are not just sending him away due to his race, are you?" Gabe asked.

Moffett, who had stood up, sat back down. After a moment, he spoke, "Maybe, in part, his race does enter the picture. I don't have enough for his ship to do to keep him busy. Even sending him out on patrol with a couple of frigates as a tender, he'd still be in port much of the time. In truth, Gabe, I don't want him ostracized. I think if he is left here on this small island it would not be beneficial to anyone."

Gabe nodded. It had cost the admiral to be truthful. He might not have been to someone else. "I, of course, will be glad to have *Lynx* with us."

Moffett stood up and shook Gabe's hand. "I will have your orders drawn up. I will also put a crew aboard *Trident* to see her over to the dock-yard. Be prepared to take on provisions in the morning."

As Gabe started to depart, Moffett stopped

him again. "Dine with me tonight, Gabe. If you like I'll send invitations to Kirk and Montgomery."

"Thank you, sir. I think that would be good. We can all get acquainted," Gabe replied.

"Right you are. Having a small squadron under your command will show the Admiralty what we think of you, Gabe. You'll come out from under this cloud. I have faith in you, Gabe." Looking at the admiral, Gabe realized he meant it.

***

ABOARD SHIP, THE SUN was finding holes in the clouds and the deck was starting to heat up. The breeze was enough to keep the sails filled but not much more. Gabe had spent the last hour going over journals, signing papers for the purser and the carpenter, and God only knew who all else. Wiping the previous captain's pen thoroughly, he put it in the desk drawer. He could hear Josh Nesbit puttering in the pantry. He and Jake Hex had taken a boat ashore and purchased enough supplies to last a month. The quick decision to put a crew together, replenish the ship, fill her holds with water and put her to sea in under three days was something of a minor miracle. At one point, a body could have walked to shore using water hoys and small crafts of every type that were waiting to come alongside of *HMS Leopard*.

Up on deck, Laqua and Vallin were talking to the new Lieutenant Bufford. From the sounds of the voices they were getting along well. Tolbert was in the hole with Cornish making sure the supplies had been loaded so as to prevent spoilage as much as possible. The dinner with Admiral Moffett had turned out well. Before the evening was over, Kirk and Montgomery were visualizing how their ships could be sent into cays and shallow waters after the privateers. *Minds on prize money most likely*, Gabe surmised. *But why not, he'd done the same*.

CHAPTER FIVE

GABE WALKED UP ON deck, Dagan and Hex followed. It was not hot and without Gabe's coat it would have been chilly. However, in an hour or so after the sun had risen, the deck planks would be hot. More than one had already seen the surgeon for blisters on their feet where they'd stepped on a deck seam where the tar was bubbling up.

As the sun started to break the horizon, Gabe could distinguish the binnacle box, the faint light inside illuminating the compass so that it could be read. Laqua had the watch and was speaking to a helmsman. Seeing the captain, the helmsman suddenly rubbed his nose with his index finger pointing. A private signal but done in such an obvious manner, Dagan had to stifle a laugh, but that was alright. The man cared enough for the lieutenant that he had tried to warn him the captain was on deck. Gabe wondered if newly made Lieutenant Laqua had thought six months ago he'd be standing watch on a warship as a lieutenant.

After all the lieutenants had gathered together, Vallin turned out to be the senior so he was now the first lieutenant. Lieutenant Bufford was only a few months Vallin's junior, so he was second lieutenant. Tolbert, who was third lieutenant, previous to the Don's attack, was still third and Laqua was the fourth lieutenant. A full complement of officers, a good surgeon, and close to a full crew, Gabe knew Moffett had been generous.

The sun continued to push the gray dawn westward, but soon it would be full day. If the horizon was clear the guns would be secured and the daily routine would start. It would be the same routine every day, barring inclement weather or an enemy in sight. The pumps would be rigged, the decks scrubbed and holystoned, then flagged dry, brass might be polished with brick dust. It would then be sail drill, gun drill, fire drill, or any other drill or combination of drills that came to the captain's mind.

The first day at sea, Gabe had run both sail and gun drills. He was satisfied with neither. He had a lot of men but as yet they had not molded into a crew. Each drill showed improvement but when it came to ship handling and gun drill, Gabe was a hard task master. Most of the men that came over today were alive because of it. Vallin must have had a difficult task master at some point, as his views had been the same as his captain. He'd quickly put new divisions together, sprinkling the new hands in messes with the old. Every gun crew had a very experienced gun captain to train members of his crew.

Leopard had twenty-four pounders on the lower deck, and twelve pounders on the upper deck, ten twenty-four pound carronades on the quarterdeck with two more on the forecastle. They would have sail and gun drills today and tomorrow and if the master, Mr. Pittman, was right they'd reach Jamaica about mid-morning on the third day.

Gabe had spent most of his career in the Leeward and Windward Islands off the Caribbean, but he'd never been to Jamaica. He had considered passing through the chain of the Leeward Islands and taking a peek at Puerto Rico to see if he could spot any Spanish ships. He would then pass through the Mona Passage between Hispaniola and Puerto Rico and go west to Jamaica, but the risk was too great. His orders were to find Lord Anthony's squadron, make him aware of Spain's involvement in the war and to place himself under his Lordship's command. With the clouds already hanging over him, Gabe thought it wise to follow his orders.

"*Lynx* and *Bulldog* are in sight, Captain."

"Thank you, Mr. Laqua. I shall be below if you need me."

"Aye, aye, Captain."

***

MIDSHIPMAN GLENN WATCHED THE last grains of sand drain through the glass and expertly flipped it over. The marine sentry who guarded the sand glasses rang the bell three times; an hour and a half had passed in the forenoon watch. It was soon after that, when the lookout called, "Land ho."

A smile appeared on the master's face. He was spot on. The lookout had spotted land. Seeing his new captain arrive on deck, Pittman volunteered, "We've sighted Jamaica. What the lookout has spotted is the Blue Mountains. Port Royal is where we will anchor. It is a large natural harbor and is protected by a spit of sand called the Palisades. Buccaneers used to use Port Royal as a base for their raids. It was once said that Port Royal was the most sinful place on earth — the only thing that ran more freely than the whores was the rum. The pirates made it a rich place as the town was filled with looted gold, jewels, and other plunders, most of it off Spanish ships. Humph, it's no wonder the Dons have joined the Colonials. Get a little revenge on the crown for giving all the sea robbers protection. Of course, the crown had merchants in place furnishing the rum and whores for the pirates to squander their plunder on."

"You seem to know a lot about the pirates, Mister Pittman," Gabe said.

"Aye, I does, Captain. I used to sail with Morgan." Gabe must have looked dumbstruck as the master smiled and then winked causing Gabe to laugh.

"Hear that, mate," one of the men said. "Sailed with Morgan 'e did. He admits it, told you the bugger was old."

"Yes, you 'id," other mate replied.

"Morgan lived back in the 1600's, it is now 1780. Well see, 'e is old then, ain't 'e?"

"Never mind, now get back to work. 'ere comes Lieutenant Vallin."

Pulling into Port Royal, it was soon evident that Lord Anthony's squadron was not there. However, Gabe was called to the flagship, *HMS Bristol.* Speaking to the flag captain, Gabe was sent ashore to the Admiralty house to deliver the news about Spain in person to the admiral.

HMS Bristol was a fifty gun, fourth rate. She was, in fact, a small ship for a flagship. Gabe thought he remembered she had been Admiral Parker's ship when he was but a commodore. Some men become very attached to certain ships and thus he'd kept her as his flagship. If Gabe's memory served him right, *Bristol* was *Leopard's* sister ship. Both were built by the Royal dockyard at Sheerness.

Gabe's uniform was plastered to him from all the sweat it took to make his way up the stone jetty and toward his destination in a sweltering heat. Gabe was guided to a large waiting room that was cool compared to outside. Gabe thought, as he leaned back in a rattan chair, *it might be the coolest room on the island.* The Admiralty house on Jamaica was much like the one on Antigua, with white jalousies over windows, marble floors, and high ceilings. He wondered if the wooden jalousies help keep the room cool.

He doubted that they'd help much if a hurricane landed and tossed things about.

"Sir Gabe," a voice called. Had it called twice? The cool had caused Gabe to get so comfortable he'd become drowsy. He jumped to his feet, grabbing his hat before it hit the floor. The clerk smiled. "It does get comfortable in here." Gabe smiled back, thinking, 'a clerk with a heart.' At White Hall, he'd have been passed over for the next in line. Of course, he was the only one waiting at the time.

"Damme, just damme," Admiral Peter Parker bellowed, when he heard Gabe's news. "With Admiral Cornwallis off chasing the French it leaves us damn short of ships." The admiral paused, as he was deep in thought. "Yes, Lord Anthony needs to know. With Grand Cayman lying under the belly of Cuba, the Dons could likely sweep down at anytime." Fumbling with a dry quill, Parker seemed deep in thought. "It's no wonder the Dons have allowed the American privateers the use of their ports," he finally said. "They've been in bed with the Americans all along, just biding their time." Gabe had kept quiet, drinking his lime juice while the admiral rambled on. "Admiral Kirkstatter was by here. He told me a less than charitable tale about you, Sir Gabe." *Damn*, Gabe thought, *will the man slander my name in every port?* Parker turned from where he'd been gazing out of his office window and faced Gabe, "One of his captains told my captain the truth of it as did Lord Anthony when he dropped anchor. Just remember, Sir Gabe, you can't always control what others may say. Just stay the course and more often than not, people will consider the source."

"Thank you, that was kindly said, Admiral."

Smiling, Admiral Parker said, "I'd ask you to dine with me this evening, but I know you're anxious to find Lord Anthony."

Gabe made his way back to *Leopard* thinking they had more than enough fresh water to last them the short voyage to Grand Cayman, but did *Bulldog* and *Lynx*. He'd have Vallin find out and then thought, *no, I will have them aboard for a quick officer's call and refreshment. There'll be plenty of time for that and we can sail on the tide.*

As Gabe was rowed out to his ship, the watch challenged the boat, "Ahoy."

"*Leopard,*" was the quick reply. Would he get used to the title before he had to relinquish command. *HMS Leopard* was a good ship...but so had been *Trident*.

CHAPTER SIX

"CAPTAIN, SIR." VALLIN TURNED as Gabe walked up to the binnacle. Vallin had learned in just a short time the captain was a hard riser and not a morning person.

After glancing at the compass, Gabe turned toward his first lieutenant and muttered, "Morning." Vallin gave his polite reply but didn't launch into some rambling report that was very obvious the minute the captain walked on deck, most of which had surely been heard or seen from the skylight or stern windows in the captain's cabin.

Rain had suddenly appeared in a downpour with a fierce driving force that made the skin sting. As quick as it came, it moved on, but the sails and riggings still dripped and drained into the scuppers. It would be hot and muggy when the sun rose. The captain looked about the ship. He knew every gun was manned and cleared for action. It never changed for Con Vallin, this uncanny feeling, almost sinister, knowing that when the sun rose you might find yourself staring at an enemy fleet ready to blast you to kingdom come. *Did the captain have these same sensations?*

Unless the captain spoke, the only audible

sounds were those of the ship as she moved like a phantom in the deep darkness before dawn. Vallin was sure his captain had walked the quarterdeck and watched too many dawns to need somebody feeding him useless information. Of course, Dagan had dropped a hint that Gabe never faced the early morning in a good mood.

Captain Anthony stood on deck, now silent after the brief greeting. His cox'n was close enough to hear any whispered word. It seemed a strange relationship, the captain and his cox'n. A bond that was not seen very often...a bond that only happens when two men have shared great hardships together or when a man saves another's life. He'd seen captains who were fond of their cox'ns but the bond was not there.

Lieutenant Laqua had hinted it seemed to run in the family. Lord Anthony's cox'n was something of a celebrity. Laqua swore he'd heard young lieutenants call Bart sir. He also hinted it would be a foolish man to invite trouble with either of the cox'ns. Nor could a man think he could be rude or try to hurt one of the Anthony's without going through their cox'n first. It was said a few had tried, but Laqua didn't know of any survivors who'd bragged about it.

At the wheel, Vallin heard a helmsman speaking to the master, "It be lightening up now."

"It will be a hot one today," Pittman, the master, was saying to the captain. "Rains gone and other than being hot, we'll have a fine day, I'm thinking."

"Do you know these waters?" Gabe asked the master.

"No, Captain, can't say that I do, but the charts say deep water unlike the Bahamas."

Hearing Pittman's voice so cracked at times, it sounded like he was a croaking bullfrog. Even by naval standards Pittman was an old hand, with a bald pate with gray white hair over his ears and down to his collar in back, his belly huge and rotund, face and hands like leather and eyes that squinted from looking into the sun for so many years, worn by years of fighting the wind, the sea, and the enemy. Surely, he'd put enough aside to buy a tavern or ale house.

"Deck thar, *Bulldog* and *Lynx* on station." After a moment, the lookout shouted again, "Sail, sail off the weather beam."

"Shall I go up?" Vallin asked his captain.

"No, give your lookout time. He must have good eyes to make out sails in this haze," Gabe said.

A few minutes later, the lookout called again, "Looks like a schooner, sir, she's changed tack and closing."

***

IT WAS COOL SITTING in the admiral's cabin aboard *HMS SeaHorse*. Maybe just getting out of the sun and into the shade of the cabin made the difference. Anchored in the harbor with George-town in the distance, the flagship had hatches open, awning and wind sail had been rigged and very little movement could be seen as the sun was directly overhead at midday.

"So all pretense of neutrality has been abandoned, and the Dons are out," Admiral Lord Anthony was saying.

"That makes it even more dangerous for our people on these islands."

"Well," Lord Anthony said, and then paused as he held his glass toward Silas for a refill of his lime juice. Once his glass was full and he had taken a swallow, he continued, "At least, I don't feel so bad shooting at the Dons and Frogs. I can tell you, I've often been in anguish when the men I've fought and killed spoke the same language as I do." Gabe, Captain Earl, and Lieutenant Mahan listened without interruption.

"Aye," Captain Earl volunteered after a moment of silence.

"You're right, my Lord, and it only adds to our problem with the privateers," Lieutenant Mahan, the admiral's flag lieutenant added.

"I agree, Patrick. In fact, I'm sure their ranks will increase with both the Spanish and French joining in. Gabe has had to deal with that this past year."

Lord Anthony then spoke to his flag captain, "Call all our captains aboard. Since *Tomahawk* has returned, they should all be at anchor." Earl gave a slight nod indicating his Lordship was correct. "With Gabe here, and *Leopard's* added weight, we'll be able to send out two patrols that will be able to oppose anything other than a fleet."

"Aye," Earl and Mahan said in unison.

Looking at his brother, Lord Anthony asked, "You don't agree, Gabe?"

"Yes sir, but I was just thinking, *Leopard* is a borrowed ship."

"No, Gabe, she is a warship in which she and her captain are under my command."

"Aye, aye, sir," Gabe replied.

Lord Anthony smiled but wondered if Gabe had too much on his mind. *Was he still plagued with Kirkstatter's accusations? Damn it all, he should have let Bart do away with the sod. Well, what was done was done. Gabe would have to act as he'd been trained or I'd have to put someone else aboard Leopard.* Not a pleasant thought, but this was not a pleasant time, it was war. When Lord Anthony realized the cabin had gotten suddenly silent, he changed the subject. "Gabe, tell us about this new officer? A black man, you said."

"Yes sir, Lieutenant Leonard Montgomery."

***

THE GREAT PYRAMIDS OF sails on *Leopard*, the flagship, and other ships sailing in formation were impressive to Lieutenant Laqua. As accustomed as he was to such sights, he wondered what a landsman would think. *Would he be in awe? What about the privateers? Would they scurry away at the sight*? He'd mentioned his thoughts to Dagan.

"No, they'll just choose their prey more carefully. That little ship that we saw, you can bet she'll spread the word. They'll pass the word along and other ships will soon be hull down spreading the word. They know the trade routes, and they know when to strike, and they are also very good at it. We have the army and the ships, but they have the knowledge. They know where the coves are, the inlets, and waterways that lead into rivers and places to hide. They know how to make use of these smaller, faster vessels. They'll not stand up to a ship-to-ship action with a ship of the line or even a frigate. But that's not their type of war. They swoop down, and as time allows, they take what they can. It is then up to us to find them," Dagan said.

"I see," Laqua replied.

"No, you don't, not yet," Dagan said. "We've been at this since '75. It's now 1780. We have been at war with the Colonials for five years. Some said it would be over in six months. It's not over yet, Lieutenant, and a lot more men will die before it ends. Think of the mates you've lost. You're an officer now because of some of those men. But remember, it could be you next. No one is promised tomorrow." As Dagan walked way, Laqua thought, *damn'd if that didn't take some of the shine off my new gold.*

***

GABE WAS SIGNING PAPERS in his cabin. He would call all hands to witness punishment soon. Not something he liked at all. The purser had

placed the man on report for cursing him and being disrespectful. Both men were from *Leopard's*
original crew. Looking at the punishment log, it
seemed the purser was involved a lot. He'd speak
with the man himself later.

Right now he was thinking of the route they
were taking. They had left Grand Cayman and
sailed east, so they would pass north of Jamaica
and just to the south of Santiago de Cuba. They
sailed between Cuba and Hispaniola using the
Windward Passage. They'd then sail through the
rough and tricky Mona Passage, round Puerto
Rico, pass the Virgin Islands and head nor-west,
sailing past San Juan and its great fort and harbor. Gil was, in reality, inviting the Dons to come
out if they were in port. *Lynx* and *Bulldog* made a
pass through the Virgin Islands looking for privateers.

A knock on the door caused Gabe to look up
as the marine announced, "First lieutenant, zur."

As Vallin entered, Gabe spoke first, "Time for
punishment."

"Aye sir."

Gabe rose and putting on his hat and coat, he
spoke, "I'm going to have a talk with that damn
purser. He'll change his ways, at least while I'm
captain."

"I've already taken Craft aside, sir. I expect
he'll change his ways," Vallin said.

"Good," Gabe replied. He was glad Vallin was
the wall between the captain and the rest of the

ship. That he'd decided to speak to the fool purser without being told to spoke well of his abilities. Did they really call Craft the crafty arse?

CHAPTER SEVEN

THE BOSUN'S PIPE ECHOED throughout the ship as the word was passed, "All hands lay aft to witness punishment." Discipline was necessary on a ship, and at times the cat had to be let out of the bag, more on some ships, less on others. Gabe's ships had always fit in the latter category. He'd trained his officers to handle matters when they could. Taking a man's rum ration for a week or making him do some extra duty was frequently enough. Craft was not one of his officers. If they stayed together long enough, the purser would find the captain would be quick to hold him accountable.

Gabe stood at the quarterdeck rail, his lieutenants made a line to his right and the midshipmen next to them. Gabe nodded at Vallin, who called, "Uncover," to the officers and crew. Gabe then opened the Articles of War, reading the necessary charges and articles that dealt with the infraction, finishing with, "He shall be punished according to the laws used at sea." Replacing his hat, he ordered, "Two dozen lashes." Not a great amount to some but enough to rip the flesh from a man's back.

The bosun had two of his mates lash the man to a grate, his shirt was stripped from his back so that he was naked to the waist. Gabe felt bile rise in his throat as the cat-o-nine tails was pulled from its red baize bag. Crawley was the seaman being punished. He was not a young man. It was said he could hardly hear. He was so thin; it looked like his skin was stretched over his bones.

"It was his hearing," Hex said, that had precipitated the infraction. The purser had spoken to Crawley as his grog was being issued. Not responding, the purser grabbed Crawley and jerked his arm causing the old seaman to drop his cup. Crawley, not knowing who'd grabbed him, cursed, "Ye damned sodomite." Now he stood at the grate. Once he was stripped and made fast to the grate, Gabe ordered, "Do your duty."

The lashes were laid on. Each lash swung with authority, a crack being heard each time the tails of the cat bit into the naked flesh. Almost like an omen, the sky turned gray and the wind quickened. The master-at-arms had just counted fourteen when the lookout shouted, "Sail ho! Sail off the larboard beam."

Gabe quickly ordered, "Stop punishment. Mr. Vallin, send a good hand aloft with a telescope. I've a feeling."

"Aye, Cap'n."

Rain started to spatter and Gabe headed below to get his coat when he realized Crawley had never uttered a sound. Turning so fast, Hex almost collided with his captain. "Have Crawley put on as a member of my barge crew as soon as he's well," Gabe said.

"Aye, Captain," Hex replied smiling. "That will make the old seaman proud."

"Deck thar, two sails."

Returning quickly from getting his coat, Gabe spoke to Jarvis Jackson, the signal's midshipman, "Message to the flag. Two sails in sight to larboard. Then signal *Bulldog* and *Lynx* to investigate."

It did not take long before Jackson was back, "Flag has acknowledged."

"Deck thar," the lookout called again. "*Tomahawk* and *Revenant* have come about and have joined the chase."

Gabe was trying to figure the angle of *Tomahawk* and *Revenant* with that of *Bulldog* and *Lynx*. "Mr. Pittman, alter course, I want to close the gap."

"You think we have them in a box?" Vallin asked.

"To early to tell, but it's worth the try," Gabe replied.

"Aye," Vallin answered, as sail handlers were called. Overhead, the sky darkened and lightning zigzagged across the sky.

"Deck thar, flag has signaled give chase, the squadron has changed tack." Vallin looked at Gabe, "Mr. Glenn is in the tops with the lookout. He's learning the signals."

"I see," Gabe replied.

"Deck thar, she be coming about," the report coming loud and clear.

Looking at the sky, Vallin swore, "It will be dark before we can bring her to action."

"Aye," Pittman agreed. "We'll be in the Exumas before long. We were off Long Island when she was sighted. She'll not get between Cap'n Jepson and Cap'n Davy, so she'll head toward the Exumas, I would wager." Pittman continued, "Maybe Great Exuma. If we lose sight of her we can forget it."

"Why is that?" Gabe asked the master.

"Too many places to hide, Cap'n. There's a cay for everyday in the year and that's just the Exumas. She could weave her way through the cays and then head for Cat Island or Eleuthea to the north or come about and head for San Salvador, Rum Cay, or continue on. She'll have a shallow draught and she's fast. She'll go places the sloops might follow, but the flag never will. Places we can't go. This is what the likes of *Bulldog* and *Lynx* are for. Not proper ships, but they'll go places we'll not dare."

Gabe watched as the British ships closed the gap. They would be cutting it close, as it would soon be dark. Vallin had climbed halfway up the shrouds to get a better look.

"*Tomahawk* has fired," Vallin shouted.

"The schooner has run up her colors," the lookout called down.

"Looks like she'll stand and fight," Vallin called again.

Across the waters a rumble was heard, almost like thunder. "That was *Revenant*," Glenn called down in an excited voice, quickly followed by another shout, "She's struck, sir."

"Aye, that she has," Vallin added.

***

THE SCHOONER LAY HOVE to under the shadow of *SeaHorse*. Her crew was under guard while her captain had been taken aboard the flagship. Gabe, Hex, and Dagan, along with a handful of marines and a dozen seamen, were aboard the schooner. The gunner, Abrahams, had the ship's crew sent forward where the marines had them covered with muskets and a swivel gun.

"A lot of men for a schooner, is it not?" Jackson, the midshipman, asked Dagan.

"Aye, lad, but this is a raider. The extra hands are to put aboard ships they capture," Dagan replied.

A thorough search had been made of the captain's quarters with nothing found. Gabe sent a few seamen below while Hex took the middy with him to search the officers' cabins. Jackson was looking under the cot when Hex pulled the pillow back and found a letter.

"Mr. Jackson, go tell the captain...no, go ask the captain if he would be so kind as to come here, please. Don't shout it out like your reporting, just speak casual like."

"Aye, sir."

Hex read the letter and re-read it to the point it ended in mid-sentence. Standing, Hex handed the letter to Gabe, who sat in the one chair in the small cabin. As he read, he began to smile.

"Did you ever write such a letter, Jake?" Gabe asked.

"No, sir, but I never had such a sweetheart who I was trying to impress," Hex replied.

Gabe handed the letter to Dagan. The man could already see his own command. Dagan laughed. The first officer in trying to impress his sweetheart had bragged about ships they'd taken, how much his shares would be worth, and where they would head after rendezvousing at Cat Island. Then they'd be home in...the letter ended there.

"When did he expect to mail the letter?" Jackson asked, and then realized his error. "Sorry sir."

"No, Mr. Jackson, that's a good question. Is there a ship at Cat Island that is headed back to the Colonies? If so, what is she carrying? Say nothing about this letter," Gabe said, his comments meant for Jackson.

"Aye sir."

Gabe put the letter in his pocket and as they came back on deck, he spoke to Jackson again, "Go see what, if anything, was found below, young sir." After a few minutes, he spoke again. This time so the schooner's crew could hear him, "A waste of time. I will go aboard the flagship and see what his Lordship plans for this vessel."

"Sink 'er, I'm thankin'," Dagan replied in a put on manner.

CHAPTER EIGHT

STEADY AS SHE GOES," Hex whispered after taking a quick glance at the compass. Gabe sat in the stern sheets as men pulled at the oars. He could remember the cynical smile on his brother's face as he handed him the letter.

"Love makes one do foolish things, doesn't it? Present company excluded," Gabe said. This caused Bart to laugh.

"I guess you propose to see what's at this rendezvous point?" Lord Anthony asked his brother.

"That was my plan," Gabe said.

"God's speed to you," Lord Anthony had said to his brother, holding up a glass in salute.

Four boats loaded with men were now rowing toward what...? A single ship? Two ships? Capture, pain, imprisonment or even death? Hex, Dagan, and Gabe were in one boat. Captain Leonard Montgomery was in a boat and Gregory Kirk another. Why had he chosen those two? Because they had sailed with him from Antigua...was that it? Did they need their names mentioned in the admiral's report, the Gazette even? He was not sure of Kirk, he might; but it would be a surety Montgomery would. In all likelihood, he'd reached his terminal rank. For some it would seem a lofty position but for most it was just the first rung.

"There's a glow ahead, sir," Crawley, the man who'd been at the grate not three days ago, said.

Turning to Hex, Gabe could just make out the raised eyebrow. Once the man was told he was part of the captain's crew, only death would have kept him aboard the ship. Lieutenant Laqua was in the fourth boat. Gabe knew the other lieutenants might think Laqua had favor but he'd tried to dispel that notion. He'd gathered his officers in his cabin to apprise them of what was to take place.

Vallin had objected, "Captain, it's my place to go."

"No," Gabe said. "I need someone aboard *Leopard* who can handle the ship should I fall. You are too important, Mr. Vallin. Unlike some," he said, as he looked at Lieutenant Laqua; hopefully, the newly made lieutenant saw through his captain's words.

As the boats neared, a second glow was sighted. Was this one on shore or was there another ship beyond the first? If there were only one ship, two boats would board from each side, larboard and starboard, forward and aft. If there were two, Kirk and Laqua's boats would head for the second ship. Hopefully, there would be no third vessel.

As they drew nearer, they could see only one

ship and the tide had her stern on. Gabe wanted to pause to ask the men if they knew what to do. But that would only show his nervousness. They were near now and Hex looked at Gabe, who nodded. The cox'n's arm rose. The signal for "boat your oars." Up front a man made ready with the grapnel, his broad back told Gabe that it was Lewis, the bosun's mate.

The grapnel shot up and over with a dull thud. It held and, as Crawley had hooked onto something with the boat hook, men scrambled up and over. Men were already on the ship's deck when a shot was fired and someone screamed. It had to be one of the ship's men as none of their pistols had been charged, Gabe hoped. Now it was his turn, up and over. Forward, the ship's men were firing at Montgomery's men.

"At them, men," Gabe shouted.

Muskets were being fired at the British and then they were used as clubs. Coming up from the sleeping berths, more men charged. Somebody fell in front of Gabe, making him stumble. As he did so, a belaying pin whooshed by, striking someone by the yell that followed. Hex, his blade flashing in the moonlight, cut sleepy men down as he barreled forward. Someone swung a musket, which caught one man, knocking him to the deck but another lunged forward with a boarding pike, impaling the enemy in the abdomen. A sucking sound was heard as the pike was snatched loose, the wounded man's innards spilling out onto the deck. More shouts were being heard as Laqua's crew had gained the deck.

Blades clinked against musket barrels, another shot went off and a man near Gabe groaned. As he fell, Dagan took his boarding pike and threw it like a spear, striking the musket man in the chest, its point protruding from his back. The British seamen now seemed to be gaining. Gabe hacked at some man's blade as another skewered the rogue. It was Crawley, smiling a near toothless smile. Blade to blade they fought. As a man made to club Hex, Gabe swung his blade down, feeling it grate on bone. The muskets were mostly quiet now as nobody had time to reload. A giant of a man clanged blades with Dagan. With a deft movement, Dagan pulled a smaller blade from his sash and rammed it into his foe. The man dropped his cutlass and grabbed his stomach, bending forward. Dagan hit the man on the chin with the hilt of his cutlass, knocking the man backwards and out.

The British, sensing victory, were now like crazed demons as they pushed and parried an attack here and there. Someone seeing it was over cried surrender, but was slashed along his ribs for his troubles. Gabe heard a splash as the man hit the water. Did he jump or was he put over?

A few feet away from where Gabe fought, Captain Montgomery had just downed his foe. Seeing Gabe, he smiled and gave a salute with his blade. *The man is a fighter*, Gabe decided. A cut and bleeding man with a coat was now facing Gabe. An officer, maybe even the captain. As he made to lunge forward, he fell to his knees. Was he dead or had the fight just gone from him?

Now, it was Gabe, who called, "Surrender. Surrender, in the King's name."

One of the privateer's men shouted, "The captain's down."

It was silent then, except for the groans and cries of the wounded. Splashes were heard, several men had jumped over the side. Someone began to load a musket.

"Let them go," Gabe ordered. "The fight is gone from them."

"Aye, from us as well, Sir Gabe," Montgomery said. He'd made it.

Looking about him, Gabe spied Kirk, wounded and holding his arm but he'd survived. A sob was heard and Gabe looked at the deck. There were many who hadn't made it, from both sides.

***

THE SHIP'S CREW STOOD in defeat. Many of the dead and wounded were their mates. None of the privateers resisted as their weapons were taken and put in a pile. Gabe walked through the corpses until he found the American officer, who was still breathing. Next to the officer lay Crawley. He'd given his all for a man who'd ordered him flogged.

Seeing the little man, Dagan spoke, "He died proud. You gave him worth. He was part of the captain's boat crew."

Gabe rose, "See if they have a doctor aboard and take this man to him," pointing at the American officer.

"Aye," Hex replied as he lifted the man.

"Mr. Laqua."

"Yes sir."

"I congratulate you, sir. A fine job, you did. Your first cutting out, I believe."

Dagan smiled; Gabe had just built respect for the fourth lieutenant. The men would spread the word once they were back aboard *Leopard*. Thinking of others...the captain takes time to think of others, after all of this.

CHAPTER NINE

*S*AIL HO!"

"Where away," Captain Stephen Earl barked, before either the lieutenant on watch or the master aboard *SeaHorse* had time to react.

"Dead ahead," the response came down. "A sloop, she be flying our colors."

Due to the contrary winds, it took the better part of an hour for the sloop to make its way to the flagship, which was now lying hove-to.

Lieutenant John Jenkins, of sixteen gun *HMS Zebra,* was greeted at the entry port by Captain Earl. After a pleasant greeting, he was taken below to the admiral's cabin.

"My Lord," Jenkins said, with a slight bow, and then getting right to the point, he bluntly stated, "The Dons are out and Admiral Kirkstatter has been taken."

"Taken," Lord Anthony said, rising from his chair. He could hardly believe his ears. "What about the ship, man, the ship?"

Jenkins was a former master's mate who had risen from the ranks. A man Gabe had spoken very highly of was still ill at ease by such a high-ranking officer as Lord Anthony. "The ship was taken as well, sir, with all aboard. It was off the coast of Florida, sir; he came upon three of the Dons' frigates. One attacked *Thorn* and the other two went after the flagship. *Comete's* rudder was blasted away and the frigates fired on the bow and stern until the admiral surrendered. *Thorn* was no match for the frigate so Captain Taylor made for the Florida coast where the shallow water kept the frigate from closing. *Thorn* had taken a beating but was still able to return to Savannah without sinking."

"What in the world made the admiral sail with only a sloop as an escort?" Lord Anthony asked.

"It's my understanding, sir, that the governor in Saint Augustine received word that the Dons were to aid a Spaniard…Mr. Bernardo de Gálvez, who is marching toward Mobile with an army. After taking Mobile, they would march on Pensacola. According to the news we received, the campaign was coordinated in Havana where a squadron of ships is supposed to reinforce this Galvez. On top of this, sir, prior to the news about the Dons, the admiral got word that the French Admiral d'Arzac de Ternay has sailed with a convoy carrying six thousand French troops from Brest to aid the Americans. The admiral sent the frigates, *Venus* and *Stag*, up the coast to spread the word."

Admiral Lord Gilbert Anthony paced the deck in his cabin. The French, the Spaniards, and the damnable privateers, were all out to wreak mischief on British shipping and he only had a handful of ships to meet the overwhelming threat. He'd have to divide his command. Not the best choice...but the only one he had.

***

GABE SAILED WITH *Bulldog* and *Lynx* as well as *Tomahawk*. He was to search out the privateers while his brother, Admiral Lord Anthony, searched for either the Frog fleet or the Dons, supposedly at either Havana or San Juan. Only heaven knew where the French might be. Gabe had tried to persuade his brother that the addition of *Leopard's* weight might be the deciding factor if indeed he happened on a fleet, be it Spaniard or French. The question, in Gabe's mind, *was what if I run up on a fleet*? He had received a direct order not to engage a superior force. It was that possibility that made Lord Anthony assign *Tomahawk* to Gabe. If a fleet was sighted, he would shadow it but send *Tomahawk* for support. Gabe recalled his brother's harsh words, "I mean it, Gabe. I'm giving you a direct order. You do not engage a superior force. We need all our ships." Those words stung but the truth was evident. With an arm around Gabe's shoulder, Gil japed, "Bart would never forgive me if he lost his favorite card player. Who would he fleece then?"

Gabe would weave his way through the Bahamas and up to Saint Augustine. Shallow waters where his ships could get in close. Lord Anthony's patrol would revisit Cuba and take a look at the

Havana harbor, San Juan, Culebra, and Vieques, and the Virgin Islands, and then they would head back to Grand Cayman but taking their time to look in the harbor at Santiago de Cuba.

Watching Gabe sail away, Bart looked at Lord Anthony and said, "Not much of a war when yew has to play hide and seek with yer enemy. I miss the days where the liners stand broadside and him that's got the best gunners wins."

"Aye," Lord Anthony agreed. "It's not the kind of war we have been trained to fight, and the reason the Americans will win this war. They will haul their wind and await better odds. Can you see a British officer doing that? No," Lord Anthony said, answering his own question. "Belief in their ships, their men, and yes, even pride in themselves. I tell you, Bart, I don't want to see Gabe, or any other of my captains lost by taking unnecessary chances."

"Aye," Bart agreed, "and lady luck is bound to run out. Dagan or not, Gabe 'as pushed it, I'm thinking."

"My thinking as well, old friend," Anthony responded, pouring himself a snifter of brandy and motioning with the decanter to see if Bart cared for one. "I'd rather see him beached than face odds like he did last year. He's a changed man, Bart."

Taking his pipe from his mouth, Bart tucked it in a pocket. "That 'e be. 'E's still trying to live up to Lord James' standards...and 'is brother's."

Lord Anthony paused, his snifter in mid-air, "You think so, Bart?"

"No thinkin to it, 'e does," Bart replied.

As per Lord Anthony's orders to the sentries, his flag lieutenant did not have to be announced to enter the cabin. Because of that order, Lieutenant Patrick Mahan had entered in time to see and hear the conversation that had just taken place. Was there another admiral in the entire Navy, who would offer his cox'n a glass and carry on a conversation about his Lordship's brother? Lieutenant Mahan didn't think so. Not in the Royal Navy, and maybe not in any Navy. But that was one of the things that made Lord Anthony special. It was why he was proud to serve his Lordship as flag lieutenant when commands had been offered, such as the just-captured brigantine. He was offered it but decided to stay with the flag. Tapping against the pantry door, Lieutenant Mahan made himself known.

"The *Tidewater Witch* is approaching, sir. It appears that she's got a coastal trader with her."

Smiling, Lord Anthony said, "Damned if that Jem Jackson don't take to the hunt. Better than some, I know who is always looking for a handout from his betters."

"Them's few what's got sumthing to hand out," Bart responded.

The small coaster's captain was a short, portly, older looking man with wisps of hair covering a bald head. His leathery face had so many lines in it, Lord Anthony was afraid it'd crack when the man smiled.

After a cheerful greeting, in which the captain gladly accepted a glass of port, he told of his news. A large Spanish ship, one as big as the ship he was now on or bigger, almost swamped him during the night. A hellish time it had been when, after the big Spaniard passed, several more of the Dons passed also. One ship threw their garbage overboard, hitting his little coaster, and laughing about it.

"Did you get the name of any of the ships?" Jackson asked, already knowing the answer.

"Aye, it were the *San Cristobal*."

"Where did they pass you?" Lord Anthony inquired.

"You have a map?" the little captain asked. Lord Anthony nodded and Lieutenant Mahan fetched one and laid it out across the table. Smacking his mouth, the captain asked if any more port was to be had. It sure as torment beat the bottled vinegar called wine he was used to. Without waiting for Silas, Bart refilled the glass. The captain continued, "I was between the Turks and Great Inagua heading to Port de Paix."

The admission of the man's destination let Lord Anthony and his officers know he'd just as much as admitted to being a smuggler. Well, that was none of Lord Anthony's concern. He asked the captain, "You would suggest they were following what course?"

"Nor-norwest," the man said. "No guessing, nor-norwest." The little captain was given a few guineas for his information and told more would follow when he had more information for his Majesty's Navy.

Once the captain was seen over the side, Captain Earl and Captain Jackson rushed back to the great cabin. "If they are headed north, they are likely to meet Gabe's patrol," Lord Anthony said, when his captains returned.

"How did we miss them?" Captain Earl said, shaking his head in disbelief.

"We sailed to Havana first. They probably sailed from San Juan," Gil replied.

"Do you think they are headed to the Bahamas, my Lord?" Earl asked.

"It's possible," Anthony replied. "But since they passed between Turks and Great Inagua, I would think they have headed to the Florida Keys, Pensacola, or Mobile."

"I'll have the master get a chart of the Gulf Coast of Florida to...to New Orleans," Lieutenant Mahan said.

"Thank you," Lord Anthony replied. He then ordered, "Send your fastest frigate to get Gabe's patrol. If they can locate him soon enough, he can meet us here," Lord Anthony said, pointing to Andros. "If he misses us there, he is to sail toward Pensacola."

"Aye, my Lord, *Phoenix* is the fastest. Frostbrier will enjoy being out from the flag," Mahan replied.

Lord Anthony looked at his flag captain, "Make sure he knows he's not out looking for prizes. If he sights the French or the Dons, he is to avoid engaging."

"Aye, my Lord, he'll know his duty."

CHAPTER TEN

GABE'S PATROL WAS FOUND sooner than later as luck would have it. Not one enemy vessel had been spotted. Two days later, after meeting up with Frostbrier's *Phoenix*, Lord Anthony's ships were spotted by *Leopard's* lookout. Both groups were approaching Andros. Dropping anchor, Lord Anthony transferred to *Lynx* to have a closer look at the island and inquire if the Dons' ships had stopped over or been spotted in their passing.

It was an honor to Captain Montgomery and the *Lynx* for the admiral to come aboard. Lord Anthony had been told by his father, Admiral James Anthony, 'If you truly want to know a man, go aboard his ship unexpectedly.'

Lieutenant Mahan and Bart were the only ones to accompany his Lordship to the smaller ship. All due honors were sounded and Captain Montgomery was beaming that the admiral had chosen the *Lynx*. The correct orders were issued and the admiral's flag was hoisted as he cleared the entry port. While time did not allow an official inspection, Lord Anthony's professional eye could find nothing amiss.

Shaking hands with the admiral, Montgomery invited his Lordship below to his quarters with a quick warning to get all four into the smallish cabin would make for close quarters. After he squeezed into the cabin, a decent wine was offered and the ship made its way into Andros. The admiral went ashore hoping that his rank might open doors and gain information faster than would be provided to the lieutenant or captain.

Yes, the Spanish ships had sailed past showing no concern for the island's fishermen or their nets. They did not drop anchor but continued to sail on by.

Back aboard the flagship, the charts of the West Coast of Florida was looked at. "I think we could send someone ashore at any of these islands," Waters, the master, said. "We may scare a few pirates to death, thinking we are raiding them, but if they were not seen at one of the islands, then it's unlikely they'd be seen at another."

"Which island would you suggest?" the captain asked.

"Marco, I think, would be my choice. I've been told there's usually a few of the blackguards there. If they did not pass Marco Island, they probably stood out in the Gulf if they did indeed come this way."

Lord Anthony nodded. "Make the necessary signals, Captain Earl."

"Aye, my Lord."

***

Several smaller ships were indeed at Marco Island. "If that's not a privateer anchored there, I'd be surprised," Captain Gregory Kirk whispered to his midshipman.

Lord Anthony had sent *Bulldog* in to shore under a flag of truce. Several seamen lounged about the beach. A few palmetto huts had been built and several tents were spread about. Several blackened spots indicated where large fires had been built. The remains of a roasted goat were still hanging from a spit over one such spot. The rogue, who had come down to meet Kirk's boat, had a British accent, and had surely been a jacktar at some point.

"Got no love for the Dons' I ain't, so I'd tell you truthful like, if we'd spied 'em, but we's been at anchor more'n a week and we ain't seen or heard of the buggers." Pirate he might be, but Kirk believed him, and so did his cox'n.

Hearing this news, Lord Anthony had all captains repair on board and bring their masters or anyone else that might have been aboard who knew the Gulf.

***

Lord Anthony made his way on deck. The dawn horizon had been empty and so he'd gone below to break his fast. The taste of Silas' strong coffee warmed his belly. The sea was still empty except for the long rollers with their white crest. The wind had picked up and you could hear it humming in the riggings.

The master laid a course for Pensacola, Florida. If the Dons were not there, they'd sail to Mobile, Alabama. If there was no sign of them in Mobile, they'd accept it, and admit that they'd made the wrong choice and the Dons had sailed north, up the coast of Florida to God only knew where. Still, Anthony felt they'd sailed to support the attacks on those ports proposed by Bernardo de Gálvez. He felt it. It made sense to take another course if their information had been correct.

With a stiff wind following, Captain Earl had ordered the topsails and forecourse be reefed. With the wind pulling the sailors' slops tight against their bodies, they scurried up to the tops, seemingly with agility and ease.

"Aren't you glad you don't have to climb to the tops in all kinds of weather, Bart?" Lieutenant Mahan asked the burly cox'n.

"I wouldn't mind a bit o' exocise now and then, but I'd not want to do it regular like. Shame 'em I would…wouldn't be fair to 'em, I'm thinkin', to hurt their feelings that way. Course should the need be there, I'd take 'em under me wing so's they'd know 'ow it s'posed to be done."

"I'm sure you could and would," Mahan responded with a smile.

"Aye Lieutenant, never worry, old Bart will pitch in and teach 'em when there's teaching needs to be done."

***

IT WAS SEVEN BELLS in the first watch. The midshipman flipped the hourglass, thinking only a half hour left and he'd be off watch. The wind had calmed down to a moderate breeze. Small waves rolled along with breaking crests and fairly frequent white caps. In the admiral's cabin, Bart was sitting on a soft cushion next to an open stern window, which caused the tobacco smoke to drift out the opening. He was smoking a corncob pipe Dagan had given him. Dagan had gotten it from the Indian Kawliga, at his uncle's horse farm in Virginia. Bart just about had it broken in. It smoked cooler than a clay pipe, but not as cool as a briarwood or meerschaum pipe. Still it was a nice gift and not a bad smoke.

Bart had just cleaned the admiral's sword and was wiping the excess oil off the blade when a cry from the lookout caused him to look up. His Lordship sat in his desk chair napping with his feet propped up on another chair.

"Deck there, sails fine off the starboard bow."

A good lookout, Bart thought, hearing the report. The captain did not have to shout 'where away'.

Lord Anthony rose up and with a smile, looked at his cox'n, "Found them?"

"Aye," Bart answered, hoping that it was the Dons. The lookout had said, 'sails, not 'sail.'

Within moments, the marine sentry stomped the butt of his musket on the deck and answered, "Mr. Prentiss, sir, midshipman of the watch."

Anthony was still in his chair when the midshipman announced, "Captain's compliments, sir, we've sighted several sails, possibly the Spanish ships."

"Thank you, young sir. Inform the captain that I will be on deck presently."

"Aye, aye, my Lord." As the midshipman left the admiral's cabin, he thought, *wait until I get to the midshipman's berth and tell them that with the Dons now in sight, his Lordship just sat there cool as you please while his cox'n cleaned his blade. Might even say he offered me a glass. They'll be envious, no doubt.*

Once on the main deck, the captain looked at the midshipman, "You, Mr. Prentiss."

When the youth didn't respond, Captain Earl called him again, "Mr. Prentiss!"

"Yes, sir."

"I'm sorry to interrupt your daydreaming, but did the admiral send a reply?"

"Oh, yes sir. I'm sorry, sir, Lord Anthony said he'd be up presently."

"Thank you, Mr. Prentiss, I will be watching you."

"Aye, sir."

"Now, get back to your duties."

As the boy rushed off, Earl wondered how many times he'd left the admiral's cabin, his mind awash from the grandeur that lofty soul enjoyed. Little did he realize the responsibility that went with the office.

Moments later, Lord Anthony and Bart came on deck. Captain Earl greeted the admiral and nodded to Bart. "We spotted them, sir. Mr. Hunt went aloft and with his young eyes was able to make out two ships of the line, a pair of frigates, and two smaller ships. Brigs, he thinks."

"My compliments to the young sir on such a fine report," Lord Anthony said.

Standing near, Midshipman Hunt beamed at the admiral's words. Prentiss could say what he wanted, but Hunt would say, 'the admiral recognized me for a fine job.' The thought never occurred to the youth that he might be visiting the cockpit instead of his berth on the orlop deck.

The Spanish ships were still not visible from the deck. "Looks like it will be a long chase," Captain Earl volunteered.

"Aye, close to evening at the earliest, I'd say," Lord Anthony acknowledged. "Speak with Mr. Waters and see if the master has an idea about landfall. They may run all the way to the coast before we close with them."

"Aye, my Lord, I was thinking the same thing. We may have a night action."

Lord Anthony nodded; a long day chase and possibly a night action. The adrenalin of sighting your enemy would long be gone by the time the enemy was brought to battle. The men would be tired and sluggish. He'd rather have a day action but unless the enemy came about to meet them, only God would decide when the action would be.

Pausing a moment, Lord Anthony turned, looked up at the sail and his flag, "Captain, signal

Phoenix...and *Leopard* to close with the enemy. They are faster than *SeaHorse*, so maybe they can stalk them."

"Aye, my Lord." *That cost him*, Captain Earl thought. Sending two lesser ships to stalk the larger ship could easily turn bad if the enemy decided to come about.

It didn't take the ships long to pull away from their positions and pass the flagship once the signal was given. For a fifty-gun ship, *Leopard* put on a good show of speed as she quickly caught up with and passed the flagship. Not as quick and graceful as the greyhound-like frigate, *Phoenix*, but enough. As *Leopard* passed, Gabe stood at the rail and doffed his hat in salute to his brother. With a sense of pride, Lord Anthony waved back.

"A fine officer, Sir Gabe be," Waters said.

"Thank you, that was kindly said," Lord Anthony replied.

Feeling suddenly embarrassed, the master excused himself and went to collect charts of the Gulf Coast.

"He meant it," Bart volunteered. "He was not trying to toady up like some."

CHAPTER ELEVEN

THE ENEMY BRIGS WERE in long cannon range. Generally, in ship-to-ship action, the smaller ships were left out of the battle. However, time was not on the side of the British ships. Gabe fired at the nearest brig with his bow chaser. Short! The next shot splashed water over the stern. With his glass, Gabe watched as there was a flurry of activity with the last ball.

Signals quickly went up, asking for assistance, Gabe guessed. *Phoenix's* guns were now in range and his bow chaser boomed as he fired at the other brig.

"Deck thar, signals from one of the seventy-four's and two frigates have come about."

"Any change with the lead ship?" Gabe called up.

"No sir! Yes sir! Yes Sir! Sir, one o' the Dons' big boys be breaking formation."

This brought a smile to Gabe, "Lieutenant Vallin, make sure that man gets an extra tot this evening."

"Aye, Captain."

Gabe fired two more shots at the brig, and then changed his target to the approaching frigates. The seventy-four was not close enough yet.

"A guinea to the gun crew who finds his target first," Gabe said.

The gun crews worked feverishly to get the guns loaded and sighted in, aimed and fired. The acrid smoke drifted aft toward the quarterdeck. The shots had straddled the leading frigate. The next rounds were true. Both guns scored hits on the bow.

"A guinea for both," Gabe shouted. "Mr. Pittman, let's come about. We've tarried long enough. Mr. Vallin, have the gunners on the starboard lower deck fire as they bear."

"Aye," Lieutenant Vallin said, and then he relayed the word to Lieutenant Laqua, who was in charge of the lower deck.

"First time I seen the cap'n run," a young seaman said to an older petty officer.

"'E ain't running, ye fool. Its tactics, what the cap'n be doing and glad you should be of it. Were 'e to sail on you'd likely be feed for the sharks 'fore long. Foolish idget," the petty officer swore, shaking his head.

The ship was filled with the sound of the gun ports opening and the rumble of the trucks as the carriages were hauled forward, sticking their large black snouts out of the ports. One after another, each big twenty-four pound cannon roared, belching flames as it spewed forth its ball. The last gun captain fired as the ship came about, unsure if they'd scored a hit or not, so dense was the smoke. Above decks the hands were cheering. The ship had completed its turn and was now pulling away from the Dons. To larboard, *Phoenix* had just completed her maneuver.

Laqua took a chance and run up the ladder. Seeing the first lieutenant, he inquired, "Did we aim true?"

"Aye," Vallin said, with a smile. "Our frigate is minus her bow and the foremast is down as well."

Seeing Laqua, Gabe bellowed, "Damned fine target practice I'd say, Mr. Laqua. Every shot told."

Laqua knew the bravado was for the men. He doubted every shot hit, but the captain said so, and so far as he, newly promoted Lieutenant Laqua was concerned they all fell true.

"Huzzah! Huzzah!" The cheers went up.

Turning to his first lieutenant, Gabe ordered, "Make sure our lookout keeps his eyes on that large Don."

"Aye," Vallin replied. "Lord Anthony is near, so we will have to come about." Gabe looked forward and, as Vallin had said, the rest of the ships were fast approaching.

"Signal from the flag," Prentiss called out. "Our number, sir, take station to starboard of flag." He then called again, "*Phoenix* number, sir, they're to take station to larboard."

Gabe had to use his glass to see the signals, dusk was approaching. He heard Vallin telling the master to bring the ship about and take station as directed by the flag.

"He's a good first lieutenant, Gabe," Dagan said. He had walked up and Gabe hadn't even noticed.

Nodding, Gabe said, "It'll be a night action, Uncle."

"Aye, I've had a feeling all along," Dagan replied. His attention now on Dagan, Gabe said no more. If his uncle wanted to expand on his words, he'd do so.

From the masthead, the lookout called down again, "They've gone about, sir. The big Don has taken station at the rear of the formation."

"To protect his brigs, the same as I would do," Gabe said.

The sun seemed to hang on the horizon for a long time, and then not unlike a candle that has burned all the way down, it gave a last wink and was gone.

"Takes a minute to get our night vision," Hex volunteered.

"Aye," someone replied.

Leopard's deck canted as she swung around to take up her station. Now it was a game of nerves.

"Shall I feed the hands by station, Captain?" the first lieutenant asked.

Gabe gave it some thought. "Have the cook and the mess man from each mess break away by section. Cheese and a cold biscuit may be all we have time for."

"Yes sir," Vallin replied, turning to issue the orders.

***

THE NIGHT SEEMED TO be eerily silent. The men had eaten their meager meal at their stations. Nobody was talking. Other than the sounds a ship makes sailing through the water, it was silent.

Overhead, an excited lookout shouted down, "To starboard, a ship, off the starboard beam." The voice was frantic. "A big bitch she be."

"Fire a broadside," Gabe ordered.

The only big ship in the squadron was the flagship, and it was to larboard. The enemy had clamped on all sails and put out its lanterns. A good trick, somebody had imagination. The cannons were hauled into place and one after another the guns fired, not a timed effort, but even with a ragged broadside some of the balls should find their mark.

"Look away, look away from the flashes," Vallin was shouting. *Glad he's on the ball*, Gabe swore to himself. *Had it been left up to me to give the order most of the crew would have night blindness.*

The enemy fired then, the flashes seen before the sounds of the cannons were heard. The tongues of flames were followed by the sounds of balls slamming into *Leopard's* side. The ship was being hit time and time again.

"Aim at the flashes, Mr. Laqua," Gabe shouted. This time, *Leopard's* guns were more uniform as they gave a deafening roar as they were fired.

"The lower deck, Mr. Vallin, have the lower

decks fire. Mr. Laqua, have a measure of grape put atop the balls." The lieutenant saluted with his sword. The enemy was firing again at *Leopard*.

"Faster," Vallin said, "three minutes or less."

Part of the bulwark was shattered, lines and riggings were cut but the mast still held. Some of the balls had entered open gun ports, plowing into a twenty-four pounder and knocking it over and on top of all but the gun captain. The screams of the wounded and dying men could be heard above the cannon fire.

"The flagship is firing to starboard," Vallin announced.

Hopefully, *Phoenix* was not in the mix. She'd never stand such an onslaught. *Leopard* seemed to lurch to leeward as the upper and lower gun decks fired almost at once. Hex was thrown to the deck and was barely missed by a red hot ball that landed just behind him, searing the deck and leaving a huge gouge in the planks. The thick smoke took the air from a man's lungs and made him cough and choke. Another ball slammed into an open port. The ball struck the carriage, sending splinters everywhere as it disintegrated. A powder boy suddenly ceased to be, his body turned into a pulp as it hit the deck, leaving little more than a bloody blob. As bad as *Leopard* was receiving, it seemed that the enemy seventy-four was getting the worst of it.

Dagan grabbed Gabe's arm and pointed to the enemy ship. A ball had struck a gun that was being loaded, igniting the powder bag and now a blaze could be seen through an open gun port. They'd have to take men away from their guns to deal with that or the entire ship would soon be on fire.

"Mr. Laqua," Gabe shouted. "Fire at the flames...direct your fire toward the flames."

Laqua had the guns elevated and aimed. "Fire as you bear," he ordered. "Fire as you bear."

Gabe counted the shots that went off. Three, three guns didn't fire. Three of *Leopard's* upper deck guns were out of action. The flames on the enemy ship grew. Shouting, curses, and threats could be heard coming from the enemy ship. She broke off the battle and swung to starboard.

"A broadside up her arse?" Vallin questioned.

"I think not," Gabe said. "There's no honor in firing on a burning ship. Let's go about setting *Leopard* to rights. The flagship is still firing; we may be called upon to assist."

"Aye," Vallin responded. "But I can hardly see a damn thing. I'm sure had it not been for the enemy's flashes, Laqua would have been firing blindly."

Across the way, the flagship was keeping up a steady barrage and further to leeward two other ships were firing. Gabe felt he should try to add assistance but they could fire on or be fired on by friend as likely as foe. No, it was better to remain on station where she was expected to be unless otherwise signaled by lanterns. Besides, he had no idea how badly his ship was faring. Vallin had the bosun, the carpenter, and their mates going through the ship, checking for damage already.

The lookout called down, "Looks like one of the Don's brigs has pulled alongside the burning ship."

"Taking off her people," Pittman said.

It was the first they'd spoken since the battle had begun. Lieutenant Laqua had climbed the steps to the main deck to ask if he should fire on the brig. The flames had her lit up. Seeing his captain standing there, Laqua turned back. The captain was not one to fire on a rescue ship, enemy or not.

Gabe and Dagan watched as boats quickly crossed back and forth between the brig and the flaming ship. Overhead, a deep rumble was heard, thunder in the distance. As the brig sailed off into the dark, raindrops began to fall; big drops that splattered when they hit the deck. Hex went below to get the captain's tarpaulin. He came back with it in one hand and a cup in the other. Nesbit had managed to heat up a cup of coffee and following Silas, Lord Anthony's servant's, example, he had added a dollop of brandy.

The flagship was no longer firing. Gabe was not sure when the further ships had broken off action. Flares broke out from the flagship and lantern signals were hoisted, heave to. The admiral would lay hove to tonight and see what the dawn offered.

Aboard *Leopard* it would be a sleepless night. The carpenter and his mates were already at it, the thud of their hammers audible on deck.

Vallin came on deck and rushed over to where Gabe stood. Without a coat on, his shirt was quickly soaked to the skin. "Nothing below the water line. They must have thought we were another seventy-four. Most of the damage is from the upper gun deck upwards. A lot of deck planking will have to be replaced." Across the water the flames on the enemy ship were diminishing. "We might be able to salvage the abandoned ship," he said. "A bit of prize money would be pleasing."

"Aye," the master agreed.

Well, things can't be too bad if they can think of prize money, Gabe thought. "At your convenience, Con, pry the purser from his hole and issue a double ration to the men. They deserve it."

"Aye," the lieutenant replied, thinking, *that's the first time a captain has called me by my first name.*

CHAPTER TWELVE

DAWN FOUND THE HORIZON empty except for Lord Anthony's ships and the abandoned seventy-four which, surprising to all, still floated. The rain had barely started when the Spaniards abandoned the ship, thinking the worst. However, there she sat, mast empty of sail and one gun port charred, but no other apparent fire damage. The larboard side, which now faced *Leopard*, was minus a big portion of her upper rails and the jib boom was gone. An anchor hung down where she'd broken loose.

"It's time," Hex spoke to Gabe.

Gabe nodded and looked about the crew, tired but victorious. Gabe looked over at Vallin. The ship lay motionless. The topgallant yards were a-cockbill. Eighteen bodies lay on the deck. Their messmates had placed them each in canvas with two cannon balls at their feet to ensure sinking. The canvas had been sewn, starting from the feet and going upwards. The last stitch placed through the man's nose to make sure he was indeed dead. The bodies were then placed on the eight man mess table and covered with a red insignia. Due to the lack of flags, the men would be buried in groups of six.

The bosun's pipe sounded for the funeral service. Gabe stepped forward as the first lieutenant ordered hats off. Gabe took his prayer book as Dagan handed it to him. Every crewman stood with head bowed. Gabe started to speak but couldn't. He swallowed and tried to take his mind off of the sobs and weeping from men who'd lost their mates.

He read aloud, "I am the resurrection and the life, saith the Lord; he that believeth in me, though he were dead, yet shall he live: and whosoever liveth and believeth in me shall never die."

Gabe then turned the prayer book to the last page where he'd written in and continued, "In the hope of hope of the resurrection to eternal life through our Lord Jesus Christ we commend to the Almighty God our shipmates..."

He then called out the names of those fallen men, six at a time. When a name was called, it was usually met with a few sobs or God bless him. It was rare a man didn't have at least one mate to mourn his passing. Pausing until the last splash was heard, Gabe finished the service, "We commit these bodies to the depths...Ashes to ashes, dust to dust. The Lord bless and keep these men. The Lord make his face to shine upon these men and be gracious unto them. The Lord lift up his countenance upon them and give them peace. Amen."

When it was only one burial, Gabe would usually read the Lord's Prayer but he felt that today brevity was called for.

Vallin dismissed the crew from the funeral service and walked over to his captain. Gabe looked at Vallin and said, "Give the men a quarter hour, and then call away my gig. Put the carpenter, the bosun, and a squad of marines in it and a long boat. You may pick a midshipman and a lieutenant to accompany us. I want to look through that ship before his Lordship calls for his captains to repair on board."

"The flagship has just finished with their funeral service, sir, but the frigate's service seems to still be going on," Vallin informed Gabe.

"Let's not start any hammering or sawing until they have finished," Gabe replied.

"Aye! Sir Gabe, I would have to be sinking before I did anything that would be considered disrespectful."

"I know that, Con."

Going below to change, Gabe told Hex to get his crew together once all services were concluded. Tonight, God willing, he'd try to write to those families who had lost their sons. Midshipman James, whose flowing blonde hair, sunburn nose, ready smile and freckles, had been standing next to Gabe as the captain's messenger when suddenly he dropped to the deck. He was struck by a ball from a marksman, who had probably been aiming at the captain, not the boy. The midshipman was but twelve. How many lieutenants waiting for that lofty goal of command ever thought of these aspects? He hadn't. Eighteen dead, most of them from the upper deck gun crews. Cornish had only reported a dozen or so wounded. Of them, most were only minor injuries.

***

A KNOCK WAS HEARD as the marine sentry announced, "Mr. Jackson, sir, midshipman of the watch." Removing his hat, the midshipman entered the cabin as his captain was putting on his sea boots. He'd worn his dress uniform for the service and now having changed he was putting on his boots.

"Mr. Vallin's compliments, sir, but voices can be heard from the abandoned ship."

"Voices," Gabe repeated.

"Aye, sir. Some of the hands think it's the ghost of them that was left without proper burial."

"Ghost, you say," Gabe repeated, trying not to snicker. "What do you think, Dagan?"

"I don't doubt voices can be heard but it's the wrong moon for ghosts. They only come out with a full moon and last night we had little more than a sliver of moon," Dagan said.

"There you have it, Mr. Jackson. Tell the first lieutenant I will be up directly and..." Gabe leaned forward and whispered, "Tell the crew Dagan said that we had the wrong moon for ghosts."

"Oh yes sir, Captain. Dagan would know." The boy then turned and rushed from the cabin.

"I wonder what stories he'll tell," Dagan asked, causing both he and Gabe to laugh.

Once Gabe and Dagan were back on deck, Vallin reported that the boats were ready. "Lieutenant Laqua and Midshipman Hunter will go over to the abandoned ship with you. Have you heard the voices, Con?" Gabe asked.

"Yes sir, but I couldn't make out what was being said," Con replied.

Nodding, Gabe said, "You'd best send one of the lieutenants over to the flag and let them know we are investigating voices from the enemy ship. And Con!"

"Sir!"

"Don't mention the ghost."

"No sir," the first lieutenant replied, smiling. "But I'm sure his Lordship would enjoy such a concern."

"Bart would anyway," Dagan threw in.

"Lieutenant Bufford," Vallin called, as he walked away. "Please carry a message to the flagship. Voices have been heard from the abandoned enemy ship. Boats are being sent to investigate."

The captain's gig led off toward the abandoned ship. They'd gone about half-way when they could hear the voices. One of the oarsmen broke time as the sound appeared to frighten the seaman.

"Mind your oars," Hex snapped. "Give way all. Jumpy bunch they are, Captain, but if one does such a foolish stunt again, he'll be working for the purser, that he will." Hex's comments caused a few snickers. Winking at his captain, Hex ordered, "Quiet in the boat."

Once they were along side, Lieutenant Laqua called, "Captain, do you recognize her?"

Gabe's mind had been on what it would take to have the ship made ready for sail. But now that Laqua had mentioned it, she was familiar.

"She's *Comete*," Dagan said. "The ship you captured and the Dons took from the admiral."

Dammit, it was *Comete*. Once the boat was made fast, Gabe sped up the side of the ship and through the entry port. Dagan was behind him and then Laqua, the carpenter, and bosun.

"Call out, Hex."

"Ahoy, mates, ahoy."

The longboat was hooked on and Midshipman Hunter came aboard, followed by the marines. "Forward, sir. I think they are forward." Moving rapidly through the ship, voices were heard as they moved toward the fo'c'sle.

"They're British," Dagan said. "They've been locked in the fo'c'sle."

The door leading into the fo'c'sle was padlocked. "You there, Sergeant," Gabe addressed the marine sergeant, "Have someone pry this hasp off."

A big marine came forth and, removing his bayonet from his musket, he picked at the wood until he could pry the metal clasp from the wood, which made a groaning sound as it gave way. The door was flung open and the first man Gabe saw was *Trident's* old master, Mr. Hayes.

"Thank God, sir, you are a sight for these old eyes."

Gabe couldn't help but smile as several of his old crew stepped forward, and there at the rear stood his nemesis, Admiral Kirkstatter. "Sir Winston," Gabe said.

"Captain," the admiral replied.

CHAPTER THIRTEEN

ADMIRAL, I THINK YOU should come see this."
Lord Anthony looked up at the smiling face of
his flag captain.

"Is it that amusing, Stephen?"

"I would say so, my Lord, although some might
call it due justice."

"Come on, Bart, let's go see what my flag captain has found to excite such a smile."

As the trio left the cabin, they ran into Lieutenant Mahan. He had just left the main deck to inform the admiral of a sighting, but a quick finger to the lips to hush him made him stand aside.

"Come along, Patrick, I can see you're about to bust a gut but let's not spoil our captain's fun." Gabe's gig, followed by a longboat, was headed to the flagship. Huzzah's had gone up as they rowed past *Leopard*.

Captain Earl handed the admiral a glass, "Look who's sitting beside Gabe, my Lord."

Taking the glass, Lord Anthony focused in and then swore. "Well damme, just damme. Captain Earl, prepare to give our visitors due honors."

"Aye, my Lord, we wanted you to see it first. There are several of our seamen in the longboat including Lieutenant Hawks and *Trident's* old master, Mr. David Hayes. Wonder, sir, just 'ow many times Gabe...Cap'n Anthony has gotta take that bloody ship?"

"Do you recognize her, Bart?"

"Aye, Admiral, just like I'd recognize me own mom. She be the *Comete*, what Cap'n Anthony took last year. Now 'e's took 'er again. Do yew get prize money twice, I'm wondering."

"You scoundrel," Lord Anthony snapped. "Think of the people."

"Oh, I is, sir. A little extra prize money would come in handy to more'n a few."

"Us being in sight didn't fit in to your thoughts did they?"

"No, but now you mentioned it I'd not turn down a guinea or two," Bart said.

Captain Earl interrupted Bart's banter. "Do you know, my Lord, what Gabe did with a six-ty-four, he's now done with a fifty gun ship. They were never made to stand in the line of battle."

"You're right, Captain, but for a lucky shot the outcome might have been much different."

"Aye, you're right, my Lord, but we can't think about 'might haves', we have to deal with what did happen. And what happened was a British captain in a fifty gun ship defeated a Spaniard in a seventy-four. We sunk one but it was an equal fight. We were supposed to win. We'd never live it down if we lost. It may be Dagan's luck or any number of reasons. But the facts are the facts.

Now, my only question is will Sir Winston have changed his mind?"

"He damn well better have, Captain, or I'll make sure he's put ashore never to command again."

"That may be done for you, sir. He will have to answer to a court martial on how he lost his ship. He can't place all the blame on *Comete's* captain."

"We'll see," Lord Anthony replied. "When he comes aboard, you can escort him down to my cabin. Then after a few minutes, duty will require you on deck. You and Lieutenant Mahan talk with Lieutenant Hawks."

"What about Gabe, sir?"

"I'm sure he has duties enough putting his ship and the...ah, prize back to rights. Tell him I expect a full report once the prize has been evaluated."

"Aye, should I have the skylight closed in case voices are raised?"

Lord Anthony thought for a minute. "I'm tempted to say let the men hear what's going on, so they'll know everyone is held accountable regardless of rank. However, closing it would be the honorable and respectful thing to do."

***

FOR THE REST OF the day the ship's company went about the work of putting *Leopard* and *Comete* to rights as best as they could. The wounded were brought on deck. Dr. Cornish thought the fresh air and sunshine would be better for their wounds than the stale air below. Gabe watched and wondered how the men could work so hard after going through such a battle as last evening.

"They are just glad to be alive," Dagan whispered. "Mourning will only worsen things. It's good we have something to keep them busy."

Busy they were. The sound of hammers and saws echoed across the water as carpenters and their mates were making progress. The sail-maker and his men had their needles out, sewing canvas and repairing sails. The bosun had his mates busy with riggings, paint and tar. At sunset, Gabe called a halt to the work. The majority of the work needed on *Leopard* was done. She was ready to sail and fight. *Comete* still needed much work but she could sail, and with a larger crew fight if need be.

Several of the ships in the squadron followed the flag's suit and sent skilled craftsmen over to help. *Phoenix* also had to have much repair. She had taken on two frigates. Jepson on *Revenant* engaged one of the frigates while Lieutenant Kirk and Lieutenant Montgomery were able to engage the brigs. Both the brigs got away, one apparently coming to the aid of the burning *Comete*; the other sailed into the darkness. One of the Spanish frigates now sat low in the water, her decks all but awash. The other drifted, mastless. The seventy-four that engaged *SeaHorse* sank in the night. The remaining seventy-four never engaged in battle and, like the brigs, disappeared in the black of the night.

"Boat ahoy!" The challenge sounded from *SeaHorse's* watch. The reply rang out by Gabe's cox'n, *Leopard*. Gabe climbed aboard the flagship, careful not to drop his reports. His brother was there to meet him. Dagan and Hex followed Bart to his quarters. A bottle of rum and three cups were all sitting on a small table.

"I know a few lieutenants that would like to have quarters like these," Hex volunteered.

"It's called position and seniority," Bart japed. "'ow's Gabe?" he asked.

"He's strained," Dagan admitted. "He's trying to write letters to the families of some of the dead. It's not easy."

"I's seen 'is Lordship fret over wording many a time. I's seen them that felt guilty that they's alive when so many 'as been put over the side."

In the admiral's cabin, Gabe enjoyed a glass of hock. The white German wine was usually kept in the bilge by Silas. That made it cooler than room temperature but not chilled. While he enjoyed the wine he marveled at how the craftsman had made the long stem. Not every glass blower was as good at his craft. Looking over his glass, he could see his brother reading his reports and making notes he would question Gabe about later. They had already discussed the Dons' poor gunnery.

"I think in the dark, they must have thought us to be another seventy-four. Numerous shots had gone overhead at the start of the engagement while ours were aimed true. The deck received a lot of damage as guns were depressed," Gabe said.

Lord Anthony then picked up Gabe's report and began to read. Nothing had been said about Sir Winston. Gil would address this subject when the time came. "So you consider Lieutenant Hawks a suitable prize master to send the *Comete* back to Antigua, do you?"

"Yes sir."

"And why did you recommend Antigua as opposed to Jamaica?"

"In truth or my official reasons?" Gabe asked. "Officially, I know Admiral Moffett assures the work done by the dockyard there. In truth, if she's sent to Antigua, you will have greater control of the ship. She would make a fine command for one of your senior captains."

"Anyone in particular?" Gil asked his brother.

"Captain Frostbrier would be my choice," Gabe replied.

"Not you?" Gil asked, surprised at his brother's answer. "What would I do with *Phoenix*?"

"Now, I'm sure you have several Captains who could fill the vacancy," Gabe said, smiling.

"Including you?" Gil asked.

"Yes sir. I'm sure I would be in the mix. If indeed *Leopard's* captain survives and is able to assume command of her."

"Do you like her?" Gil asked and then added, "I

know a lot of people who feel the fifties have no place in line of battle. They do a fair job in places like the Caribbean where you deal with shallow waters. Do you think *Leopard* would have opposed a seventy-four in the daytime?"

"No sir, I'm under no illusions."

"Then we agree," Gil said, sounding more like the admiral than the brother. "I'm having all of the captains to dinner tonight and go over the reports we've been able to get from several of our officers and seaman who were being held aboard *Comete* while the Dons had her. It's a shame so many of her officers were killed. Her captain and two lieutenants died in the first exchange according to Lieutenant Hawks."

CHAPTER FOURTEEN

SEAMEN GATHERED ON THE fo'c'sle. The sun was going down, the darkness bringing a breath of coolness from the heat of the day. The sea seemed to be getting up as *Leopard*, *Bulldog*, *Tomahawk*, and *Lynx* sailed in a loose formation.

They had just sailed past the Florida Keys and soon would head on a northerly course up the coast of Florida to Savannah. There, Sir Winston Kirkstatter would report to the Royal Governor. The two would then decide if Sir Winston would remain on station, using a frigate as his flagship and awaiting instructions from the Admiralty, or he might decide to sail back to England in the next dispatch vessel.

Lord Anthony had taken statements from Lieutenant Hawks, the master, Mister Hayes, and the gunner. The statements along with the admiral's report would be delivered to the admiral in Jamaica.

Sir Winston had been aloof but was not vocal as he had been toward Gabe at Barbados. Bart, never one to hold back his thoughts in the privacy of Lord Anthony's cabin, bluntly stated, "'E came in like a lion, now 'e's going back like a lamb. 'E's all aback, that'n is."

Lord Anthony frowned at the liberty taken by his cox'n, but in truth he agreed. Still, he hated to see the admiral humiliated. Had he been notified that Spain was now an ally of the Americans, things might have turned out differently...the almighty if.

***

ON BOARD *LEOPARD*, HEX with his mandolin, and a couple of seamen sawing away at their fiddles had a jaunty little jig going.

> *Singin', blow, ye winds, in the mornin',*
> *Blow, ye winds, high – ho!*
> *Clear away yer runnin' ger*
> *An' blow, me bully boys blow!*

No sooner had the three musicians ended the tune when a seaman called out, "Hex, be a good mate and play the one about the mermaid."

Hex plucked at a string tuning his instrument, "It'll cost ye a swig of yer grog. Ye grog face villain."

This set several seamen to japing with their mess mate. Hex plucked once more, turning the tuning key until he was satisfied. "Half your ration it is now." Then without waiting Hex and the fiddle players started.

> *'Twas Friday morn when we set sail*
> *And we were not far from the land*
> *When the Captain, he spied a pretty mermaid*
> *With a comb and a glass in her hand.*
> *Oh, the ocean waves do roll*
> *And the stormy winds do blow*

While we poor sailors go
Skipping on the top
And the lubber lie down below.

"You have a happy ship, Captain."

Startled, Gabe turned. It was Sir Winston. "Aye, Sir Winston, but I can only claim a handful. The rest sailed under *Leopard's* original captain."

"Nevertheless, Sir Gabe, they are yours now," the admiral responded using Gabe's title. "They would give their all for you. I wonder what it would have been like had I a man such as you." He then turned and left as silently as he appeared.

"I think that was as close to an apology as you will get," Dagan whispered. Gabe looked into his uncle's eyes; piercing eyes that seem to look right into a man's soul.

When Dagan did not continue, Gabe spoke, "Come below with me, Uncle. I could use a cup of cocoa and one of Nesbit's pastries."

***

"LAND HO!"

"That will be Grand Cayman," Pittman, the master advised.

Gabe was not sorry to finally be back at the rendezvous point. Gabe and the company of ships had met up with John Jenkins and *Zebra* at the northern border of Florida, almost to Georgia. Sir Winston had transferred to *Zebra* and Gabe was almost sorry to see him go. The admiral had asked to use the service of Nesbit, understanding that while the man was Gabe's chef and servant, he was also a man of education. He had had Nesbit make a fair copy of his report to the Admiralty, in which he was highly commendable of Gabe.

He'd ordered Nesbit to not present his captain with the copy until he, the admiral, had taken his leave from the ship. Reading the report, Gabe felt vindicated and was only wishing something could have been mentioned in regards to Lord Skalla.

After transferring the admiral to *Zebra*, Gabe sailed to Bermuda and then the small squadron weaved its way through the Bahamas. They spotted a fast schooner off the Grand Bahamas' Island, but before *Tomahawk* could be ordered to investigate, the ship had clamped on more sails and was over the horizon in no time. They stopped at Nassau but left on the evening tide. They then made a sweep through several of the Bahamian Islands and cays, sending the smaller ships to look in at Eleuthera Island, which was very long but hardly a mile wide; Cat Island, San Salvador Island, Rum Cay, Long Island, Crooked Island, and finally Acklins Island before turning westerly passing Ragged Island, around Cuba and then southeast to Grand Cayman. *Bulldog*, *Lynx*, and *Tomahawk* had taken turns, often circling the islands before meeting back up with *Leopard*.

They met several fishing boats along the way. The ship would heave to and they would buy some fish, crabs, and small lobsters from the fishermen. The King's gold loosened up tongues where threats would have gained nothing. The islanders were amazed to find *Lynx* commanded by a black man. Feeling a kinship with Lieutenant Montgomery, they offered up more information than might have otherwise been obtained, even with the spreading of gold coins.

The forenoon watch was being relieved. Lieutenant Bufford had just assumed the watch when the lookout called out again. Lieutenant Tolbert paused to hear the information before going down to a quick meal and nap. "Deck there! Flagship at anchor." *Damn, time for a bite but not for a nap*, Tolbert thought.

The water in the harbor at Georgetown was a deep blue. A white sandy beach seemed to stretch on as far as the eye could see. Gulls hovered overhead and then plunged into the harbor's still water after some small fish. Gabe could soon see the flagship and others of the squadron.

"Let's look lively," Gabe said to the master and Lieutenant Bufford. "Make sure the guns are unshotted when we fire the salute. I'd hate to be on the admiral's bad side for holing his flagship."

"Aye, sir."

Lieutenant Laqua had walked on deck, and seeing the rail lined with seamen, he snapped, "Mr. Jackson, clear those idlers away from the rail."

"Aye, sir," the midshipman replied and hurried to carry out his order.

"May we begin the salute, Captain?" Lieutenant Bufford asked. Gabe nodded.

"Open ports, remove tampions," Bufford bellowed. "Mr. Abraham, you may commence the salute."

Abraham, the gunner, walked from gun to gun, counting out the timing using the old 'if I weren't a gunner, I wouldn't be here, number one fire'. The guns crashed out, firing the traditional salute. The slight breeze that blew caused the cannon smoke to drift toward the flagship.

"I wouldn't be smiling were I you," Dagan said. "He may have a glass on you. If he sees you sneering, you might find yourself pushing wares from a bumboat."

"Aye," Gabe replied, trying to hide his smile. "Mr. Vallin!"

"Aye, Captain."

"Pending my visit to the flag, if we are to remain in port a few days you may allow liberty."

"Aye, sir...ah!"

"Is there something else, Mr. Vallin?"

"Yes sir. I'm not familiar with the captain's view on 'wives aboard ship'."

"No wives, Mr. Vallin. I would hate to receive urgent sailing orders and have to weigh wives before we weigh anchor."

"Aye, Captain."

Hearing the captain's remarks, several of the seamen laughed. "What's 'e mean, weigh wives?" one of the newer hands asked.

"Johnson, you slack-arsed idler you," a petty officer rebuked the man. "What kind o' bloody lubber, are ye anyway? Gawd!"

Now it was Hex who had to smile. He looked at Dagan and swore, "He'll latch on to some double poxed doxy and spend what little money she doesn't take on mercury treatments."

"Better have one of his mates stir him toward the surgeon's mate. See if he has a cundums for sale," Dagan replied.

"Aye," Hex agreed, but secretly thinking, *not before I check on it first*.

CHAPTER FIFTEEN

Marie Galante was exotic: a black-eyed, black haired woman whose skin was the color of a light coffee. A cup that was long on cream. A woman who was as bewitching as anyone Jacob Hex had ever seen; a widow...a young widow, whose husband was killed in a duel fighting with a previous suitor. That both men were killed enhanced the gossip that this woman was indeed a witch. A woman who Bart would swear made it necessary to put a Bible under your pillow to ward off the spells she could cast on a man. Hex was no different than any other man; perhaps being at sea weakened his ability to think straight. The minute he walked into the tavern and saw her sitting by an open window he was smitten.

The sign above the door proclaimed the establishment to be The Forbidden Siren. The picture drawn below the name was that of a mermaid.

"Somebody didn't know about sirens," Dagan said. "A mermaid has a woman's upper body and a fish's lower body, whereas a siren has a bird's body from the waist down."

"Neither would do a poor sailor's humors much good, would they?" Hex joked. That was before he saw Marie.

After finding a table, the two ordered a tankard each and roast kid. While listening to Dagan, Hex found himself stealing glances at the witch woman who boldly looked back. Soon, she picked up a guitar and sang a sad ballad of the sea.

A smile on Dagan's face, he said, "No siren did ever so charm the ear of the listener as the listening ear has charmed the soul of the siren." Hex stared at Dagan dumbstruck. "Shakespeare," Dagan answered Hex's unasked question.

Not five minutes later, Marie walked to the table. Grasping Hex's hand, she looked at Dagan and said, "You'll excuse us, I'm sure."

Rising, Dagan bowed and answered, "I'm sure."

After taking a few steps, Hex stopped and turned, "You'll see after the captain, won't you?" Still smiling, Dagan nodded his affirmative.

The next day, Hex went aboard *Leopard* to be greeted by the master, "Where you been, Hex? Dagan's doing your duties."

"Aye," was Hex's only response.

Gabe was sitting at his desk signing papers for the purser. "Captain," Hex spoke. Looking up, Gabe paused with his quill in mid-air.

"Yes," Gabe said.

"I would like to have a few days leave if it wouldn't be an inconvenience, sir," Hex replied.

Damn, Hex is being so proper, Gabe thought. Not that he'd ever been anything else, but this was different. Almost like the first time he'd spoken to him about being the cox'n. "Of course, Jake, how many days do you want?"

"Ah...how long will we be in port, sir."

"A week, I'd guess," Gabe replied.

"A week then, sir," Hex said.

"Alright, but make sure Dagan knows how to find you."

"No worries, sir, I will stay in touch," Hex replied.

Ink dripped from the quill on to the report Gabe was to sign. "Damn," he snapped.

"Sir?" Hex stopped and turned.

"Nothing, Jake, have a good time," Gabe said.

Smiling, Hex replied, "I intend to, Captain, I intend to."

***

A KNOCK WAS GIVEN and the marine announced, "First lieutenant, sir."

Vallin came in and handed Gabe a note, "A man is here from the island's chief resident, Sir. He states he's to wait for a reply."

Reading the note, Gabe looked up at Vallin, "There's to be a ball at the chief resident's house this evening, Con. We, you and I, are invited."

"Hmm, might prove interesting," the lieutenant said.

"Oh no," Gabe said, shaking his head. "First, my cox'n and now my first lieutenant overflowing in humors."

"Shall I inform the man we will accept the

chief resident's invitation?" Vallin asked.

"Aye, I'm sure his Lordship would frown did we not show."

***

A LINE OF CARRIAGES were parked along the jetty. Looking at Vallin, Gabe said, "It seems we are to be transported in style."

"Unless one of those carts further back is for us," Vallin joked.

"If it is we'll find this tavern where Hex spends his time," Gabe responded. "I'd love to see the woman who has snared my cox'n anyway."

A young, black livery servant stepped up to Gabe and Vallin. His breeches were red while his coat and vest were white with red trim and a red collar. He wore white silk stockings. His shoes were black with silver buckles. Taking a look at Gabe's card he opened the door to the carriage.

"The driver will take you to Pedro Saint James, sir," the livery servant said.

As they got in the carriage, Vallin commented, "An educated servant."

The carriage moved along at a good clip, and Gabe was dozing when the carriage turned down a road shaded by mango and mahogany trees. The horses seemed to strain as they pulled the carriage up a rise where it stopped. A footman opened the door and the two stepped out to see a three story house built of coral stone and wood. Huge white pillars helped hold the house up where the stone walls ended. Looking about,

Gabe could see where pineapples and bananas were planted. The walkway was lined with palm trees, and with tropical plants planted between the trees. A great lawn covered the area to where a bluff dropped away but giving one a spectacular view of the Caribbean.

"Magnificent," Vallin said in awe of his surroundings.

As Gabe and Lieutenant Vallin approached the huge doors at the chief resident's house, two handsomely attired footmen appeared and opened the doors. Once inside the foyer, a servant took their hats. A cacophony of music and voices filled the room.

Vallin leaned over to Gabe and whispered, "Sounds like a cage of monkeys I once saw." Gabe smiled but didn't respond as the majordomo took his card and announced, "Sir Gabriel Anthony, Captain, *HMS Leopard*." A few people looked his way and clapped. Vallin was then announced.

One man, somewhat more elegantly dressed than the others, walked toward Gabe, "Gabe, Sir Gabe."

"Yes."

"I'm William Eden. Thank you for joining our festivities."

"Is there a special occasion?" Gabe asked.

"Yes, my wife's niece has just turned twenty-one."

"My congratulations," Both Gabe and Vallin said in unison.

"May I present my first lieutenant, Con Vallin."

"Vallin! I seem to recall a Vallin on my trip to Scotland," Eden said.

"Possibly my father or grandfather," Vallin responded. "My father, like his father, is Lord Fergus Vallin of Glasgow." Seeing the puzzled look, a look that Con was used to, he explained, "My father was somewhat of a wayward youth. My mother, his first wife, was an Indian princess. She had the misfortune to die in childbirth."

"It's with sorrow, I hear of your misfortune. Still you come from a good family," Eden paused as if unsure whether to continue and then went ahead, "You will find there are many cases where a son has been sent to the islands, where he is accepted without question by most. A number of them without the benefit of his parents being wed." Gabe winced. If Eden saw it, he made no move or comment.

A woman with a young lady in tow walked up. Mr. Eden introduced his wife and niece. "Dear, other carriages have arrived," Mrs. Eden informed her husband.

"We will talk later," Eden said with a smile. "Get these nice gentlemen a glass, will you?" Eden requested, speaking to the niece.

"This way, please," she invited. The young lady wore a gown of pale blue. It was cut wide and low, showing off a pair of suntanned shoulders and an ample amount of the tops of her breasts.

They were just as tan as her shoulders. She wore a necklace of diamonds that sparkled when the light hit them. The tanned neck and shoulders seemed to attract more attention than the diamonds. She turned taking both men, one on each arm, and walked to a table where glasses were being filled.

"We have a fruity wine, a rum punch," and leaning forward, she spoke in a whisper, "a weak rum punch, and a punch made with melons, bananas, and oranges." Leaning forward as she did made both Gabe and Vallin look at the unblemished view. Gabe recovered but she caught Vallin, "You'll not find any punch there."

"My apologies, mademoiselle," Vallin muttered. "Your beauty is breathtaking."

Smiling, the beautiful creature said, "Not mademoiselle. Hannah. My name is Hannah Bodden."

"I'm Con Vallin and..."

"I know who you are," Hannah interrupted. "I listened when you were announced."

"Are we to understand that this is your birthday?" Gabe asked.

"My birthday celebration, Sir Gabe. My birthday was several days ago, but we had to wait until today for the planters."

"I see," Gabe replied.

The music stopped again and the majordomo announced, "Vice Admiral, Lord Gilbert Anthony, Commander and Chief of His Majesty's Navy in the Caribbean."

Thinking that this was the opportune time to make his departure, Gabe bowed to Hannah, "My apologies, Hannah. There are some pressing matters that I need to discuss with Lord Anthony." Vallin's eyes lit up when his captain made his departure.

Hannah looked at Vallin, "I'm not stupid. He left so we could be alone. That's his brother," she continued. "He can talk to him anytime."

"I'm afraid that we are caught. Do you mind?" Vallin asked.

"No," Hannah replied, handing him her glass. "I'll be right back."

Not wanting to be seen holding two glasses, Con sat one down. Just before Hannah returned, a woman, who appeared to be in her thirties, walked over and gave Con a smile. Her gown was even bolder than Hannah's. It was cut very low and when she leaned over to get a glass she could have easily reached standing up, Vallin thought, *she may as well have had nothing on.*

"Mrs. Patton, how nice to see you," Hannah said.

"Oh, dear child, you have grown into such a young lady. Soon you will be a woman." The statement was made with Mrs. Patton's eyes darting toward Vallin.

He bowed and said, "A pleasure." Mrs. Patton made an exaggerated bow, flashing her wares once more.

Hannah put her arm through Vallin's and said, "You promised to introduce me to the admiral,

Lieutenant." Walking away, Hannah asked, "Can you believe that brazen woman. No more than a tavern's whore showing her wrinkled tits. Mine are much prettier."

Raising his eyebrows, Vallin thought, *a different breed these island girls*. "Where did you go?" he asked politely.

"To have your place card changed, so you'll be sitting by me. But if I catch you with that whore, I'll have it thrown away and you'll do without," Hannah replied.

Without what, Vallin wondered, but didn't ask.

CHAPTER SIXTEEN

SEEING CAPTAIN ALBRIGHT AND Captain Neil at William Eden's house was really no surprise but when Albright shook the admiral's hand, he leaned forward and said softly, "We need to talk when it's convenient."

"You are welcome to come aboard my ship," Anthony replied, wondering what was on Albright's mind.

"No, that would be noticed. Let's walk outside for a smoke. There are chairs and a swing that overlooks the ocean. I'll meet you there in half an hour if his Lordship is agreeable."

When Anthony nodded, Albright walked on. Should anyone be watching it looked no more than a greeting. Seeing their host, Anthony made a point in telling Eden what a wonderful meal they'd eaten.

"Are you a card player, my Lord?" Eden asked.

"No, my flag lieutenant is a fair hand." He said this while clapping Mahan on the shoulder.

"I'm average," the lieutenant responded.

"Well, we have several guests who enjoy a game. Perhaps, you'd like to join in."

"I'd be glad to, but I'm afraid that I didn't bring any money with me," Mahan said.

"I will loan you enough," Eden said. "These men are poor players so you should not have to worry. I think they play cards so that they have an excuse not to dance."

As Mahan walked away, Anthony engaged Eden in more conversation. "I'm curious as to the title Chief Resident."

"In truth, it has no authority. Grand Cayman comes under the authority of the Governor of Jamaica. When the island feels we have a need in addressing the governor, I usually lead the delegation. The Boddens, Hannah's grandparents, was one of the first families to settle on the island in the early 1700's. The island has mahogany, cotton, sarsaparilla, and of course the turtles. The turtles are not as many as they once were, but they still remain a fair way of support for many."

"I see your blacks tend to be educated," Anthony said.

"That is true, my Lord. Most of the islanders on Cayman do not believe in slavery and I expect it to be done away with before too many more years," Eden replied.

"By educating some of the slaves, you will have set in place educated men who can help others of their race make a living," Anthony said.

Eden's wife walked up, "William, you simply must come watch Hannah dance with this dashing Navy officer. My pardon, my Lord."

"No, go on," Anthony replied. "I think I will

take in a bit of the evening air and smoke one of these cigars you've so graciously provided."

"Come along, William," his wife said.

"Enjoy the cigar," Eden replied, speaking over his shoulder as he was being pulled away.

***

SILAS HAD CUT UP melons, mangos, bananas, and pineapple. This was placed into small bowls and cups of sugar were put between every third bowl. Cold biscuit and cheese was also laid out. A rum punch was served. This had been made early that morning, poured into jars and placed in the bilges to cool. Most of the fruit had come from the grounds of Pedro St James. Anthony made a note to himself to be sure to thank the Chief Resident for his generosity.

Gabe had been summoned prior to the other captains. Once aboard the flagship, Gabe was greeted by Stephen Earl. "Have Dagan brought aboard and then send your boat back to *Leopard*." Earl's order was out of the ordinary, but Gabe spoke to Dagan, and then to his temporary cox'n, who gave the boat crew their instructions. Once in the admiral's cabin, Gabe and Dagan were told to have a seat. His Lordship soon appeared followed by his flag captain, Stephen Earl; his flag lieutenant, Patrick Mahan and Bart.

Without being offered refreshment, Lord Anthony motioned for the group to sit. "Where is your cox'n, Gabe?" Anthony asked, coming right to the point.

"I gave him a few days off," Gabe responded, wondering what this was about and what had Hex gotten himself into.

"Do you know where he is?"

"In general, but Dagan could tell you exactly. May I ask what this is all about?" Gabe asked.

"I have been given reliable information that this woman, who has enticed your cox'n, is in league with the privateers. Ships were seen leaving the north side of the island and Marie Galante was seen on the beach talking to one of the captains. We have reason to believe this woman may be using Hex in hopes of gaining information related to the ships' movements and such."

Gabe rose in defense of his cox'n, "Sir, I don't believe that my cox'n would ever divulge any information, in regards to our ships."

"Bart said the same thing," Anthony admitted. "In fact, no one in the cabin thought him to be culpable. Nevertheless, today at lunch I will announce the squadron will depart for Jamaica. From there, we will send out patrols looking for the French. This is in fact true. A vessel was sent from Jamaica with the news. We will all weigh anchor at the same time but once we reach Jamaica, you Gabe, *Bulldog* and *Lynx* will set a course for the Bahamas. Dagan and Bart will go ashore tonight and loudly fetch Hex, making sure they let anyone who will listen know their thought on visiting Jamaica where the rum runs free and the women freer."

***

LORD ANTHONY'S SHIPS HAD just set sail when the sky turned grey. The watch was miserable, first the heat and now a misty rain. Steam rose from hot decks as the misty rain cooled them down.

"The ropes are sure to swell," Vallin said, pointing out the obvious.

Pittman gave a nod but didn't otherwise speak. He knew that the rain soaked riggings would have a time of it passing through blocks and sheaves. In all likelihood, he'd have to send someone to clear the blockage.

Land was just below the horizon when a cry came from the lookout, "Sail ho!"

"Where away," Vallin shouted in a voice so strong the speaking trumpet was not needed. "Heave to!" Vallin ordered.

Just before they set sail a message from the admiral had told them to expect a fishing boat once clear of land. The boat carried a special passenger. Once the boat, a fishing smack, pulled alongside a nimble young man leaped across the short distance between the smack and *Leopard's* side. Grabbing the man rope, he climbed up the battens and through the entry port. Before he could be taken below to the captain's cabin, a sail was hauled up the smack's single mast. The smack came about and headed back toward Grand Cayman.

Gabe had sent for his cox'n, Vallin, the master,

and Dagan. After cooling refreshments were served, Gabe introduced the young man.

"This is Jeremy Albright, Captain Albright's son. If you recall, it was Captain Albright who requested Lord Anthony to send a squadron to the area. He and several others had been used most terribly by privateers. Mr. Albright, I turn it over to you."

"Thank you, Captain. The boat which brought me to your ship belongs to a fisherman, a friend of my father's. He does most of his fishing in the North Sound and Rum Point, over to North Side and Old Man Bay. Our fishing boat is a regular sight and most fishermen are usually a closed mouth group, so nobody pays them much attention. About a year ago, several of us was asked if we'd like to run a load of turtle meat and other food products to Cat Island."

Vallin went to speak, but Gabe shook his head not to interrupt. Taking a drink from his glass the boy paused and then started talking again. "We pulled into Cutlass Bay near Bain Town. Several ships were anchored there. As we unloaded our fish and turtles, a steady line of men carried crates and things to a hole in the ground where a hoist had been set up."

"A cave?" Gabe asked.

"That would be my guess, sir. I'd stepped off the trail to relieve myself and when I stood up I was face to face with a rogue."

"'What are you doing?' he asked.

"'Relieving myself', I replied. He shoved me aside and looked at the spot, using a torch to see. Grabbing my collar, he shoved me back toward the beach and said, 'Next time go down the beach a ways. Somebody will likely step in it here.' I apologized and ran back to our boat."

"How does Marie Galante enter into this?" Gabe asked.

"Well, she sells her rum cheaper than most and she's always got plenty. Besides, her husband, who was a Frenchman, was known to associate with pirates and smugglers. Men would come in and talk about when they were sailing, what they were carrying and the next thing you know you can't remember seeing them for a while. Most men would tell everything they knew once Marie sat with them and sang a song or two, and gave a sailor just enough to look at or a slight touch and they'd be all mouth."

Gabe understood what effect a woman, especially a beautiful woman, could have on sailors. Looking to his cox'n Hex, Gabe asked, "What was your impression?"

"She could easily be a temptress. I was with her day and night for several days and she did ask leading questions about how long we'd have together and when would we be leaving, would we be going far and could she expect to have me back before long." What Hex didn't say was the questions usually came before or after they'd been in bed together. Just that morning after a vigorous tryst, she had embraced him whispering she didn't know how she could survive without him. She hoped he'd be back soon. Fortunately he didn't know, otherwise she had seemed so genuine that he'd most likely have told her without thinking.

"You were with her every night?"

Hex went to reply and then thought for a minute before he answered. "Most nights, but my second night ashore, she begged off stating she had business to attend to. She was back before dawn and woke me as she...as she made ready for bed."

Everyone smiled not at what was said but what Hex didn't say.

CHAPTER SEVENTEEN

THE SMELL OF RUM was obvious as Gabe, Dagan, and Hex walked through the seamen's berth spaces. No doubt, a seaman had given his mates a little extra of their rations knowing they were in for a long night...a night in which some might not return. The men were gathered in little groups enjoying what little rest they could before being called to man the boats.

"You be going wid us, Cap'n?" a seaman asked.

"Of course," Gabe responded. "You don't think I'd let you have all the fun ashore, did ya?"

The little group laughed. Gabe always liked to walk among his men when such an assignment came up. It helped to let them know he'd be at their side.

"Reckon they's any loose plunder where we be going," another seaman asked.

"I don't know," Gabe replied. "If any is found make sure you share with your captain. I'm married with a family now. Any married man will tell you, trying to satisfy a woman's desires takes a might of doing." This got another laugh from the group.

"That's why ole Ned's got so many mates,

Cap'n. He pays the rent while we's keeps 'er clothes up."

There was more laughter. Ole Ned was a sixty year old seaman who claimed he had a wife and seven children.

"Said he'd went to sea to get away from the lot." The remark of his mates keeping her clothes up caused all to laugh including Ned.

"I've no worries, Cap'n. Brown,'e ain't used 'is wedding tackle in so long 'e's forgot what it's for 'cepting to piss," Ned said.

Gabe had reached the ladder to go up on deck. He turned and said, "Keep close and keep your ears open tonight. Any plunder you find better fit in your pocket, otherwise it'll have to be inventoried." He started up the ladder and then turned and paused. "Brown, wasn't that you with two of those wenches at the Forbidden Siren. From the looks of those lusty young ladies, you must have something to charm them. I doubt that Hex, young bull that he is, could have satisfied the two at one time."

"It were a man-sized job, Cap'n, but I couldn't let the reputation of *Leopard* be questioned like some I knows."

"Glad to hear," Gabe replied as he disappeared up the ladder.

"Two of 'em was it?" a young seaman asked. "You 'ad two doxies at once?"

"You 'eard the Cap'n, Billy. Is ye deef?"

"That was well done," Dagan said to Gabe once

they were out of hearing of the men below. He knew Gabe had not seen Brown with anyone, let alone two wenches. But now Brown could boast of his prowess and it'd keep his and the others' minds off the action to come later that night.

***

GABE WAS STANDING IN his cabin looking out the stern windows. There was a sliver of a moon hanging over a flat glassy sea. It would be a dark night. So dark it should hide the boats rowing ashore. Thinking of the three boats that would be going along on the raid, Gabe hoped it wouldn't be too dark.

From the map, that he, the master, young Mr. Albright, Lieutenant Vallin, Lieutenant Greg Kirk, Captain of *Bulldog*; and Lieutenant Daniel Bufford, *Leopard's* second lieutenant, had gone over, the row into Springfield Bay should be an easy pull. The cave was just a stone's throw up on the beach. A small settlement, Bain Town, was further up on the rise, but it was nothing more than a fishing village.

Everyone was gone from the cabin now except Lieutenant Vallin. "Captain, you will forgive me, sir, but you have no business going on the raid."

"Con, my conscience would never allow me to rest otherwise. Besides, I need you to carry out the actions against the privateer ships if they are still anchored off Devils Point.

The anchorage at Devils Point, according to young Albright, was just to the west of Devils

Point. The nearby beach was almost white powder and the water a bright blue. The privateers, having been raided at the Bight, had moved their anchorage to the southern tip of Cat Island. French's Bay was plenty deep for the privateers. *Lynx* would go in closer and if all was as expected would try to cause as much havoc as possible under the cover of *Leopard's* big guns. If possible they'd cut out a ship, if not they'd set fire to a ship and cut its cable in hopes it would drift into the other anchored ships. They'd taken a small fishing boat early that morning and with Montgomery aboard had sailed past Devils Point. The return trip that afternoon found another privateer had sailed in, so four were at anchor. The captain of the fishing boat was given five guineas for the use of his boat. The sum was far more than he'd have made in a month. All he had to do was stay out of sight from now until the raid was over.

***

ABRAHAM, THE GUNNER, WAS checking the swivel guns he'd rigged in the bow of *Leopard's* two longboats. Hopefully, *Bulldog's* gunner was doing the same. The swivel was charged with canister and powder under a canvas. If it came to a fight it would be close range and the canister would be deadly. The rasp of steel was heard as the seamen each drew a cutlass from the blade barrel.

"Grab your blade and muster aft," Midshipman Jackson ordered the men. "Go get yourself a pistol."

The accuracy of a pistol was suspect unless in the hands of a qualified person. However, most seamen jammed the barrel in the gut of their foe and pulled the trigger. The pistol was then used as a club or dropped, hopefully to be picked up and collected later, after the fight.

Marine Lieutenant Hobart was talking to his sergeant, undoubtedly making sure everything was ready and ensuring no muskets were loaded. It was time. The marines were in Bufford's long-boat with Midshipman Jackson. Gabe was boarding his longboat when a swell caused the boat to rise up and then out. He was in danger of falling in the water when a pair of hands grabbed him roughly and pulled him aboard.

"Gotcha Cap'n," a seaman said.

"Shove off, pull handsomely," Hex ordered as Gabe settled in the stern-sheets. Gabe tried to relax his mind that kept running away...did someone remind the seamen and marines not to load their muskets and pistols. A primed weapon going off at the wrong time by a nervous or itchy trigger finger could cost all their lives. *Too late to worry now*, Gabe thought. To say anything would be a sign of distrust and point out his nervousness.

As the men rowed, Gabe realized his eyes were now accustomed to the dark as he could plainly see the men up forward in the bow. Looking aft, he could see the next boat astern. White spray was visible as oars were pulled and lifted.

Overhead, a few stars shone down on the black sea. Looking over the backs of the straining oarsmen, Gabe took the small shaded lantern to look at the compass.

"On course," Gabe said as Dagan was closing the light.

"'Eadland, sir," one of the forward seamen announced, his voice just above a whisper.

Holding onto Dagan's shoulder, Gabe rose slightly. He could see surf as it rushed up on the beach and pulled back. Looking astern, he could see both boats were there. Things began to move quickly now. The longboat's bow ground into the sand.

Hex hissed, "Boat oars."

The tide then surged in and swung the stern around almost turning the boat over. Several seamen jumped over, and were able to pull the bow around. A couple of them were running up on the beach with the bow rope. The rest of the men jumped overboard in knee deep surf. They'd made it, excited, some fearful, but all silent. As the second boat ground up on the sand, seamen from the first boat took hold and pulled it forward so the seamen and marines could unload and gather.

The marine sergeant was setting up a perimeter while the third boat was beached. The boats were pulled far enough up on the beach that they'd not be subject to the tide. Leaving two seamen per boat to man the swivels and keep the escape route open, Gabe moved the men forward to where sea grass and mounds of sand offered cover. Captain Kirk, Lieutenant Bufford, and marine Lieutenant Hobart all gathered around Gabe.

"I sent my corporal, an old poacher, forward," Hobart volunteered.

The corporal returned in a few minutes, his boots crunching in the sand as he neared. "There are a couple of tents further up and a fire that's burned down to embers. What I take is the cave is a bit further back. They've got canvas rigged up like it is covering the entrance. There are women with the men." Not waiting for them to ask how he knew, he said, "Wash be hanging." This brought a smile from the men.

Nodding Gabe said, "We'll wait until *Leopard's* guns wake 'em up and then we'll attack." This drew smiles. What Gabe meant was when the big twenty-four pound carronade and cannons blasted off; it'd wake up everyone for miles around. Until then they'd sit and wait.

Several of the men had found a comfortable place in the sand and lay back. All was quiet and everything was going to plan.

"This might be even easier than we hoped for," Hex whispered.

When a dog started barking, Gabe swore, "Damn you, Jake, you had to say something, didn't you?" Now several dogs had taken up the howl. "Oh hell," Gabe said. "Lieutenant Hobart, send your men to the left flank. Lieutenant Bufford, your men to the right. Now let's be at them before all surprise is gone."

CHAPTER EIGHTEEN

WHAT'S GOT THAT DAMN dog so stirred up," snarled a man, naked from the waist up and with no shoes on, as he pushed the tent flap aside and stepped out. A black woman, completely naked, walked out behind him and called to the dog. Another tent flap opened and a man walked out. He was wearing pants and a long nightshirt.

"Can't you keep that dog quiet?" Inside the tent a woman's voice called for him to come back in.

At the edge of the dune, the dog stood growling and barking at the men hovering just below it. Taking a lantern from a post, the half-naked man yelped as he burnt his hand. The handle had gotten hot from the heat rising from the flames. The man cursed his stupidity and misfortune. He walked back and got a shirt from inside the tent. The lantern's glow still gave enough light for the men to appreciate their fortune as the woman seemed comfortable standing there nude.

"Plunder?" one British seaman whispered to his mate. A nod and a smile was his answer.

The man returned to the lantern and, using his shirt as protection, he picked up the lantern by the handle and turned up the wick. Hobart got Gabe's attention and using his finger to indicate dispatching the man with a blade. Gabe shook his head giving an affirmative. Two men slithered further up on the dune, daggers in hand. As the man came forward, he held the lantern up high with one hand and his pistol in the other.

Just as he reached the crest of the dune a marine rose up and threw his blade, knowing his aim was true. The second man threw his knife, the blade sinking deep into the growling dog. With the knife stuck in his throat, the privateer dropped the lantern and tried to pull the blade from his neck. He took a stumbling step forward, his mouth open like he was trying to speak. Sinking to his knees, the man then fell over the dune. As he died, his finger pulled the trigger on his pistol.

Gabe was not sure which came first, the bang of the pistol or the woman's scream. Whichever it was, was enough. The surprise was shot. No more waiting for the sound of *Leopard's* guns.

As the privateers rushed from their tents, Gabe stood and ordered, "At them lads, at them." Doing so, he aimed at a man with his pistol and shot him in the chest.

Shots fired in a volley by Hobart's marines cut down men emerging from their tents. Interestingly, Gabe was surprised to see the naked woman still standing. So far, with musket balls flying all about, she'd not been hit. Further up, more men emerged. Awakened from their sleep, they'd armed themselves very quickly and rushed to join the fight. Hobart's marines had reloaded and sent another volley of swarming death into the pack of privateers. Privateers were picking out targets and firing. Their accuracy not near as telling as the marines, but some shots found a target. Gabe heard a man go "ummph"as he was struck by an enemy ball. The silence that followed meant the privateers' guns were empty.

"At them lads, quick, before they reload," Gabe yelled.

Shouting and screaming the British seamen and marines charged, with a few hanging lanterns giving off just enough light to silhouette their foe. Something hit Gabe in the shoulder with a thud, spinning him around. A spent pistol had been thrown at him, jarring his shoulder and causing great pain. Had it been his right arm, he'd have dropped his sword. Using the sword to keep him from falling he was unprepared to defend himself from his assailant. However, Lieutenant Kirk was close by. Seeing the man attack the captain, he fired his remaining pistol. The man fell, shrieking as he hit the sand, his blood turning the white sand dark.

Hacking their way toward the cave, seamen, marines, and privateers fought. Face to face and blade to blade, amid shouts, cries of pain and curses. A few more shots sounded when someone had reloaded a musket or pistol. Hex was tangled up with not only a large man but a bare chested woman who was trying to stab him while his focus was on his other attacker. Dagan smashed the woman in the back of the head with the pommel of his sword, felling her with a single blow. *She'll have a headache when she wakes*, Dagan thought. Now, Hex only had to worry about his single attacker.

Dagan, a man of medium height, suddenly found a very tall man facing him. A shadowy form, the man was with clenched teeth and a sword in each hand. The tall man swung down hard, and the steel blades clanged as Dagan blocked with his own. As the blades grated, the giant of a man gave an evil smile and swung his other blade. Dagan was barely able to parry when he had to duck as his enemy gave a vicious swing with his second sword. Knees down on the ground, Dagan looked up. His foe had reared back to finish the battle using both blades. Seeing his opening, Dagan, one hand on the ground to balance himself, lunged with his blade. Up under the ribs and into the man's chest, blowing out his lungs and skewering his heart. Dagan's blade would have been wrenched from his hand as the giant fell backwards, had his strap not been around his wrist. As the man fell backwards, the blade made a sucking sound as it pulled loose, followed by a gush of foul air from the spurts of blood.

All around the British seamen and marines fought, the British pushing their enemy back,

back toward and then beyond the cave's opening in the ground. Men fought, reeled and staggered as the battle lust turned them into a craze banned of demons. Finally, the few surviving privateers turned and ran from the melee.

Given out and trying to catch his breath, Gabe ordered the marine lieutenant to set up a picket line. Seeing Hex, hands on his knees, blood all over his clothes, Gabe asked, "Are you hurt?"

Gasping, Hex nodded no, and then looking at the blood, he said, "Not mine."

Jarvis Jackson, the midshipman, appeared unharmed but his face was blackened and smudged from firing his weapons.

"Mr. Jackson, if you will have a detail of men find and light as many lanterns as they can, so we can see what, if anything, is in those tents."

Two seamen were looking down at the body of the nude woman. Her luck had run out, she had been shot from behind, probably a wild shot, but regardless she now lay face down in the gritty sand.

Shaking his head, the seaman Brown shook his head, "What a waste. That's one wench that was denied the pleasure of me company." Seeing the glint of metal as a lantern was hung up on a pole, Brown bent down and removed the gold bracelet from the dead woman's wrist. *A small remembrance*, he thought as he slid the plunder into his pocket. Gabe pretended not to see the dead privateers being removed of any valuable trinkets, chains, gold crosses, and knives.

Dagan called to Jackson as he emerged from a tent, "Guard this tent until the captain can inspect it. Hex, you may need to stand guard inside the tent until the captain can come."

Not comprehending Dagan's words at first, it dawned on Hex, when he noticed a bulge in Dagan's pockets. *Ah...*he thought, *what did Dagan call it...retirement*. As he entered the tent, Dagan walked over to the cave entrance where Gabe was. It was more a cavern than a cave...an underground cavern, the perfect place to store bounty.

Gabe looked at Dagan and said, "Not much here other than military supplies, powder, shot, uniforms and the lot."

"What are you going to do with it?" Dagan asked.

"Set it afire, I'm thinking," Gabe replied.

Dagan nodded, "There's a chest in the tent that has specie in it."

Looking at Dagan's pockets, Gabe asked, "Who else has seen it?"

"Hex is guarding it."

Gabe grunted, "I hope you don't fall overboard on the way back to the ship, you larcenous scoundrel." Calling Lieutenant Kirk over, Gabe instructed him to set fire to the cavern's contents. "I can't see ruining the cavern by blasting it so spread everything out, put holes in those barrels of coal oil, and when everything is soaked good, throw a torch down the hole and let it burn."

"Aye," Kirk replied. Like the captain, he didn't want to see one of nature's miracles destroyed.

CHAPTER NINETEEN

Lieutenant Leonard Montgomery, Captain of *HMS Lynx*, had just had a very similar argument with his first lieutenant that Captain Anthony had had that same evening.

"This is something I must do," Montgomery said. "I need you to be ready to pick us up once the raid is finished." What he didn't tell his young, white first lieutenant was that if he were to ever rise beyond his present rank, it would have to be by doing something daring so that his name would stand out in the admiral's report. Otherwise, he was at his terminal rank. He only knew of one other black naval officer, who had made quite a name for himself and he was still a lieutenant. The move upwards for a black man was unheard of, so far.

John Perkins, once a ship's pilot aboard *HMS Antelope*, was now the captain of the *Punch* schooner. It was said that he'd already captured over three hundred enemy vessels. His crew and fellow officers had nicknamed him 'Jack Punch'. He was a favorite of Admiral Sir George Rodney. The admiral had promoted him to commander but it was disallowed by the board.

Knowing this, Lieutenant Montgomery felt privileged just to have a ship. Yet to get to the next rank would take an act so dangerous that the board would have to take note. Finding himself an officer under Lord Anthony was definitely a bit of good fortune. Lord Anthony was a fair man, who would give a man credit for his accomplishments, regardless of his color.

***

THE OARS ROSE AND fell as the oarsmen put their backs into it. A tiny dot in the distance was probably a lantern hanging beside the mainmast or possibly by an open hatch leading down to the seamen's messes.

Speaking to the cox'n, Montgomery whispered, "That light is your point." As they came closer, Montgomery warned his men, "Don't stare at the lanterns. You will lose your night vision."

Up front in the bow of the boat, a man rose with a grapnel. As the sleeping ship loomed before them, the cox'n ordered, "Boat your oars."

The tide was running in their favor. As the cox'n put the tiller over, the longboat swung around. The bow man let go with the grapnel, pulling the rope tight, the grapnel lit into the rail and held fast. The longboat slewed as the slack was taken up on the rope. Men jumped for the small ship's rail, and then up and over. So far, there hadn't been any alarms sounded.

As more and more climbed aboard, Montgomery sent them to find and silence any crew members aboard. He and his cox'n entered the captain's cabin to find it empty. In the gun room, a man was sitting down, with his head back, mouth open, and passed out from drink. In his lap, a woman sat with her head against the man's chest. She, too, was passed out. He shook the man, but neither he nor the wench stirred.

Speaking to his cox'n, Montgomery said, "Better throw her over the side. Hopefully, the water will rouse her. She will surely die if left aboard this ship." He then ordered his men, "Gather everything that will burn and spread it about the decks. Pour on oil or, if you have to, sprinkle gunpowder in the mix, that will catch it on fire."

The men moved swiftly but silently. Soon piles of hammocks, canvas, rope, and tar were put in piles on the main deck and the berth deck.

"Cut the cables," Montgomery ordered. Immediately, the ship began to move with the current. "Fire the ship," Montgomery hissed.

Seamen nodded and rushed to do their task. On the main deck, a seaman took a hanging lantern and smashed it on the deck into a trail of gunpowder which led to piles gathered around both the mainmast and the foremast. With a whoosh the gunpowder caught hold and ran the deck to the first pile and on to the next. The piles blazed up and more tarred rope was thrown on the pile for good measure. Quickly, the flames grew until they raced up the tarred ropes and into the riggings, furled sails and soon the shrouds were ablaze.

"Abandon ship, into the boat," Montgomery ordered.

As the men rushed to the longboat, the flames grew hotter as they leapt skywards. Others were now aware of the roaring inferno. Fear of the impending collision drove captains to send men to their ship's guns. Cannons were quickly loaded and run out, firing independently. Great sections of the rails were blown skywards and sharpshooters were firing at Montgomery, their balls peppering the deck near the wheel, but it was too late. Montgomery kept station at the wheel, steering the inferno toward the anchored ships. Cables were cut and sails loosened but this only made the situation worse as ships drifted together, causing yard arms to tangle as they collided.

The fire ship was lighting up the sky enough so that the gunners aboard *HMS Leopard*, had something to aim at. Vallin ordered the upper deck cannons to open fire on the beach and any vessel sighted. As the big guns roared, people on the beach, who had been wild-eyed, unbelieving observers, now ran inland, away from the deadly hell of *Leopard's* guns.

On board the fire ship, the current wanted to turn the ship so Montgomery had fought the wheel in spite of the intense heat. His face and hands felt like they were on fire. Unable to stand the roaring furnace any longer, he lashed the wheel, hoping the rope would not burn and part too quickly. Hearing his men shouting his name to hurry, he turned just as the deck planking burst into flames, the seams acting like a fuse or runners allowing the flames to run the length of the ship's decking. His hands were burned and painful so Montgomery tried to use his arms to crawl over the stern rail where amid the crackling flames and shouts of his men, he dangled. He tried to look below to see the boat but the smoke had caused his eyes to water so much that his vision was blurred. Rough hands reached up, and grabbed hold of his body and plopped him down in the boat.

"Out oars, shove off, handsomely now lads, else yer arse'll be scorched before ye knows it," the cox'n shouted.

The fire ship soon drifted into the mass of tangled ships. Ship after ship succumbed to the flaming hell that the fire ship brought with it. Panic and terror gripped the anchorage that less than an hour ago was peaceful and silent.

As the other ships caught fire, the sky lit up so that the *Leopard's* gunners were now picking out their targets. Flames shot out gun ports and up the masts; and riggings were so bright the men who had raided the cavern at Bain Town paused in their rowing to watch the spectacle.

"I'd not want to be aboard any of those ships," a voice spoke out.

"Nay, me neither," several men replied in unison.

Dagan placed his hand on Gabe's knee, knowing his thoughts and feelings about the men on the ships. "War's not always pleasant," he whispered.

Seeing the emotional toll the night was taking on his captain, Hex ordered, "Lively now, sooner we gets back to the ship, the sooner we gets a ration, I'm betting."

Smiling, Gabe thought, *Hex knows how to speak to the men, how to motivate them.* As the men started rowing, a loud boom was heard as it echoed across the water.

"Powder room," somebody volunteered.

"Hope the sods got off," somebody else said.

"'E ain't feeling nothing now if 'e didn't," another chimed in.

"Silence!" Hex snarled.

***

THE NEXT MORNING *LEOPARD* stood in as close to the shore as prudent. Charred timbers and debris floated out with the tide. Between Montgomery's fire ship and *Leopard's* guns not a ship floated. One of the ships had sunk close to the beach; water sluiced over its deck as the waves raced in and out. Satisfied their task was complete; they sailed back to Grand Cayman. After arriving, Gabe had the captains repair on board.

Once everyone had greeted each other and been given a drink, they sat down at the table.

"I've finished my report to the admiral," Gabe announced. "Four ships destroyed, along with large amounts of powder, shot, small arms, large quantities of rum, and other plunder. I'd say that we had a very successful raid."

"Was all the rum destroyed or did Hex confiscate it?" Kirk asked.

"To the best of my knowledge, it was done away with," Gabe replied to Kirk. "But if he or Dagan approaches you with a good deal, I'd be suspect." This brought the chuckle that Gabe knew it would. Most of the captains knew Hex had been a smuggler in his former life. "I think the admiral will be glad that we only lost one man and that there was only eight wounded," Gabe said, getting back to business. "Not a bad night at all."

Looking at the captains, Gabe remembered how everyone had been dirty and sooty. All of them looked about done in, but Montgomery looked the worse. The intense heat had caused blisters on his face and hands. The coat sleeve on his right arm had been charred and ragged looking.

Calling Doctor Cornish to look at his fellow officer, Gabe joked as Montgomery was being evaluated, "Damme, but you look a sight, Leonard."

Trying to smile hurt so much, Montgomery made a motion with his hand and arm that he knew Gabe would understand. Once Cornish was through with his administrations and had departed, Gabe took a leather purse from his pocket and after hefting it a time or two, he gave it to Montgomery.

Leaning forward and speaking in a whisper, Gabe explained, "We found a chest full of specie. A small amount was lost transporting it to *Leopard*. Dagan would call it retirement. In this case, I call it just reward. Just don't tell anyone."

Montgomery did manage a smile and nodded. Now back at Grand Cayman, with bandages still on his hands and arm, Montgomery still looked in pain but he smiled at the comments about Hex so that was a good thing.

After the meeting, was over, Lieutenant Vallin was seeing the captains over the side. As planned, Dagan stepped up next to Montgomery and said, "A moment if you please, Captain." Following Dagan back to the captain's cabin, Montgomery found Gabe at his desk. Nesbit brought him a glass and he sat down when Gabe motioned for him to do so.

"Admiral Anthony has been pressured to leave a ship, a naval presence as it were here at Grand Cayman when I sail," Gabe said. "He left it up to me as to who gets the assignment, you or Captain Kirk. I wanted to make the offer to you first to accept or decline."

Montgomery looked at Gabe for a moment, and then asked, "Does my color have anything to do with the offer?"

"Yes...and no. The First Resident made a comment to Lieutenant Vallin that struck true. Mr.

Vallin is the son of a Scottish lord. His mother was an Indian princess. Lieutenant Vallin has found that being a half-cast, he was not as readily accepted by anyone at home other than his father. Here in the islands, he is readily accepted. At the Chief Resident's party I saw you were well received. Therefore, I leave it up to you but you must decide quickly. If you stay, you will be looked upon as the authority. You will have to investigate and deal with the Galante woman, and let her know she's being watched. You may even have to deal with privateers so I'd keep a close look out and have some gun stations built."

"How long will I be here?" Montgomery asked.

Gabe shrugged, "Until Lord Anthony or some other competent authority relieves you. A year, or maybe until the war is over. I don't know but I'd plan on a year. I will tell you that I'm sending a letter to the Gazette mentioning your name, and one to my brother-in-law recommending your promotion. Hugh is in Parliament. You may never get your swab. I don't know, but you will always have my friendship."

"Thank you," Montgomery said, trying to control his emotions. "I will take the assignment." Shaking Gabe's hand, he said, "I wish there were more like you."

PART II

The Fallen Midshipman

So many fallen comrades...now line the deck
A once proud ship...now a floating wreck
The ship's men will put her...back to rights
The chore I face...will take all night.

Another shrouded soul...goes over the side
And I feel guilty...cause I'm alive
It's the hardest letter...I've ever had to write
A battle won...but what the price

To say he did his duty...sounds so trite
When telling her...of his sacrifice
I'm sending her...a lock of his golden hair
It's not much...but it shows I care.

—Michael Aye

CHAPTER TWENTY

THE BOAR'S HEAD WAS one of the finer taverns in Kingston and Port Royal. It was not up to the standards of Scolfes or the George Inn back home in Portsmouth, England. But for Kingston, Jamaica, it served a higher quality of patrons than the other dives of note close to the port. At a rectangular table with benches on each side that would sit four sailors sat Lieutenant Laqua, who had just risen from the master mate's ranks; and Bart, the admiral's cox'n, who in his uniform looked more like an officer than Lieutenant Laqua; Jacob Hex and Dagan. The latter two looked more like civilians in their dress than Royal Navy sailors.

"Don't let it bothers you," Bart was saying. "You bedded the wench, gave her a bit of fruit from yer loin, and sailed away when yer ship weighed anchor. Yew didn't die-vulge no secrets to my way o' thinking."

"But she used me," Hex said. A burden he'd suffered since he'd been made aware of Marie Galante's activities with the privateers.

"She could have used me all she wanted," Lieutenant Laqua volunteered. "The only remorse that I would have had would have been when I had to give it up."

"That's no error," Bart chimed in.

Dagan had kept silent. He, alone from the others sitting there, felt he understood. Jake had felt there was more to their whirlwind relationship. For Hex, it had almost been love at first sight. She was an exotic creature to be sure. She was all woman and knew how to dress to drive a man insane. Just seeing her, she had, in fact, stirred Dagan. How she picked out Hex was in itself a mystery. However, both he, and more importantly Gabe, had believed Hex when he swore he'd not said anything that she and her privateer friends could use. That Captain Neill and the Chief Resident, Mr. William Eden, seemed more inclined to doubt Hex, was why he felt so. His honor had been impugned.

"Oh, Hex, let's have another set and then we's can pass the time wid a run at the cards," Bart interjected.

"Not likely," the three men said at once, as they watched Bart absently do one handed cuts with a single hand.

"Pay 'em no 'tention. Back in 'Bados this young planter said to me...'e said, 'Bart, your feet stink, your breath's bad and you don't love Jesus.' Now, you all knows I've a close place in me heart for Jesus so I jus' clopped 'im a good'n side 'is noggin and thought no more bout it, I's didn't."

Now Hex, Dagan, and Laqua were laughing.

"See, old Bart'll get yer mind offen yer troubles, so how bout that game?"

Laqua rose, "I can't, I told Lieutenant Tolbert and Lieutenant Bufford I'd meet them."

"Too good for the likes o' us now yew be a lieutenant, I see," Bart said.

"No," Laqua responded. "I didn't want to bring you guys down by hanging around you. Besides, Bart, I haven't been paid for lieutenant yet so I definitely can't stand your style of playing."

***

THE ADMIRAL, HIS FLAG captain, and the captains in Lord Anthony's squadron had been invited to dine with Admiral Peter Parker, who was the naval commander of the Jamaica station.

In a moment, when they were alone, Admiral Parker spoke to Lord Anthony, "I've sent out dispatch vessels to let Cornwallis know the Dons have joined in. He's left the island vastly undermanned."

"Therefore, Gil, your stopping over is luck as I see it. With your squadron in and out as you've been, it may lead our enemies to reconsider attacking Jamaica. It might not prove to be such a suitable endeavor," Parker exclaimed.

"I'm glad we've been able to put forth a show of force, Peter. While I've left a good captain in command back at Barbados, I can't help but feel the need to return. I've left a sloop of war at Grand Cayman. It is not a great warship, but it may cause a privateer to have second thoughts about cutting out merchant vessels. Besides, it does give the island's people a sense of protection and hopefully will make them feel they're not abandoned."

"Aye, now let's go greet our officers," Peter replied. As the two rose, Peter put his hand on Lord Anthony's arm. "By the way, Gil, how did Kirkstatter react when he found out it was you and Sir Gabe who rescued him from the Dons?"

Pausing to collect his thoughts, Gil spoke, "Let's just say he was a changed man."

"I'll bet," Peter answered. "Humble pie will certainly change a man."

***

CON VALLIN SAT AT the tiny desk in his cabin. The mail boat had stopped over and there was mail from Grand Cayman. More importantly, there was a letter for him. The mail had been delivered to the flagship and a boat was sent from there to each ship that had mail. When the ward room servant had informed him of the letter, he thought it might have been from his father or fellow officer.

That was until Patch, the one-eyed servant, had volunteered, "It smells good too, Mr. Vallin."

Taking a whiff of the envelope, Vallin knew who the letter was from...Hannah Bodden. It was the same perfume she had worn when they had gone riding in her uncle's carriage the day after her birthday celebration. Had it just been the two of them, it would have been much nicer. But even with island society that was too much and a friend had gone along for the ride. Hannah had promised she'd write as soon as she'd received a letter from him. Reading her letter, Vallin found himself smiling. She might be an angel but her spelling was lacking.

My deer Lieutenant Vallin,

I had hopped to hear from you by now. I reelize you are off chasing pirates and may not have had time or you may be dead, killed by a pirate. I thought I simple must find out.

The letter went on for a page and a half. Her closing remarks made Vallin's heart race.

I find that I have been compleetly smitten with you. I would like to know if you feel as I do.

Do I?, Vallin wondered. *Am I 'smitten' with the young lady? Sure I am, but is it love or lust? I'll answer that in time*, Vallin thought. For now, he'd just answer the letter.

***

GABE WAS SITTING AT his desk reading a letter from Faith. She'd had a letter from his mother stating she might come to visit. She wanted to see her grandchild. A cave had been discovered on the island, and Admiral Buck had said they may take a day trip to go see it. He stated he'd take his cox'n, Crow, and Lum could come along and all of us girls and we could take lanterns and see the cave and maybe have a picnic. Faith had gone on to say she'd gotten his letter and Admiral Moffitt's saying he was sent to find Gil's ships and kill the Spaniards. Gabe found himself chuckling.

"What's so funny?" Dagan asked. Gabe handed him Faith's letter. Reading the letter, Dagan began to frown but before he could comment, Hex knocked and came in.

"Sir Gabe."

"Yes."

"I got a letter from the...ah...woman on Grand Cayman," Hex reported.

"Marie Galante?" Gabe inquired.

"Aye sir," Hex replied.

Gabe looked at his cox'n and realized that this was not the usual Jake Hex. This man was a subdued person. The Jake Hex he'd always known was far from subdued. He'd never seen him so meek. "What does it say?" Gabe asked.

"I haven't opened it."

"Why not?" Gabe asked.

"I just thought I'd let you do it or at least I would open it in front of you," Hex said.

Dagan put Faith's letter down on Gabe's desk. "Jake, I've told you, neither Gabe nor I, nor has the admiral or anyone who knows you, doubted your honesty, loyalty, or integrity."

Sensing where Dagan was coming from, Gabe added, "Jake, I trust you as much as I do Dagan and my brother...and in some ways more than I would my wife." This brought a smile to Hex's face. "You open the letter and if there's something there you want me to see you can show me."

Hex nodded, and then sat in one of Gabe's leather cushioned chairs. He read the one page letter, and then he looked up at Gabe and Dagan. "The wench says she took up with me to gain information, but found that she felt something about me that was different than the other men. Therefore, she didn't pry me for information. Information she was sure I would not have given anyway. She had heard about the raids and by now I must know she was involved. One of the privateers was her brother. We sunk his ship. She said she was not trying to justify her actions by telling me all this, but wanted me to know how she felt about me and that our loving was real. So far, she's not been arrested but her business is all but closed. She just wanted me to know the truth and that she was sorry if I was hurt by her actions." Silence filled the cabin for a long minute.

"I'd say I believe her," Gabe offered.

"Aye," Dagan added. "This damnable war causes people to do some strange things. Jake, if I were you, I'd fold that letter up and put it in your chest. Things may not have turned out like you would have wanted it too, but I'd say you enjoyed something a lot of men would die for. A woman, who respected you enough not to want to cause you problems, yet cared enough that she gave you what she had...herself."

"Thank you," Hex replied and walked out.

"That letter was a Godsend," Dagan said. "Were it not for Betsy, I'd be envious."

CHAPTER TWENTY ONE

A CONVOY APPROACHING JAMAICA WAS not an unusual sight. The island could expect three or four a year. However, with the war going on and the possibility of privateers wreaking havoc among the merchant ships, it was a cause for celebration when the convoy was sighted.

The joy was twofold. For the islanders, it was the replenishment of needed goods and that occasional frill that had been special ordered. More often than not, it was for some planter's wife, some sweetheart or young bride. But it was a joyous occasion for the escort vessels, ships where the captain, officers, and crew were under constant stress. Stress related to the enemy raiders who now hunted in packs. Stress related to sailing a ship with less than a full crew in all types of weather and the stress of trying to keep the grocery captains sailing in loose formation without the escort commander having to send one of his warships to harass some laggard.

This convoy would be the last of the year before the hurricane season. Therefore, it brought with it the reality that the island would have to be self-sufficient for several months. Other than the small coastal ships, the islands could expect nothing that they were not able to produce themselves. Today's convoy carried a large quantity of war supplies. Among them were ten cannons that would be unloaded there at Jamaica, and then ferried to Grand Cayman to be used as shore defense.

When Lord Anthony was first made aware of the arrival of the cannons along with sufficient powder and shot and that a ship was requested to ferry the guns to Grand Cayman, his first question was why didn't the ship that brought them from England take them? It would be a lot simpler and he'd send an escort vessel, two if need be. But the ship's master was concerned he'd never make it to Grand Cayman, offload his cargo, and be back before the convoy weighed anchor and sailed on to Savannah and then north, ultimately ending up in Nova Scotia.

"More like the bugger's 'fraid he might miss out on a night of wenching, I'm thinkin," Bart snorted. "'E ain't thinkin wid the 'ead on 'is shoulders, I'm bettin'."

"Bart, don't be unkind," Lord Anthony said.

"Nay, jus' truthful and that's no error."

Mahan, Lord Anthony's flag lieutenant, had learned two things since he'd held his position. Nobody, not even his Lordship, got in the last word with Bart, even if it was just aye or nay. The second thing was Bart had a knack of cutting through the bull and getting to the truth of the matter. Mahan could not remember Bart being wrong. Don't say it in front of him, Lord Anthony had told him one day when he mentioned Bart's knack to him.

"Well, don't let him hear you say it, Patrick, he's already got a big enough head," Lord Anthony had said.

While he had taken the admiral's advice, he thought, on this occasion Bart summed it up perfectly himself. He'd been listening to the purser whine about how bad he had it in a thankless job. Bart had taken the pipe he was smoking from his mouth, sniffed hard, cleared his throat and spit once over the side. Then in a firm, frank, level tone, he said, "Stow it mate, its Bart yer talking to. Ain't you learned by now ye can't bullshit a bullshitter? Now, bugger off to some 'ole sumwheres." Mahan had about laughed out loud in spite of himself. He'd told Lord Anthony, who just shook his head, about the conversation.

"Language he probably picked up one of the times we were in the colonies," Lord Anthony said.

Lord Anthony was still considering the request from Admiral Peter Parker to allow one of his ships to go to Grand Cayman, as an escort though, not as a ferry service. Bart was right. The sod could haul his own damn cargo, cannons or no.

If he missed the convoy sailing off, he was sure one of the sloops' captains would not mind a few days up to Savannah and back, out from the admiral's clutches as it were.

A knock and stamp of the sentry's musket butt plate on the deck caught Lord Anthony off guard. He was not expecting anybody and the sentry didn't formally announce the flag captain, flag lieutenant, Bart, or any of his staff.

"Sir, Lord Skalla from the Foreign Service Office."

Lord Anthony rose and went to greet his visitor. He'd last seen Lord Skalla just before he was recalled to England after Admiral Kirkstatter's complaint had been received. Now that Skalla was back, it meant he was no longer under a black cloud. Greetings were exchanged and Skalla stated he was enroute to Nova Scotia but didn't comment further.

After a minute or so of chit-chat, Skalla asked about Gabe. He was surprised when he learned Gabe was in port and expressed a desire to see him and possibly the three get together for a meal. Skalla then went on to say that the first lord stated in the presence of Parliament that he had every confidence in Sir Gabe and all the Anthony's, in fact. "I think the whole thing would have been forgotten about but for a few. It seems that possibly some of the Anthony's biggest enemies lay within the boundaries of our own shores. This one fellow made such an arse of himself that your brother-in-law gave him to the count of ten to cease his banter and apologize or be prepared to meet him on the field of honor. Of course, the Gazette sided with Sir Gabe and stated that anyone who found fault in the mission could not in truth consider himself an Englishman. I have several copies that I brought along including the report from Admiral Kirkstatter."

"Kirkstatter," Anthony repeated. "He wrote the Gazette?"

"Aye, Lord Anthony, that he did. He told how his ship had been captured, unaware the Dons had joined in with the colonies. He gave a detailed account of how Gabe defeated a seventy-four with a fifty-gun."

Anthony interrupted his guest, "Sir Gabe will tell you it was lady luck more than skill."

"No matter, Kirkstatter retracted his negative comments about Sir Gabe and went on to say England was lucky to have not one Anthony but three who have served so well."

"That is something I'll admit. I must write him and thank him on behalf of the family," Anthony said.

"You don't know?" Skalla interrupted.

"Know what?"

"The same vessel that brought Admiral Kirkstatter's reports and letters also brought news of his death. I'm sorry, Admiral, I thought you knew. Admiral Kirkstatter committed suicide," Skalla replied.

"Damnation, we hadn't heard. Gabe will be sorry to hear this. The admiral and Gabe made peace with each other."

"I would guess, my Lord, that death looked like a better option than to be humiliated constantly by his run of bad luck."

"It could have happened to any of us," Anthony half-muttered. "Silas," he shouted.

"Aye, my Lord."

"Pour Lord Skalla and I a glass. I think a bit of Manning's bourbon might be in order. Then find Lieutenant Mahan, and tell him his company is requested in my cabin. Now, when you've done that, Silas, roust out Bart from wherever he's fleecing honest seamen and tell him I require my barge."

"Aye, sir. Bourbon, find lieutenant and Bart in that order."

Anthony nodded, then leaning over he whispered, "He'll smell of bourbon himself by the time we get our drinks, if you happen to catch a whiff of his breath."

CHAPTER TWENTY TWO

THE WIND WAS FROM the southwest. *Leopard* was racing along under full sail. All around, men were following routine. Petty officers were supervising working parties along the main deck while others worked above. Forward, the bosun had one of his mates splicing lines and greasing spare tackles, and still another group seemed to be inspecting the guns for rust.

Gabe leaned against the fife rail and puffed on his pipe. He had been given some new tobacco by Lord Skalla. It was a very mellow tobacco and smoked cooler and without the bite some of the island brands tended to have. He was not sure he favored it above a good cigar, but Lord Skalla was right in his assertion of the quality. It was a mixture of Virginia burly that was soaked in Jamaican rum and then cured. A pleasant smoke when one had the time to relax and enjoy the smoke. But with the need to pack, light, use a tamping tool and relight the tobacco, a cigar was much more convenient. Plus, the Cuban cigars were a fine smoke if you didn't get one of the darker leaf cigars. Gabe had found he could hardly stand after smoking one of those. As he puffed on his pipe, he thought of Lord Skalla's arrival in Jamaica. He was certainly glad to see his friend and was doubly glad neither he nor Lord Skalla had been called to task over their activities in the Indian Ocean. Admiral Kirkstatter's final letter had calmed the fires he had stirred.

Gabe had felt a sense of pride upon hearing that his brother-in-law, Hugh, had stood up for him as he had, although he didn't want Hugh fighting any duels for him. He had a family to think of. Gabe had also been very sad to hear about Admiral Kirkstatter's suicide. Would he have done the same thing? *I might have retired or resigned my commission and moved away from England, but to kill one's own self?* "Honor and dignity," Dagan had said. "Sometimes death may seem desirable when a man loses his honor and dignity." The thought had crossed Gabe's mind to write his widow and express his sorrow. *Would she accept it in the light in which it was written or resent him for it? I'll write it*, Gabe decided.

Finishing the bowl of tobacco, Gabe decided to go below. He noticed Tolbert kept looking his way. Was he making the lieutenant nervous being on deck? Did Tolbert think the captain was evaluating how he stood his watch? He shouldn't, he had proven to be a good officer. A cry from above caused everyone to look up. Once the lookout identified his sighting as a coastal trader, the men went back to their tasks. No prize money this time.

Walking into his cabin the same pile of papers that needed signing yesterday hadn't vanished and indeed seemed to have grown. Nesbit, without asking, brought Gabe a glass of lime juice. Gabe sat down at the desk but did not pick up his quill. Instead, he wondered why he had volunteered *Leopard* to escort the merchantman to Grand Cayman. He didn't have to. In fact, Gil had mentioned in passing he was going to have Captain Roger Frostbrier's thirty-six gun frigate, *Phoenix*, escort the ship. However, recalling the look on Con Vallin's face when discussing the letter he'd got from the Bodden girl, Hannah, and how he would have liked to spend more time with her, made Gabe volunteer to escort the ship. Having a brother that was a vice admiral ought to provide such a fine captain, such as Sir Gabe Anthony, a few perks anyway.

Since Frostbrier had not been given orders yet, Gabe got the assignment. Besides, it would be nice to see Leonard Montgomery again. Lord Anthony, in deference to Admiral Parker's request that they stay in Jamaica a bit longer, had set their sailing date a week from Saturday...eight more days. Reports had come in from coastal traders and the frigate that had been on patrol, that both French and Spanish vessels were being sighted in increasing numbers. Lieutenant Mahan had talked to the captain of the merchant ship that was carrying the cannons and explained that he would find less competition and lower prices on Grand Cayman, for both his carnal and culinary desires.

Reporting back to Lord Anthony, Lieutenant Mahan said, "I knew if I appealed to his belly, we'd make strides."

"Humph," had been Bart's reply. "Iffen yer 'pealing to 'is belly, yer aiming too high, I'm thinkin´."

Mahan was sure the cox'n was right but didn't feel it polite to admit it.

***

THE CRUISE TO GRAND Cayman was a short one. Immediately upon arriving, Gabe had himself taken ashore. Seeing a local merchant on the walk in front of his ship, Gabe inquired about transportation to the Chief Resident's home.

"I will send a rider on horseback," the man said, explaining Mr. Eden had just left. Knowing island time as he did, Gabe knew 'just left' could mean anything from five minutes to an hour.

Standing under the stoop of the shop, Gabe looked down at the beach. Jarvis Jackson was standing in as cox'n. The midshipman had had the gig pulled up on the beach, and had the crew standing under the shade of a tree, such as there was. Fishing a guinea from his pocket, he walked down to where Jackson and the crew stood.

Giving the coin to Jackson, Gabe said, "Take the men to the tavern. You can see the sign just down the street. Buy the men a wet, not more than two each, mind you. I don't want them arse over kettle and dumping us over going back to the ship."

"Aye, Captain. Watch them I will," Jackson replied.

Each of the crew was smiling at their good luck as they passed by. Finding a crate, Gabe stood it on end under the tree and prepared to wait on the Chief Resident. As he waited, he watched the merchant ship come as close to shore as she could. Her draught was too deep to come alongside of the pier. The unloading and hauling would have to wait until the Chief Resident arrived and set up the ferrying process.

Once on land a major of artillery and his company of men would see to the emplacements. The major and his men had been given passage on *Leopard* so as not to cause the grocery captain more expense. Another boat had shoved off from *Leopard*. Smiling to himself, Gabe thought, *I know who that is.*

As *Leopard's* lookout had sighted Grand Cayman, he had stated that he didn't see any other ships at anchor.

"Must be out on patrol," Gabe had said.

"Aye Captain, but patrolling for what is my only question," Vallin replied. This caused the master, Mr. Pittman, Lieutenant Laqua, Dagan, and even Hex to laugh.

"Mr. Vallin," Gabe called, speaking in his 'captain's voice'.

"Aye, sir."

"I am certain we will be at anchor for three days minimum. Therefore, I see no reason we can't allow the men ashore as you see fit."

"Thank you, Captain, and as to the watch?"

"As per my in port policy," Gabe replied.

"Aye Captain."

"Ah...Mr. Vallin."

"Yes sir."

"Being the first lieutenant, once the ship is secured to your satisfaction, I'm sure you can find something to occupy you for the next three days. I also see no reason during that time that would require you to sleep aboard."

"Thank you, Captain." Gabe had just given his first lieutenant the ultimate gift.

"If he can't charm that young lady in three days, he's not the sailor I think he is," Dagan joked.

"Aye," Gabe answered his uncle. Leaning forward so that only Dagan could hear, Gabe whispered, "I have a request to make of you."

"You don't have to ask," Dagan replied, knowing what the request would be. "I'll go over with Jake. We'll see if this Galante woman is at her tavern, or even if she's still in town. Once we know something, I'll get word back to you." Dagan then told Gabe that he'd taken the liberty of having young Jackson assigned as the temporary cox'n. Jackson was not the oldest, but did appear to be the brighter of the mids.

I wouldn't mind having him on my ship, Gabe

thought. "Thank you again, Uncle."

Dagan looked at Gabe for a moment, "Jacob Hex means a lot to both of us, Gabe. If the woman is on the island I'll find her. After that, it's between Jake and her." Gabe shook his head in understanding.

CHAPTER TWENTY THREE

THREE DAYS AFTER ENTERING port, the merchant ship sailed back to Jamaica, being escorted by *Lynx*. Spoilage from several barrels of pork had been found and now the beef was nearly gone. *Lynx's* crew had supplemented their rations with turtle meat, but that grew old quickly. *Lynx* needed her stores replenished and that could only be done in Jamaica. So Gabe sent the ship back, killing two birds with one stone, so to speak.

The artillery major had done a good job. A powder magazine had been built using palmetto logs and covering it with a plaster made from seashells. Palmetto logs had also been used to form a barricade of sort to give the people firing the cannons a means of cover.

"The palmetto log is made of a soft fibrous wood," the major explained. "Instead of bursting when hit, the soft wood tends to absorb the impact." Gabe and William Eden had been most impressed.

Try as they may, Marie Galante was not to be found. One man stated he saw her walk out into the ocean but never saw her come back again. No one else could remember when they'd last seen her. Captain Montgomery had said he'd gotten much the same information and wondered if she, like Admiral Kirkstatter, had committed suicide.

Dagan didn't think so. "She might have walked out or swam out never to be seen again but that doesn't mean she's dead. I think she realized she'd never do well on the island again and left. Sometimes it's better to vanish without a trace," he said.

Gabe agreed with Dagan. He hoped Hex would be inclined to agree with Dagan's theory also, rather than she'd taken her own life.

"Who knows, she may surface again when the war is over," Dagan stated.

***

A KNOCK AT GABE'S door was followed by "Mr. Hunter, sir, midshipman of the watch." The sentry made the announcement without the stamp of his musket butt on the deck. He'd learned that the captain cared little for excessive noise. "Mr. Laqua's compliments, sir, you have a note...an invitation. The messenger is waiting for a reply if you're not too busy, sir."

After a moment of waiting, Gabe asked, "Am I to have the note, Mr. Hunter?"

The youth got big-eyed and then stammered as he passed the note, "Sorry, sir, my apologies."

"Nesbit," Gabe called.

"Yes, Sir Gabe."

"Do we have any refreshments available? It

seems the sun has gotten to Mr. Hunter. His cheeks are flushed most severely."

"Aye, shall I serve him in the pantry, Sir Gabe, while you read your correspondence?" Nesbit asked.

"Yes, that will be fine," Gabe replied.

"Come along, young sir. My, you do look flushed." As Nesbit walked away he looked at Gabe and smiled a knowing smile.

***

WILLIAM EDEN SAT UNDER a thatch roof porch at the Turtle's Nest Tavern having a drink with Gabe. "It's not something you'll find at home in England or even in the colonies. I've tasted similar concoctions on Jamaica and Nassau. It's made using the sweetened juice of a coconut, mixed with rum. I've also had variations using pineapples and bananas. The pineapple is not bad, but I'm not fond of the ones with bananas. The times, rare times I might add, that we've added ice or poured the contents in a pitcher of ice, the taste is even better. I'm convinced if ice were constantly available, my wife would become addicted to the drink. I must warn you though, Sir Gabe, this drink has a way of catching up with you before you know it."

"Thanks for the warning," Gabe replied. "It certainly is a pleasant drink. The first time I've had rum with any of those extra ingredients."

"I'll have the man here mix you up some to take back to the ship. I must tell you though; it doesn't keep long in this heat," Eden said.

I'll have Nesbit put it in the bilges to keep cool, Gabe thought but didn't mention it.

"The major," Eden started again, "tells me he will finish with the emplacements today." Gabe raised his glass in acknowledgement. "Those guns, or cannons I guess is a better word, will certainly help several of our citizens sleep better at night."

A small breeze gave a momentary bit of comfort from the sun glaring on the harbor waters. Gabe had removed his uniform coat and hung it from the back of his chair, his hat lying on the table in front of him. He'd been waving a fan made from a palmetto leaf to keep cool, but the little breeze did more than all the fanning Gabe had done. Possibly it was the rustle of the breeze that brought the tavern's proprietor out. The breeze died with his approach. *Damn man, must you chase off the breeze*, Gabe thought.

"May I get you gentlemen anything else?" the man asked.

"Yes," Eden replied. "Make Sir Gabe a jar of both the coconut and pineapple rum."

"Yes sir." The man wheeled to do as bid, mentally calculating the sale.

Once the man was gone, Eden started again, "With the guns, we will now have to train a militia of sorts to work them. Captain Montgomery has volunteered his gunner's mate to train our militia. No one has yet thought about that, Sir

Gabe." Leaning back, Eden stretched his legs and then casually propped his feet on an empty chair. Without realizing it, Gabe followed suit after taking another taste of his drink.

"Another thing," Eden started to say and then thought it funny and chuckled. "Another thing, Sir Gabe, for those guns to really be of use, we'll need to set up a night watch and a way to alarm the volunteers when they need to be manned. Ah...the desire for a means to defend ourselves. Now that we have it, who will be willing to volunteer? May have to train some of the free men. Pay them wages, I expect."

Gabe saw the humor in Eden's commentary. "Well, Mr. Eden, with the guns just being there, it ought to help some sleep easier."

"You're right, of course, Captain. Do you see Jamaica sending a company of soldiers here?" Eden asked. Then seeing Gabe's amused look, Eden answered his own question. "Not before hell freezes over, am I correct?"

"I think that sums it up," Gabe said smiling. "Damn, is this stuff getting to me? Suddenly, everything seems funny."

"In truth, aside from the privateer, who used Captain Neil and Captain Albright so sorely, we've not had any problems," Eden said. "In fact, this McCollough is a chivalrous sort. He sent a well-mannered officer ashore with a list of food stuff and coin to pay for it all. He was not among those at Cat Island was he, Sir Gabe?"

"No, sadly enough he wasn't. Nor was he at any of the other ports we looked into. In spite of many of his crew freely naming various rendez-vous ports, we found no trace of Captain McCollough or his ship, *Rattlesnake*. I think those with loose lips were doing just what the captain ordered, throwing us off. McCollough hasn't been as successful as he's been by letting his crew run off at the mouth," Gabe replied.

"I wondered," Eden admitted. "I think it was just a bit of bad luck that he happened into Georgetown at all. Had Neil and Albright not went aboard his ship, asking what business he had, they may never have been treated so harshly. When I think about it, Sir Gabe, and you can see for yourself, we don't have a lot to entice these daring buccaneers. Were it not for cotton, turtle meat, wood and sarsaparilla, we'd go hungry. As it is, Jamaica takes the majority of our few products in trade. Would you care for a good cigar, we have both Jamaican and Cuban seed tobacco?"

"Cuban would be nice," Gabe answered, thinking now the small talk is over and Eden is ready to get down to business.

After the cigars had been lighted and a few smoke rings were blown, Eden spoke again, "Sir Gabe, I would like to speak to you in a confidential manner, if I may?"

Holding the cigar between two fingers, Gabe lifted the glass at his hand and finished its contents. "Without knowing the subject it would be hard for me to promise confidentiality," Gabe said.

Eden thought this over for a few seconds. He nodded his understanding and then started speaking. "Your Lieutenant Vallin," he said, "is he the kind we could trust with my niece's hand?"

Gabe took the cigar from his mouth and looked at the tip, seeing that he had an even burn. He leaned back a second and then answered, "I have to admit, sir, I've only known Lieutenant Vallin for a few months. I have it from a good source that his family is well respected in Scotland and England. They are held in high regards by the crown prince himself, I'm told." Gabe didn't think it necessary to say his resource was Lord Skalla of the Foreign Service Department. "You are aware of Lieutenant Vallin's lineage. I understand his father gives him an allowance of one hundred guineas annually. I also know he's done rather well in prize money and he's been mentioned in the Gazette. From reports sent in by his commanding officers, I can say without hesitation that he is a first rate seaman and naval officer. Should this war last much longer, I can easily see him captain of his own ship. Were he in England, he probably would have already been given a command. As you know from your party, Mr. Eden, Lieutenant Vallin conducts himself as a gentleman."

"I must agree with you there, Sir Gabe. I appreciate your candor. I assume you know and understand the reasons I asked."

"Yes, I do," Gabe replied in a firm voice. "Had I not known I would have taken exception to the question."

A chill went down Eden's back when Gabe spoke. Eden thought to himself, *I don't think I want to be the one who causes this man exception.* The visible scars and streak of white in his hair didn't come from playing whist or going to the theater.

"Thank you for understanding my reasons, Sir Gabe." Looking at his guest's glass, Eden asked, "May I offer you another glass?"

"I think not, Mr. Eden. I'm to dine with Captain Montgomery aboard *Lynx* tonight. I don't want to stumble and fall going up to the entry port."

"Does that happen?" Eden asked. "Do men fall into the water?"

"Not often," Gabe replied with a smile, "but a few have gained the deck with a wet shoe or britches leg."

"No more then," Eden said. "I couldn't have our brew causing you to embarrass yourself. I will call for your libations to be taken to your ship. I had hoped, Captain," Eden said, using Gabe's rank and not his title, "that you would dine with us tonight. I have the feeling an announcement will be made. I think...I know Lieutenant Vallin would have liked for you to be present. I will pass on your regrets, of course."

Gabe stood and as he reached for his coat, he felt dizzy. *Is it that damnable drink, this cigar or both?* His head cleared quickly.

As he put on his coat, he noticed Eden smiling, "Sneaks up on you doesn't it?" He reached out to shake Gabe's hand and then held it a second longer before he released it. "I want to tell you, Captain, that Captain Montgomery is doing well. His being here is a blessing and has put many of our citizens' minds at ease. We are honored to have him here."

"Thank you," Gabe responded. "I'll pass on your kind words."

CHAPTER TWENTY FOUR

IT WAS NOON AND time to eat, but more importantly, it was time for the grog issue. On some ships the fife and drums announced the time, but *Leopard* had only a fair to middling drummer. They did have a fiddler, who could saw his strings and was a favorite among the hands. When the bosun's mate piped up spirits, the fiddler jumped in with a saucy rendition of Nancy Dawson. The cooks from the different messes quickly made their way to the rum tub to draw rations for their messmates.

Joshua Nesbit had witnessed the rush of men on numerous occasions. The sound of men's feet on the deck at the prescribed time gave a hint to the importance of the grog issued to the men. Thinking aloud, he said, "I find it hard to comprehend why men will rush to obtain such swill." Not realizing Gabe had walked within hearing, his laugh caused Nesbit to turn.

"Not up to your standards?" Gabe asked.

"Begging your pardon, Sir Gabe, but to answer your question, no. Though, as with anything I guess one would acquire a taste if there's nothing else available. But why not something other than diluted rum," Nesbit said.

Taking time to think, Gabe finally responded, "It's my understanding that it started as a replacement for beer or wine, which didn't keep well in these climates. Not only did the rum keep, it seemed to improve with age."

"I see," Nesbit said. "One more question, Sir Gabe. How did rum become grog?"

"My father, Lord James Anthony, said Admiral Vernon constantly wore a boat cloak made from grogram. He was soon to be nicknamed 'Old Grogram'. It was he that decreed the rum issue be diluted one to four. From that time on, the drink was called grog."

"I see, sir. As I recall, Lord Anthony's cox'n sets great store by the drink," Nesbit said.

Gabe laughed again. "Bart loves his 'rumbustion' alright, but unless it was in a pinch I doubt he's drank grog in years. My brother told me once that Bart always went to sea with two chests. One of which had a distinct clink of glass when handled roughly."

"I'd hate to be the sod who handled it too roughly," Nesbit replied with a smile.

"You and me both," Gabe admitted. "Hopefully, the man could swim, as Bart would surely toss the poor soul over the side."

"Would you care for a glass of something a bit more satisfying than the grog, sir? I've prepared a light meal for you knowing a proper meal sits heavy on a man in this heat," Nesbit asked.

"Yes, something with a chill on it if you will,"

Gabe replied. He leaned back in his desk chair waiting on his refreshment. With luck, they'd be in Port Royal before the sun went down.

***

LORD GILBERT ANTHONY, VICE Admiral of the White, stepped down from the carriage followed by his flag captain, Stephen Earl. They had been invited to dine with Admiral Peter Parker and Lady Parker at their private residence atop of what was to be called Admiral Mountain.

Sitting high up as it did, there always seemed to be a refreshing breeze. Tall palm trees were situated along the roadway up to the house and were also planted where a shade graced the porches. Arriving as they did, without anyone noticing their arrival, the voice...agitated voice of a woman could be heard.

"Cornwallis makes no bones of the woman being his mistress. She was his slave for heaven's sake, now he treats her like an equal."

"She's a doctress," Parker said, trying to calm his wife.

"She's his mistress," Lady Parker said again.

"She is his housekeeper," Parker said, trying to calm his wife.

"I bet she cleans up," Lady Parker threw back.

At that time a doorman, whose attention had been on Admiral and Lady Parker, noticed the guests had arrived. Speaking so that his voice carried, he rushed to the door announcing that the guests had arrived.

Anthony and Earl were shown in, to be greeted by a flushed Peter Parker. Shaking hands with Anthony, he whispered, "Why women can't let well enough alone is more than I can understand."

Anthony smiled back but didn't say anything. Lady Deborah would not have had second thoughts on the subject. She would not have approved, but would have felt it was not her place to make judgments. Thinking on it, Lord Anthony thought his wife was the most diplomatic woman he'd ever met. More so than his mother and his sister, and though he'd not say it, far more than Faith. Livi, Admiral Buck's soon to be wife, was much like Deborah. Maybe it was from all the years in the islands. If the war kept going and they continued their stay in the West Indies, would women like Lady Parker and Faith have a change of heart? Only time would tell.

***

THE EVENING MEAL WAS outstanding. A turtle soup, followed by garden vegetables that Lady Parker said their gardener grew on the grounds.

"We've set up a cistern to hold rain water and we use that to water the garden," she told her guests.

A rack of lamb had been fixed island style with both a sweet and spicy flavor. This was set off by hot bread cooked to a golden brown. A bowl of fresh butter sat on the table to spread over the tasty bread. They had coconut custard for dessert.

After the meal, the men retired to a side porch to light up cigars. The porch was situated on the east side of the house away from the setting sun. A zephyr caused the fronds of the palm trees to rustle. Parker was telling Anthony that he'd be going back to England soon.

"My wife is most anxious to return, whereas, I have mixed emotions," Parker said.

"I've been told you are in line to pick up Vice Admiral," Lord Anthony stated. He'd heard this from Lord Skalla.

"It has been mentioned," Parker admitted, "but I've learned not to trust rumors."

The sound of a galloping horse could be heard. Admiral Parker rose up and said, "Who could be using a horse so ill, galloping up here?"

"Must be important," Lord Anthony said.

"Aye," Parker agreed.

A young naval lieutenant dismounted from the horse. The reins were given to a servant, who walked the winded, blowing animal before watering it.

"Sir," the lieutenant said, handing a note to his admiral. "The *Porcupine*," seeing Lord Anthony's questioning look, he added, "armed merchantman, fourteen guns has just returned to port. She relates she just barely avoided capture by a French brig."

"One brig?" Parker asked, with annoyance in his voice.

"No sir, the brig was on the far side of a large

convoy. The captain stated his lookout thought he could make out both French and Spanish sails."

"I see," Parker said. He then asked, "Has Cornwallis been sighted?"

"No Admiral, but one of Lord Anthony's ships was entering port, HMS *Leopard*."

"Good," Anthony responded. "Admiral Parker, we will set sail at first light."

"Thank you," Parker replied.

Turning to the lieutenant, Anthony said, "I'd like to talk with *Porcupine's* captain."

"We thought you might...or Admiral Parker might," the lieutenant said.

Parker waved his hand in deference, "Lord Anthony has the ships, I don't."

"There's a few in port," the lieutenant replied, trying to be positive.

"Humph...the best I could do with those is scuttle them at the entrance to the harbor, and block the entrance. Otherwise, they'd make a nuisance and little more to a frigate or ship of the line. Lord Anthony, I'll have the carriage brought around while I tell Lady Parker I'll be gone. Lieutenant, let your horse rest for a while. I'll see that Lady Parker offers you some refreshment. After that, you can return to Port Royal," Parker said.

"You are most kind, Admiral," the lieutenant replied.

As the carriage pulled away, Parker leaned over to Anthony and whispered, "Lieutenant

Smyth comes from a good Kent family, but he's somewhat of an embarrassment to them. His father is an old friend, so I've found a place for him here. There's no concern on my part of leaving him alone with Lady Parker as he much prefers the Windward Passage."

Shocked, Anthony said, "You allow him to serve?"

"In a manner of speaking. Before we left England, I sat him down and told him his sexual preferences would not be tolerated on my navy base. What he did in Kingston was none of my business, unless it came to reflect on my command or the Navy in general. He knows he will never rise above lieutenant. He has...associates in Kingston that tell him with his education and knowledge of Navy organization, he could get a job with the Honest Johns and post to India, where his particular activities would not be an impediment. He might even be able to return to England as some haughty nabob," Parker replied.

Anthony nodded his agreement but his mind was on the convoy. He was glad Gabe was back. *Leopard's* weight would surely be needed...if they found the convoy. *Damn*, he thought, *what would I give for better information, something to do away with the 'ifs'?*

CHAPTER TWENTY FIVE

THE MORNING MIST GAVE temporary relief to what promised to be another scorching day. Gray clouds hung low over Port Royal Harbor but Pittman, *HMS Leopard's* master, promised they'd clear by mid-morning. As *Leopard* was the last ship in harbor, she would lead Lord Anthony's squadron out of the harbor.

When Lord Anthony, with Admiral Parker, returned to *HMS SeaHorse*, a general message for all captains and first lieutenants to repair on board the flagship was sent out. All of Anthony's ships were already provisioned and ready to sail, including *Leopard*.

Flag Captain Stephen Earl would have been very surprised if any ship in the squadron had not been fully ready for sea. He had known his lordship for a long time and found him to be a firm but fair commander. Yet any officer whose ship was not prepared to sail against the enemy would likely find himself on the beach. Knowing *Leopard* had just returned to port, he inquired privately if Gabe had any dire needs such as fresh water before sailing.

"No," Gabe had replied. "I wouldn't want to

sail to England with our supply but we've enough for this task."

Leopard was now easing out of harbor. She would reduce her sails and await orders as to her position once the squadron cleared port. Frostbrier, on *Phoenix*, would no doubt be out forward, trying to locate the enemy. *Tomahawk*, under David Davy; and *Bulldog*, under Greg Kirk would undoubtedly be on the flanks but in sight of the ship.

As the anchor was catted home, *Leopard's* sails bellowed out. The wind was sufficient for working the ship. Small wavelets lapped against the hull as *Leopard* picked up speed.

"We'll pick up a gentle wind once we are clear of the harbor," Pittman volunteered. "We will make five or six knots, unless I miss my guess. As close as we are to hurricane season, it would not surprise me to pick up a moderate breeze by noon."

Gabe merely nodded his acceptance. He'd learned long ago that there was little to be gained by disagreeing or doubting the master.

Freshly promoted Laqua had the watch. He'd relieved Bufford. While Bufford was senior, Gabe had on occasion found the man lacking in conduct. His wardroom comments about Laqua had been mentioned by the servants. Thus far, Gabe, who had been informed by Hex of the behavior, had said nothing. He still remembered the midshipman's berth and how with time the bullies tended to get their comeuppance. Vallin had said nothing and after the way he took the purser to task, Gabe felt he would intervene if needed.

Gabe feeling a bit of devilment inside him, walked over to where Laqua stood talking to a petty officer in his division.

"Morning, Captain," Laqua volunteered.

"Good morning, Mr. Laqua. I see my faith in you has not been a waste. You keep a good watch and I notice your gun deck is spot on."

"Thank you, Captain. I will do my best."

"No doubts, Mr. Laqua. I think I shall go below, as you seem to have all in order."

Dagan had just stepped through the companionway and over the coaming when he heard Gabe's comments. Knowing why Gabe said it, Dagan was not sure it would serve the intended purpose. It would definitely let everyone know Laqua had the captain's eye. Possibly he might even be considered a protégé. But should Laqua fail, it would be brought to the forefront. It could even cause jealousy and where an officer might have helped or given a word to the wise, it might now be held back. Gabe had been the brunt of many unkind words growing up. Now, he tended to come to the aid of those he felt were being treated unfairly. It would on this occasion certainly let the wardroom officers know Laqua held his present rank in part due to Captain Sir Gabriel Anthony, brother of Vice Admiral Lord Anthony. Well, it was done now. Only time would tell if the remarks would help or hinder Laqua.

***

LORD ANTHONY'S SQUADRON HAD all cleared port and was standing out to sea. A signal was given for *Leopard* to take station behind and to larboard of the flagship. Once the maneuvers for taking station on the flag had been completed, First Lieutenant Con Vallin requested to exercise the hands-on gun drill.

Gabe gave his approval and jokingly added, "No live fire. I don't want the admiral to think we've mutinied."

This brought laughter from all around. Heading into harm's way, it was a good idea to exercise the guns. Keeps the hands occupied mentally and physically. Besides a little extra drill might just mean the difference in surviving.

Seeing Dagan, Gabe walked over and asked, "What say you, Uncle? Will this be a fruitless chase or will we come to arms?"

"To arms, I think, but the real battle lies ahead and not from the enemy's cannons," Dagan replied. He then turned abruptly and went below.

"Damnation, why did I have to ask?" Gabe cursed silently, and then went below for something to drink. Maybe, the coffee would still be warm.

***

RETURNING TO THE MAIN deck, Gabe was approached by the first lieutenant, who had his watch in his hand. *HMS Leopard* rated as a fifty gun, fourth rate ship. On the lower deck, she mounted twenty-two twenty-four pounders; on her upper deck there were twenty-two twelve pounders. She carried two twenty-four pound carronades in the forecastle, and four six pounders on the quarterdeck. Thus, *Leopard* actually mounted fifty-two guns plus swivels.

"I think we will only exercise the great guns for the first hour," Gabe said to Vallin.

"Aye sir."

Gabe then spoke to Bufford, who was in charge of the lower gun deck. "We will start with your division first, Mr. Bufford."

"Silence," Bufford bellowed. No conversation of any kind was allowed. Silence immediately fell over the starboard section of the lower gun deck.

Midshipman Jarvis Jackson stood by Bufford, he would take command of the gun deck if Bufford were to fall. The gun captains were all experienced seamen and a gunner's mate was assigned to each battery of four guns on *Leopard's gun deck*.

The crash of waves against the hull could be heard as the gun crews awaited the word. One man was biting his fingernails while another repeatedly licked his lips. One old gunner moved a chew of tobaccy to the other side of his toothless mouth.

Bufford finally ordered, "Open your gun ports. Cast loose your guns." With a squeal and grinding sound the guns rolled back on the tackles. "Level your guns."

The sponger heaved his handspike under the

gun breach. As it rose the gun captain placed a wedge under the breach to hold it level.

'Out Tompion' was ordered by the gun captain. The first sponger took out the tompion and passed it to the second sponger, who hung it amidships.

"Sponge your guns." The sponger had to lean out of the gun port to insert the sponge and work the handle. The first sponger rammed a wet sponge down the barrel. The gun captain made a show of placing his thumb over the touch-hole while the sponge was being removed, creating a vacuum in the gun to extinguish any sparks had the gun just been fired.

"Load cartridge." The powder boy passed the powder charge to the first loader.

"Ram cartridge." The rammer rammed the charge home.

"Load ball." The shot and wad man passed a selected round and wad to the loader. The wad was placed between the cartridge and round.

"Ram round." Round and wad were rammed against the charge. The gun captain inserted the priming wire into the touch-hole, making a hole in the cartridge bag. He then primed the gun.

"Run out." The side tackle men strained as they run the gun up to the side of the ship. The gun captain then sighted the gun using an elevating screw or quoin.

The gun captain then stepped back and yelled, "Fire as you bear." This ended the gun drill.

"Time?" Gabe barked.

"Three minutes and a half," Vallin proclaimed. Gabe eyed him suspiciously. Smiling, Vallin said, "By this watch, sir."

"I'd take it to a clock maker when we return to Barbados," Gabe replied. "Continue the drill, Mr. Vallin, until it's less than three minutes by your chronometer."

"But, sir," Vallin feigned insult. "This watch was made by Harrison, one of England's finest."

"Humph," Gabe snorted. "You had better learn to tell time then. Under three minutes by your watch, Lieutenant, under three minutes."

The drill was in Gabe's own opinion a full minute longer than the three thirty proclaimed. If the morrow's horizon provided a convoy, they would need the speed...the speed, practice, and above all accuracy.

CHAPTER TWENTY SIX

A RELENTLESS, SLEETY RAIN MADE standing watch a misery. The rain was bad enough, but the unusual cold that came with it was unmerciful. Pittman ducked into the wardroom for something to warm his bones and then he'd go back on deck and face the elements.

"Unusual weather is it not, Mr. Pittman?"

"Hurricane season," the master responded. "All types of oddities come with it, but this shat makes me nervous about what comes next."

"Hopefully we'll be back in Antigua," Lieutenant Tolbert said, picking up on the conversation as he walked into the area. Lieutenant Laqua had just relieved him so he could get a little something to ease the effects of the elements.

"I thought you had the watch," Vallin said, almost as an accusation.

"Lieutenant Laqua gave me a minute to freshen a bit...warm up as it were," Tolbert replied.

"Be thankful that Bufford is not relieving you. He'd be late," Pittman said, looking at Vallin.

"Did I hear my name?" Bufford asked. He'd been in his cabin.

"Just saying what a fine sort Laqua was to relieve me for a spot," Tolbert said.

"Humph! He's just seeking to make a place for himself among his betters," Bufford replied.

"I think not," Vallin responded. "I think he's made a place for himself. He's a lieutenant just like you, the last time I looked."

"Captain's arse licker, that's what he is," Bufford said.

"Enough," Vallin snapped. "Not another word. I've tolerated your ways too long, thinking that you'd come around. Lieutenant Laqua is a fine officer and a welcome member of this mess. I shall not tolerate another insult toward him. Do I make myself clear...do I, Lieutenant Bufford?"

"Aye."

"Very well, that ends it," Vallin said.

Finishing his drink, Pittman smiled to himself. He had started to wonder when or if Vallin would come around. Bufford had made a great arse of himself. Hopefully the day would never come when he would have to serve on a ship Bufford commanded.

On deck, the wind whipped the waves so they'd lost their blue tint and were almost as gray as the clouds. Laqua held on to the binnacle, his knuckles white from gripping so hard. Rain stung as it hit his face and made seeing almost impossible. The tarpaulin helped with the stinging rain but did little to keep one dry. Two men were on the wheel and they were having a time of it. Seeing the master, Laqua smiled.

"On course?" Pittman asked.

Laqua answered by pointing to the compass. With the ship rolling like a pregnant whale, the helmsmen were doing a good job Pittman nodded again and stiffly made his way to the chart room. As he pulled the door shut, he noticed Tolbert was back on deck, ready to assume his watch. *Laqua was a good sort*, he thought. Being a master's mate, he'd had a lot of training by men who knew the sea. As long as he didn't forget it, he'd make a good officer. *It'd been better had he become a ship's master like me*, Pittman thought, but then he was biased.

***

ON THE LOWER DECK, a seaman was telling his mates how the first lieutenant had told that pig, Bufford, off. "I was trading with Smilley." He was one of the officer's servants. "Lieutenant Tolbert was relieved by Laqua so's he could get a wet and everyone was making what a nice chap 'e were, when ole pig face, Bufford, told as 'ow they was all bloody daft. He said Lieutenant Laqua didn't belong in the officer's mess wid 'is betters, all lofty like."

"'ou do 'e think 'e is?" a seaman named James broke in. "Laqua is not a bad bloke, not even for an officer."

"Well Vallin, 'e up and told 'is bleeding lordship, pig face Bufford off," the seaman continued.

"Better watch out," James interrupted again. "'e'll 'ave you in blocks afore long."

"Aye," another said. "'owever this cap'n don't 'old wid the cat-o-nine tails as 'sums does."

"Well, old Vallin, 'e made no bone about voicing 'is 'pinion about Laqua."

"You 'eard all this?" one of the older mates asked.

"Aye, every word. Me and Smilley was tucked down in the pantry but it was plain as day. Couldn't see pig face, but 'e was fair fuming 'e was. He waited for Vallin to leave before 'e said anything. He was an unhappy lookin' man when 'e passed us by," the seaman said.

"'e didn't see ya?"

"Not so I could tell. Probably thought I was just a servant like Smilley."

"Reckon 'e'd take a poke at Vallin?" James asked.

"Not unless 'e wanted 'is arse kicked, to my way o' thinking. Lieutenant Vallin doesn't 'pear to me like a bloke you'd mess wid."

"Aye, and there's sum I'm thinkin' who'd 'elp 'im over the side, I reckon."

"Say 'e'd done it on purpose like, if we says anything. We could be so bleedin' lucky. More than one 'as fell over on a night like this un."

"Some un is coming," a voice hissed.

It was Midshipman Jackson making his way to the midshipmen's berth. He smiled and greeted the men as he passed. They were all in his division and he was well liked.

"Thar be another one pig-face Bufford 'arps on. Maybe 'e'll get 'is soon."

"We can only 'ope so," someone said. "Jackson be one o' the better snotties."

"Aye, 'e takes to you learning 'im, 'e does."

***

ONE OF THE ADVANTAGES of being an admiral is that you don't have to go on deck in all the elements thrown at you. The admiral's staff also was able to appreciate the same advantage. Captain Earl stopped at the entrance of the admiral's cabin and hung his tarpaulin and drenched hat on a peg before he entered. The marine sentry frowned and took a side step as water dripped from the hat and tarpaulin, making pools of water on the deck that ran back and forth with the roll of the ship.

"A bad night." This was the third time the captain had come down to report to his lordship.

I'm tired of standing, the marine thought. It could be worse though, he could be on deck and drenched like the seaman. He heard Silas ask if the cap'n wanted a cup of coffee. *I'd like some myself*, the marine sentry thought, knowing it'd be laced with brandy. If you took a deep breath, you could catch a hint of the brandy's odor...*Lucky sods. We get grog and they drink the good stuff.* He knew because Silas had slipped him some, time and again. But not tonight, too much coming and going to chance it.

"Nothing yet, Stephen?" Lord Anthony asked.

"No sir," Stephen replied.

It had been a guess, a wild guess as to what

course the enemy had taken. *Porcupine's* captain had said they were headed nor-nor-west off Dominica when he was spotted and chased. They were headed for the colonies, Anthony was sure. His only question was whether they would sail on, or stop at Guadeloupe. 'I don't think so,' *Porcupine's* captain had said when the question was asked. Neither did Captain Earl, Admiral Parker, or himself. Which route? That was the big question. Did they pass between the Virgin Islands and Saint Kitts, taking the Sombrero Passage? Did they pass between Puerto Rico and Hispaniola? Anthony was sure they didn't sail close enough to Jamaica to take the Windward Passage between Cuba and Hispaniola. He did not rule out the possibility that either San Juan or Havana might be possible ports.

He'd sent Frostbrier's *Phoenix* to look in at Havana and meet up with the squadron north of Puerto Rico, sailing on a northerly course toward the colonies. If he found the enemy at San Juan, he'd send either *Bulldog* or *Tomahawk* for Frostbrier.

Sinking in one of the admiral's leather chairs, Captain Earl thanked Silas for his coffee. "Do we shorten sail as we pass through the passage and have a look-see into San Juan with the dawn?"

"As you think best," Anthony said, showing he trusted his captain's judgment.

Porcupine's captain had recommended the Mona Passage be avoided. "It's a treacherous business during the day, and I'd never try it at night."

Separating the islands of Hispaniola and Puerto Rico, the Mona Passage connects the Caribbean Sea to the Atlantic. It was the shortest route but had a dark reputation. The eighty mile stretch was prone to unusual currents created by sandbanks stretching out from the islands on either side. To make matters worse, three islands, in the passage itself, caused shoals and a variation of the wind, which always seemed to be coming off the bow regardless of the direction you sailed. In addition to the tricky currents caused by the islands of Mona, Monito, and Desecheo, tall, rocky cliffs towering two hundred feet above the sea made a wind tunnel of sorts, where even on a calm day they swirled at fifteen knots and more, with the sea five feet or higher on a beautiful day. Bart recounted how some of the older Jamaicans had told of pirates throwing women they'd raped or who were menstruating into the sea, to watch and see how long they survived before circling sharks took them.

"A bad business, if it's true," Earl remarked.

"Aye," Bart answered. "I believe it, 'aving met some of the bloody buggers."

Earl finished his coffee and then got ready to go back on deck. The wind, which had been shrieking through the riggings, had lost some of its intensity. "The master promises clearing on the morrow," Earl announced on the way out.

"Hopefully, the enemy has faced the same elements we have," Lord Anthony replied.

"Aye," Earl responded. "At least, we don't have a lot of grocery captains slowing us down."

Bart smiled; it was the same regardless of navies. Convoy duty was hated by one and all. "I think I'll finish me pipe and this wet and then call it a night. No need for ole Bart's help. Cap'n Earl has it under control, 'e does. Course 'e ought too, as much time as I spent teaching 'im when 'e was a youngster." *Learned mostly*, Bart thought, as he turned up his cup.

CHAPTER TWENTY SEVEN

LIEUTENANT DAVID DAVY, CAPTAIN *HMS Toma-hawk*, stood at the taffrail puffing on a Cuban cigar that had been given to him by Con Vallin, Gabe's first lieutenant.

"Light it when you have time to enjoy it," Vallin had said. "You'll never smoke a finer stick of tobacco." He went into the specifics of how it should be lit. "You don't thump the cigar's ash, you let it fall off on its own accord." And then with a straight face, Vallin had asked, "Do you know the secret of why a Cuban cigar is so much better than any other in the world?" Davy replied it had to do with the soil, the growing conditions and the rain. "No, no," Vallin cut Lieutenant Davy off quickly. "Tobacco leaf is tobacco leaf. Some are definitely better than others but the Cuban cigar is special because of the way it's rolled."

Davy had seen many a cigar rolled but couldn't tell much difference between the individual rollers. Vallin smiled, shaking his head. "I thought you a worldly man, David. The cigar, that fine cigar, the upmost in taste and pleasure comes only in this specific brand. Now the truth. Do you know why they are so much better?" Without waiting for Davy to answer or reply, Vallin charged on, "It's because, my friend, these cigars are rolled between the thighs of fourteen year old virgins."

Davy could not believe what he was hearing and looked thunderstruck. Vallin clapped him a good one across the shoulder as he burst out laughing. "You'll never smoke another virgin Havana without remembering that," Vallin said, getting his laughter under control.

Davy smiled good-naturedly and wondered if Bart had told the tale to Vallin. It sounded like something Bart would cook up.

"Deck thar," *Tomahawk's* lookout called down. "I see a light, almost a blinking light, sir."

"Where away?"

"Amidships larboard side, sir. It comes and goes, it does, sir."

A little frustrated, Davy tossed the half-smoked cigar over the side and bounded up the shrouds before his lieutenant could offer. Making the lookout's platform, he was a touch out of breath. "Damnation, I used to run up the ratlines."

"You 'um still pretty quick," the lookout said.

"Where is this blinking light?" Davy asked.

"Look yonder amidships, sir. Just keep yer eyes on it."

Before the lookout finished speaking, Davy saw it. It was only for a moment, and then it was gone and returned in a few minutes. Davy watched it again and again. He turned to his lookout, "A double tot for you, Smythe, tell the purser it's the captain's orders and I'll brook no argument."

Smiling, the old lookout knuckled his head, "Thank ye, Cap'n."

Davy went down a backstay but slowly. "Come about, Mr. Ruby. We've spotted the convoy."

***

IN LORD ANTHONY'S CABIN, Lieutenant Davy explained, "At first, I didn't know what it was and then I realized it was the stern lamps of a ship rising to appear and then disappearing as it fell in a trough. I looked at it through the night glass and it was not one ship's stern lamps but many. I think it's the enemy convoy."

"Good work, Lieutenant," Lord Anthony praised Davy. "It's almost dawn. Go back to your ship. Captain Earl, get with the master and plot a course to intercept the enemy using Davy's sightings."

"Think we'll see them with the dawn?" Earl asked.

"Maybe a straggler, but I'd think it'd be later. We are not far off their course, now," Anthony said.

"Aye," Earl replied as he went to get the master.

***

The dawn was clear to the horizon and the men were released from quarters and went about their daily routine, only today an air of excitement was about the ship. The enemy convoy was in the making and that meant prize money. No one thought they might be killed. It may happen to a mate but not to them.

On the quarterdeck, Lord Anthony watched as a seaman cleaned a scope of salt stains. The sun's rays were breaking through the early morning haze. The swells were not as steep as they'd been during the squall last night. The wind had lessened but it still was a fresh breeze.

SeaHorse seemed to rise and fall as she climbed one wave and then fell into the trough. *Would they see the enemy when the early morning mist cleared away?* The squadron lay comfortably on the starboard tack, headed north-westerly.

After *Tomahawk's* sighting, Lord Anthony had sent Frostbrier's *Phoenix* to the front. Frostbrier was an experienced captain with a level head. Maybe Gabe was right in thinking the captured *Comete* would be a good step up for Frostbrier.

Tugging on the chain of his watch, Lord Anthony was thinking a cup of Silas' special coffee might prove satisfying. He beckoned to Bart and as the two started down to his cabin, the lookout called down, "From *Phoenix*, sir, enemy in sight."

I know the lookout can't read the signals, Anthony thought, and then realized Earl, who was expecting the enemy to be in the offing, had sent a midshipman aloft with the lookout. The youngest of the mids would recognize the signal for enemy in sight.

After pausing a second, Anthony replied, "Come on, Bart, let's get out of Captain Earl's way so he can prepare his ship."

"Aye," Bart mumbled.

***

CAPTAIN STEPHEN EARL TOOK another step up the ratlines and, bracing himself, tried to focus on the distant ships. Doubts went through his mind. It was a big convoy and therefore had to have sufficient escort ships. *Would they be a match?* Mentally, he tried to do the arithmetic. *Tomahawk* and *Bulldog* could wreak havoc among the merchant ships. Jepson's *Revenant* would hold its own against any ship of similar size. That left the *Phoenix* with thirty-six guns, *Leopard* with fifty guns and *SeaHorse's* seventy-four guns to deal with the rest. It would depend on Lord Anthony's tactics. Did he want to damage the convoy, which was a certainty, or did he want to destroy the enemy war ships? *David and Goliath*, he thought.

CHAPTER TWENTY EIGHT

Fᴿᴼᴹ *Pʜᴏᴇɴɪx*, sɪʀ, ꜰᴏᴜʀ ships of the line and a frigate, estimates thirty merchant ships and transports...transports?

"French troops to help the Americans?" Flag Lieutenant Mahan questioned.

"Aye!" Captain Earl and Lord Anthony both said it in unison.

"From Phoenix, sir." There was a pause as the signal's midshipman seemed to be checking his book. When he felt assured, he repeated, "From *Phoenix*, sir, Comte dé Gichen."

"How the devil does he know that?" Mahan asked.

"His first lieutenant is part French," Earl replied. "He probably studies the flags."

"Captain!" Lord Anthony spoke with authority. "General signal, please 'Prepare for battle.' When you've made the signal, make another to *Revenant*, *Bulldog*, and *Tomahawk*, 'Attack convoy.' And then to *Phoenix* and *Leopard's* numbers, 'Form on flag.'"

"Aye, aye my Lord," Stephen replied.

***

Lᴏʀᴅ Aɴᴛʜᴏɴʏ ʜᴇʟᴅ ᴏᴜᴛ his arms as Bart helped him in his waistcoat. "Nice target," Bart muttered as he took down Lord Anthony's sword and clipped it on. He went to the cabinet, took out a brace of pistols, powder, and shot. They were a matched pair, a gift from Lady Deborah.

Silas stood to the side, "Anything else, my Lord?" He had held up the bosun's party, who were waiting to carry the admiral's furniture to the hold.

The partitions would then be struck down. Silas would go down and assist the surgeon and his mates. Bart winked at Silas, who smiled. They had been through it before. Each knowing this might be the last battle. The odds were bad, everyone but a fool knew it.

On deck, the wind was steady. Seeing the admiral, Captain Earl gave him his telescope. Anthony could now make out the French warships. "Sixty-fours, I believe, Stephen."

"Aye, at least two of them," Earl replied. "One is carrying dé Gichen's flag."

Anthony glanced at their flag. "Our country's flag, Stephen, is it not a majestic sight?"

"Aye, my Lord," Earl answered with a lump in his throat. He was looking at Lord Anthony's flag on the foremast.

"Alter course three points to larboard, steer north-by-west please, Captain," Anthony said.

"Aye sir," Earl responded.

SeaHorse's seamen hauled on the braces, while others freed the main course as bosun mates scrambled about, shouting at first one man and then another. As the wind filled the sails the deck canted and men had to hold on. Lord Anthony grabbed a rail.

Earl, seemingly unaffected by the leaning deck, watched the compass. "Steady, steady as you go," he ordered the helmsmen. Bart looked aft and watched as Gabe had *Leopard* following in the flagship's wake.

"Load and run out," Lord Anthony ordered Earl.

From somewhere forward, a seaman shouted "Us'll show 'em, three cheers for the admiral."

Lord Anthony felt a chill run through him as the cheers went up. *Our men will take this day*, he thought...*they have to*.

The gun ports squeaked in protest as they were hauled open, and the black snouts were hauled in place.

"Brail up the courses?" Captain Earl asked.

"Aye, Stephen, she's your ship."

Tomahawk, *Bulldog*, and *Revenant* were now among the convoy. Cannons fired and water spouts appeared.

"Damme, but that Frog will hit his own ships," Mahan swore. To prove his words, one of the French merchantmen veered to starboard, trying to get out of the line of fire. Doing so, he ran directly into another ship amidships.

"The Frogs be doing our work for us," Bart snorted.

"*Bulldog* has blasted a transport rudder,"

exclaimed David Neal, the first lieutenant.

"Possible head money," the master ventured.

One of the sixty-fours, the one with dé Gichen's flag, had come about. A French frigate had already come about and appeared to be headed toward the ships attacking the convoy. Earl was about to ask if Lord Anthony wanted *Phoenix* to intercept the French frigate.

Lord Anthony almost as if reading Earl's unasked question said, "George will have to handle that one." The French sixty-four was now bearing down on *SeaHorse*.

"Stand by to larboard." Johns, the second lieutenant, was pacing up and down the gun deck, making sure for the tenth time that each gun was ready. "As you bear," he shouted. "Watch the admiral."

Earl raised his sword. When Anthony nodded, he roared, "Fire," as he sliced down with his sword.

The forecastle carronades and *SeaHorse's* cannons spoke with authority as orange flames leaped out of the gun's muzzles. Anthony cringed at the deafening roar. The tearing of wood and shouts of men could be heard as ball after ball slammed into the French sixty-four. However, the Frenchie got in her licks and *SeaHorse* shuddered as enemy balls slammed into her.

SeaHorse's first broadside had been grape on top of ball. Mahan saw with horror the number of French sailors lying about on the sixty-four's deck, as the ships passed through the battle smoke. Another ship was now almost on *SeaHorse*, her forward guns firing, causing *SeaHorse's* deck to jar, throwing Mr. Neal down. As he tried to stand he fell again; his arm was broken. Bart rushed over to help the lieutenant and through the smoke he saw the enemy ship was alongside.

"Fire," Earl shouted as the starboard guns now spit forth their death and destruction. On the gun deck, Lieutenant Johns and a midshipman yelled encouragement to the gunners who went about their work in a rapid but methodical manner. Sounding like thunder, the foremast on the enemy ship was hit. The mast leaned and then toppled over, bringing with it riggings and stays. As the mast toppled over the larboard side the ship veered. As it did so, Gabe on *Leopard* crossed her stern and poured a full broadside, one gun after another up the arse end. The ship seemed to rumble and leap out of the water, breaking in half and sinking. A loud cheer went up from the British seamen.

"Silence," Earl shouted. He was glad to put an end to one ship but hated to see lives lost in such a fashion.

Coughing from all the smoke, Mr. Waters, the master, shouted, "The breeze has died."

Phoenix was now alongside the first French sixty-four. Neither ship was firing and they seemed to be drifting apart.

"The Frogs must think that *Phoenix* is too small," Mahan volunteered.

"More afraid that we'll bring the ship around and blast her, I'm thinkin'," Bart replied.

"Captain Earl, let's take advantage of the lull and put our ship back to rights," Anthony ordered.

"Aye, sir. I've already sent for the carpenter and gunner. We have two guns out of action that I know of."

Leopard was within hailing distance. Taking up a speaking trumpet, Lord Anthony called, "Captain Anthony, are you able to continue battle?"

"Aye," Gabe answered.

What a dumb question, Lord Anthony thought, *what else would he say*. Reforming his question, Lord Anthony hailed again, "Do you need assistance of any kind?"

"Only from the Almighty, should he choose to favor us with a wind," Gabe replied.

"Rascal," Bart snorted.

The wind did not return. All through the night, watches were set up to guard against boat attacks. Repairs were continued and by dawn tired men were fed, one watch at a time. There was still no wind...

CHAPTER TWENTY NINE

THE WIND RETURNED WITH the dawn, light and perverse at first, but gave way to a steady, gentle breeze.

"Damme, but the Frogs are catching the wind first," Captain Earl snarled.

The French ships' sails were filling sufficiently to work the ships. *Do we put boats in the water*, Earl wondered to himself, but dismissed the idea immediately. In a few minutes, he was glad of his decision as the sails began flapping as they filled with the wind. A cheer went up among the hands. Taking his glass, Captain Earl made a quick survey of the squadron and noticed all the ships were catching the wind.

"The wind has returned, I see," Lord Anthony said to Captain Earl. The captain was so intent on checking the squadron he'd not heard the admiral walk up.

"Morning, my Lord," Earl responded.

Nodding his reply, Lord Anthony's attention was now on the French sixty-four. She and *Phoenix* had been engaged when the wind had died. "Make signal to *Leopard*, 'Assist *Phoenix*, engage enemy,'" Lord Anthony ordered.

"Aye," Earl replied. He turned to relay the message to the signals midshipmen. The mid had been standing close by and had heard the order and was busy putting the signal together to be hoisted.

***

DAGAN SAW THE SIGNAL from the flagship. He, like Gabe, had been expecting the order and had said as much. Gabe had already made the necessary orders to his first lieutenant. Vallin was now busy getting all ready to carry out the signal when it arrived. Therefore, *Leopard* was ready to come about and bear down on the enemy.

On board the flagship, Mahan volunteered, "Damn quick, I'd say."

Bart smiled, "'spected it, 'e did. Taught 'im well, I did."

Lord Anthony standing behind Bart swore, "Do you take credit for everything, you scoundrel?"

"Only when it's due," Bart answered with no hint of apology.

"Ignore him, Patrick," Lord Anthony hissed. "Next thing, you know, he'll take credit for the wind."

Bart thrust out his chin and said, "I's did talk to the Almighty bout it, that's a fact."

Anthony shook his head but didn't reply. In his own way, Bart probably did send up a prayer.

***

ON BOARD *PHOENIX*, FROSTBRIER had gotten his ship underway. It was unusual for a frigate to engage a sixty-four. The weight of the sixty-four's smallest gun was larger than *Phoenix's* largest gun. Twelve good hands had been sent to the deep when the wind had died last night, to prove it.

Now, the signal to engage the enemy flew aloft. *Leopard* was charging down to do just that. While Frostbrier was senior to Gabe on the captain's list, *Leopard* took command, being the larger ship. The two ships were now in hailing distance as they converged on the Frenchie.

"Attack the stern, the stern," Gabe shouted through the speaking trumpet.

Frostbrier waved signifying he understood. *Leopard* would attack broadside to broadside, hopefully keeping the French occupied while he inflicted what damage he could on the minimally protected stern. Good strategy if it worked, but just as the sixty-four's cannons outweighed *Phoenix*, so did they outweigh *Leopard*.

The sixty-four was late in taking advantage of the wind, but even so *Leopard* and *Phoenix* were making only four to five knots.

"She's either a lubberly ran ship or she's been in port so long, she's got weeds as a sea anchor," Pittman, the master, said.

"That or she wants us to catch her," Vallin answered.

It appeared the sixty-four was making little more than steerage way. Gabe had heard the interchange but didn't join in. He wondered, like

Vallin, why the ship was not making more sail. "Mr. Pittman, I don't like it. I think Vallin is right. Yonder ship is too slovenly for my liking." Gabe continued to watch and there was little activity on the Frenchie.

"Mr. Pittman, I think yonder ship has every gun double-shotted and is just waiting for us to come alongside." Vallin didn't speak but felt Gabe was right. "Get the hands ready, Mr. Vallin. Mr. Pittman, I want to put *Leopard* hard over on my command."

"You will be exposing the stern, sir." Pittman knew his captain knew that but as master, he felt it was his place to warn him.

"Aye," Gabe replied, "but it's a much smaller target."

"Damn this wind," Vallin swore. A rare exhibit of nerves by the first lieutenant.

Dagan stood by Gabe as he had done so, so many times. "Ready, Uncle?" Gabe asked with a smile.

Dagan's only reply was, "Watch her gun ports."

Jacob Hex, Gabe's cox'n, stood a step behind his captain; his finger beating against the hilt of his cutlass. Like Vallin, he was nervous. He trusted his captain but a sixty-four in the making meant the odds were against them...with or without *Phoenix's* help.

Slowly *Leopard* gained until they were almost alongside. It was not the stern most gun port that swung open, but one forward. Gabe had expected the stern most port to open first, but it probably had an officer standing with the guns where the forward division of guns didn't.

"Now! Hard over, Mr. Pittman."

The helmsmen spun the wheel with all their might. The rudder bit and *Leopard* swung to starboard as the French ship's gun ports opened. Large black snouts were run out, spitting orange flames as they did so. Gabe felt the ship shudder as first one and then a second French ball hit *Leopard*, but surprisingly no others hit. The deafening roar caused the sea to churn as French balls plunged into the water.

"Hold her," Gabe ordered.

As *Leopard* slowly came around, *Phoenix* was firing into the enemy stern, one cannon at a time. *Leopard* came about in a relative short time but it seemed like forever.

"Get the forward guns working, Mr. Abraham," Gabe ordered the gunner. Shouting down to the gun deck, Gabe shouted to Lieutenant Bufford to be ready. An unnecessary order as Lieutenant Bufford was ready.

Every gun was double-shotted with a measure of grape. As *Leopard* pulled alongside, he shouted, "Fire, fire as you bear." One by one *Leopard's* guns roared and leapt back, straining the eye bolts as the double-shotted balls hurled forth against the enemy.

"Captain, Captain," Hex was shouting. "They've surrendered."

The white flag was indeed flying over the Frenchman. In fact, Hex had seen her go up just as *Leopard's* guns spoke.

"Cease fire! Cease fire!" Gabe shouted to the gun deck. A midshipman was sent below to pass the word in case Lieutenant Bufford had not heard.

"*Phoenix* buggered her a good one, I expect," Pittman swore.

"Aye, but it was *Leopard* who took their mind off the frigate," Vallin returned, not wanting *Leopard's* part to be belittled.

"Signal Frostbrier to board her," Gabe ordered.

Leopard came about and hove to, awaiting Frostbrier's report from the French ship. In a moment, he came to the rail. "Captain Earl, we have everything under control." Vallin thought he'd misheard, 'Captain Earl.'

"Aye, something's amiss," Gabe answered. "Do you have a surgeon?" Gabe called. "We have need as men are down. Mr. Vallin," he whispered to his side, "quietly pass the word to fire when I say 'men down'."

"Aye, sir." The orders were whispered along.

As Frostbrier didn't reply, Gabe called again. "The surgeon, sir, we have men down." He had given all the warning he could. "Fire, fire!"

Swivels, carronades and cannons all fired. The force of which seemed to shove *Leopard* over and caused the deck to shudder. When the smoke drifted away, Gabe could see no movement.

"Lieutenant Vallin, take the marines and a boarding party to the Frenchie." Gabe impatiently waited for *Leopard's* people to row over and board the enemy. As Vallin was boarding the ship, Frostbrier rose up.

"Are you injured, Captain?" Gabe shouted across the water.

"No, you warned us in time with your 'men down' comment," Frostbrier replied.

Within a few minutes, Vallin was at the bulwark. "We've secured the ship, Captain. Our last broadside killed the captain and first lieutenant."

"Just as well," Gabe said. "I'd have hung the Frogs for being so devilish."

"Hear that lads," an old topman said. "'E'd 'ave hung the Frogs. Aye, that be cap'n we got. 'E don't truck with no Frog dishonoring 'im or 'is people, 'e don't."

"'E wouldn't 'ave 'ung no officer," a young seaman responded.

"Thas yer youth speaking, me thinks. You ain't been wid Sir Gabe long as I 'as. 'E treats you good till 'e's crossed; and then look out. 'E breathes fire like a dragon when 'e's pissed."

"Humph," the young seaman snorted.

"Think not, does you? Well, I's got two rum rations what says you don't want to cross him." Waiting a moment for the seaman to reply, the topman snorted when the young man didn't reply, "What I's thought."

CHAPTER THIRTY

A QUICK SURVEY OF THE French sixty-four showed she was in poor shape. *Phoenix's* attack on the stern had caused enough damage but *Leopard's* onslaught finished her off. They divided the surviving officers and crew between *Phoenix* and *Leopard*. The gunner from *Leopard* then went aboard the beaten ship and fired a cannon ball through her bottom. The ship settled and then slipped from sight.

"It always makes me melancholy to watch a possible command sink," Vallin confided. Before the master could think of a suitable reply, Vallin made his way forward.

It was during the first dog watch that *Phoenix* and *Leopard* caught sight of Lord Anthony's squadron. *HMS SeaHorse* was at the front with Jepson and Kirk's ships to larboard and starboard. *Tomahawk* was in the rear of the formation.

The signal midshipman made his way to the quarterdeck. "From flag, sir, make more sail."

Gabe choked back an angry reply and then thought that's Stephen Earl's attempt at humor. "We're out sailing the flag now."

From the mainmast lookout, a call came down. "Flag's firing on the Frenchies."

Vallin rolled his eyes. "That's a hellish waste of information. Who else would he be firing on?"

Now the roll of thunder could be heard as *Leopard* continued to reach. *Weather or guns*, Gabe wondered.

As if reading his mind, Dagan volunteered, "Cannons, I believe."

"Signal from flag," the signals midshipman called again. "Engage the enemy."

Lord Anthony had realized that *Leopard* was overreaching the squadron. His signal gave Gabe the authority to attack the convoy and not fall into formation.

"*Phoenix's* number," the midshipman called again. "Engage enemy."

"Lord Anthony wants us to attack while he plays watchdog in case dé Gichen's fleet decides to attack our ships again," Gabe said.

"Aye," Dagan replied, "but I fear we're losing the wind again."

True to Dagan's prophecy, within the next hour the wind died, picked up and died again. But not before a handful of merchantmen had been taken.

On board the flagship, Lord Anthony's frustration was apparent. Everyone except Bart made themselves scarce. Even a cup of Silas's brandy-laced coffee did little to restore the admiral from his ill humors.

At times, the wind would tease the ships. A limp pendant would gain life, flap about a few minutes and then die as the wind fell. *Tomahawk* picked up a small breeze but it was gone by the time the sail handlers were called.

Lying close to *Bulldog*, Lieutenant Davy and Lieutenant Kirk passed the time throwing targets in the sea and firing at them; at first with muskets and then as bravado took hold, they attempted it with pistols. Captain Gregory Kirk had a matched pair of dueling pistols with rifled barrels whereas Captain David Davy had only sea service pistols. The results were Captain Kirk easily won the match but promised a rematch when they could compete with equal weapons.

Captain George Jepson on *Revenant* had engaged the surgeon in a game of chess. Aboard *Leopard*, Jacob Hex had broken out his guitar and entertained the crew with several jaunty tunes. Listening to his cox'n reminded Gabe of the days that he and Stephen Earl had enjoyed playing little tunes, often just on the naughty side. *Damn, that seemed like a long time ago...before this damnable war. How many lives had it cost*, Gabe wondered. *And in the end...would it have been worth it?*

Dagan pulled his shirt from his body. It was soaked with sweat. The deck seams fairly oozed and gripped at his sea boots. The actions against the French convoy thus far had been dismal. But no one could blame Lord Anthony. There could be no action without the wind. Would a day come when ships would not be at the mercy of the wind? Not in his lifetime, but perhaps one day. Looking across to the other ships in the squadron, Dagan found he had to squint and put his hand over his eyes to see past the sun's glare. The seamen had moved again in their attempt to find a bit of shade. One seaman was taking advantage of the lull. He'd gotten with a petty officer in his division, and was writing a letter with the petty officer's help. Was it to his parents, his wife, or some lover?

Thinking about lovers, Dagan wondered how Betsy was doing. Letters were few, due to this damnable war, but her last letter still proclaimed her love. How he missed her. So much so that it made him angry. One day soon he thought, one day soon.

***

"MIDSHIPMAN OF THE WATCH, suh," the marine sentry announced. Lord Anthony was sitting at his desk, feet propped in another chair with the stern windows open hoping to catch a zephyr. The midshipman took it all in as he stood before Lord Anthony. "Captain's compliments, sir. The Frogs...ere the French, appear to be catching the wind. At least it appears so."

"Thank you, young sir," Anthony said. "Let's go on deck and see."

"Aye, aye sir."

Anthony stood and looked at his uniform coat and left it hanging on the back of the chair. *It's too damn hot for that*, Lord Anthony thought. Besides, anyone not recognizing him without the coat was beyond help at any rate.

On deck, the sun was dimmed by slow moving gray clouds. Anthony could feel a slight coolness...a small breeze touched his face, a fleeting kiss with the innuendo of a breeze in the making.

"Mr. Waters feels like we are in for a squall, sir," Captain Earl reported. "The French appear to have already benefitted from the wind and have gotten underway."

It was a quarter of an hour later when Lord Anthony's ships picked up a gentle breeze. Slowly, the squadron was able to work their ships. With a leading wind and all the sail drawing, the pursuit of the French began again.

As the wind freshened even more, Captain Earl had the royals broken out. Seeing the look on the master's face, he asked, "You disagree with the royals, Mr. Waters?"

"No, Captain, not for now. I was just wondering how long before we have to take them in." Overhead, the gray clouds continued to build and were moving along at a fast pace. "It's the weather that bothers me, Captain. Hurricane season it is and we've been seeing very little in the way of squalls. Makes me wonder if we might not be in for a big storm. The mercury will rise a bit and then fall, rise a bit and then fall but each time it's fell a little further."

"Do you think we're in for a big blow?" Earl inquired.

"Not today, Captain. It's just a feeling I've got."

Captain Earl didn't reach his lofty rank by ignoring the master. Seeing Midshipman Black, he called him over. "Take a glass and go aloft. Keep your eyes open."

Two pair of eyes in the tops would not be amiss; especially when one pair was young eyes. The French were over the horizon before Lord Anthony's ships caught the wind. The captured merchantmen had been sent to Jamaica. Earl was sure that while it was against regulations, some of the ships' food would wind up as ship stores for Admiral Parker's ships. Looking up as he stepped over the coaming to go to his cabin, Earl realized it had grown much darker.

***

FOUR P.M., THE FIRST dogwatch. The shrill of pipes still hung in the air and the echo of bare feet on the deck and ladders had just died away. The French convoy still had not been sighted, making Anthony think that once over the horizon they'd changed course. He'd spread his ships out to patrol a greater expanse but still no sighting. The promised squall had arrived. Short lived but violent in nature.

Captain Earl, the master, and Lord Anthony were now looking at a chart spread out on his lordship's dining table.

"We should sight Bermuda in the morning, my Lord," Waters, the master pointed out. "If we've not seen them by then, my guess is they made for the coast."

The papers found aboard one of the taken merchant ships had indicated Norfolk and York-town as destinations. However, with so many places along the coast to offer sanctuary and so few British ships patrolling the French could have slipped in anywhere.

Making up his mind, Lord Anthony pecked the chart with his finger. "If we've not spotted them by tomorrow, we will pull in at Bermuda, replenish our fresh water and return to Barbados."

"What about the prize crews at Jamaica?" Waters asked quickly.

"Ah, yes," Anthony replied with a smile. "I recall a master's mate you took pride in, a protégé, I recall was sent with one of the prizes."

"Aye," Waters replied. "One I'd like not to lose. Should I fall, he'd be the one to take my place."

"We'll not leave your student adrift," Anthony promised.

"Thank you, my Lord. Not just for me, but for ole *SeaHorse*, as well."

"Sail ho! Sail ho!" The cry sent Captain Earl scrambling.

"My pardon," Earl said, as he sped on deck.

SeaHorse's first lieutenant was on deck when hatless Earl gained the quarterdeck. "Just off the bow, sir, several sails. I've sent Mr. Prentiss aloft."

"Thank you, Mr. Neal. I'm sure his Lordship will be on deck directly. I'd not want to be lacking in information when he arrives."

"Warships, sir," the midshipman called down. Then after a beat or two, Prentiss called down again. "British warships, sir. The lead ship is flying an admiral's flag."

***

ADMIRAL LORD WILLIAM CORNWALLIS' force consisted of two sixty-fours, two aged fifties, and a thirty-two gun frigate. With Anthony being the senior, Lord Cornwallis was rowed aboard *HMS SeaHorse* as the two squadrons lay hove to. He had sighted the French convoy and attacked the transports. Word had it that the French troops commanded by M. dé Rochambeau were headed to North America to ally themselves with the Colonials.

"It appears it's us against the world," Cornwallis said bitterly. "The Colonials, the Frogs, now the Dons and, if Lord Skalla is to be believed, the Dutch are throwing in with the rest."

"Is Lord Skalla with you?" Lord Anthony asked.

"No, he went with *Janus* back to Jamaica. She has been used most abusively and was sent back for repairs."

"Do you feel we've anything to gain by continuing the chase?" Lord Anthony asked.

"No, in truth, I don't," Cornwallis admitted. Again bitterness had crept back in his voice.

CHAPTER THIRTY ONE

Admiral Peter Parker welcomed the combined squadrons of Vice Admiral Lord Anthony and Rear Admiral Lord Cornwallis. He had news for Cornwallis that may or may not be what he wished to hear. He was being recalled to England. Most would think it was welcomed news, but in this case, Parker was not sure. It would mean leaving his mistress, behind...or would it? Parker had heard of men taking their mistresses back to England. Mostly it was accepted. But, a former slave? Even if she was a doctress, it would be pushing it.

***

Lord Anthony invited all his captains to dine. For the most part the group was all good-natured, and all on more than one occasion had been the brunt of a practical joke by one of the others. Lieutenant Davy, Captain of *Tomahawk*, had hidden a snake in his coat and when he'd visited *Bulldog*, and went to shake hands with Captain Kirk, he had the wiggling serpent in his hand and it coiled itself around Kirk's arm.

Kirk slung the snake off his hand and it crawled across the deck toward the marines, who were hopping about trying not to break formation. Finally, a mid down on his knees grabbed the snake, which with its tiny teeth latched onto the mid's hand. Howling, the youth shook his hand and in doing so he slung the snake over the side where it swam away. The cries and laughter could be heard on several ships anchored close by. Davy, with a smirk on his face, swore he didn't know how the snake had gotten in his coat sleeve unless it had been attached to *Bulldog's* man rope unknowingly.

"Damn you," Kirk had said. "See when I give you a second chance with target pistols again."

"Good thing 'e didn't try such a trick on Jep," Bart had told Mahan. "Otherwise, 'e may 'ave had to eat the bugger."

By the time all the captains were seated and *SeaHorse's* youngest midshipman had given the loyal toast, the meal was served. With supplies available from Port Royal, the meal was lavish. Silas had the help of a couple mess men, so he used a recipe from Gabe's servant, Josh Nesbit, and prepared a turtle soup. The soup was so tasty, the bowls were cleaned. Next came a rack of lamb garnished with a glazed sweet orange sauce. New potatoes, carrots, garden peas, and hot bread filled the table. Dessert was a medley of bananas, berries, and pineapple with a sweetened cream to dip each piece of fruit in. The fruit and cream could also be poured over sweet bread. Like the main course, the dessert, another one of Nesbit's recipes, was a hit.

After the meal, Lord Anthony brought out the cigars and brandy. Thinking of how young virgins rolled the cigars between their thighs made Lieutenant Davy enjoy the cigar even more; so he shared his new found knowledge with the rest of the captains. Gabe was sitting to the left of his brother so that when Lord Anthony asked where Davy had come up with such a tale, Gabe answered, "I'm afraid my first lieutenant, Con Vallin, being the worldly man that he is, imparted this knowledge to our Lieutenant Davy."

"And he believes it?" Lord Anthony asked.

Smiling, Gabe replied, "Well, let's just say it leads to pleasant thoughts." Lord Anthony smiled as he spun his cigar in his mouth, wondering how long they'd be able to enjoy the Cuban cigars now that the Dons had sided with the Colonials.

Clinking on a glass with a spoon, Lord Anthony was able to get everyone's attention. "Gentlemen, I believe we've done as much damage to the enemy in these parts as we can. They, at least, know the British Navy will not stand by while its citizens are attacked and abused. Now, before we're overrun by soiled maidens and angry fathers, we'll weigh anchor in the morning and sail for home." This brought a round of applause and cheers.

"Captain Kirk, you will sail in company with Captain Anthony to Antigua, where sad as I am to lose her, we must return *Leopard* to her rightful commander, if he is well. If so, Captain Anthony and his men will return to Barbados aboard your ship. Admiral Moffett will ultimately decide as to what course of action will take place with *Leopard*."

Gabe had known his time aboard was limited. But he would miss *Leopard*. She was a good ship and had been perfectly suited for the type of warfare they'd been engaged in. Some said the fifty gun ship, like the larger sixty-fours, would soon be discontinued. Obsolete. They couldn't stand in line and trade broadsides with the newer seventy-fours like *SeaHorse*. The powers that be at the Admiralty were deep water sailors. They didn't understand the need for ships to fight in the shallow waters of the Florida Cays, the Bahamas, or even between some of the West Indies Islands. Gabe already knew their answer was the frigate. They were getting bigger and heavily armed. Soon the small twenty–eight gun frigates would be gone as well; maybe the thirty-two's also. Thirty-six and thirty-eights were now coveted commands. Would he get one? Was *Phoenix* planned for him? Gil had been closed mouthed about his plans, something of a rarity. He usually confided in Gabe most of his plans, frequently after the evening meal when the wives were gossiping or playing with the kids. Macayla was turning into a little mama and liked to help with James.

Dagan had also been quiet of late. He had told Gabe when asked, that he'd not gotten any feelings in regards to what might be next. "I'm sorry," Dagan had answered. "My mind has been on Virginia." What he meant, Gabe knew, was Betsy, General Manning's daughter.

It amazed Gabe at times how both he and Dagan's loves had come from the Colonies, the enemy. So did Dagan's comment about its hard to kill an enemy you don't hate. Other than a few rogues even the Americans didn't like, it was hard to bring war against your wife's country or your love's country.

CHAPTER THIRTY TWO

VICE ADMIRAL LORD ANTHONY stood on the quarterdeck with Bart just to his right. No one questioned Bart's presence. The admiral was there, therefore, Bart was there...forever, at his Lord's side. The ship was a beehive of activity. To a landsman it would appear like mass confusion. Men were at the capstan bars, others gathered below the masts. Petty officers growled at a seaman here and there. Captain Earl looked at Lord Anthony who nodded. No word was spoken but Earl knew the admiral was ready to get underway from his mere nod.

"Mr. Neal, get the ship underway."

"Aye, Captain."

As the orders were passed, the boatswain mates started their divisions. "Hands aloft, loose topsails."

As the topman went aloft, Captain Earl ordered the bosun, "Break out the anchor, Mr. Hyde."

"Heave," Hyde ordered smacking his hand with his cane to emphasize the order. As men heaved and strained their backs, the capstan started turning, and soon the dripping cable made it on board, brownish water falling to the deck. Another order, 'loose headsails', went up once the cable was inboard. High above the deck, canvas was released coming down swiftly.

Looking up at the men spaced out on the swaying yards, Anthony spoke to his cox'n. "Remember your days in the tops?"

"Aye," Bart answered, "them was the good ole days. Not sorry they's in the past, though." Anthony eyed his cox'n; it was not often he'd make such an admission.

"Anchor's aweigh, sir." This from Neal, the first lieutenant. *SeaHorse*, free of her anchor, started to swing around. "Man the braces," he ordered.

The orders were repeated by the bosun's mates. "Look lively, you lubbers. The admiral stands yonder. Barnes," a bosun's mate yelled. "You look like some old woman."

The anchor was soon catted and made fast. The sails were drawing and *SeaHorse* surged away.

"Let her run, Mr. Neal," Earl ordered. "Let's take advantage of the wind."

"Aye sir."

The master looked over at his helmsman, "This ain't no scow, this be a *SeaHorse*."

***

ONE BY ONE, THE squadron's ships followed the flagship out of the harbor. The ships seemed glad to have the wind and with little effort were making eight knots. By mid-morning, a misty rain fell that lasted until noon. The mist soaked the sails and the ships picked up another knot. The sun finally broke through the clouds and the canvas and deck planks seemed to have steam coming from them.

Gabe was in his cabin signing the mountain of papers the purser and his secretary had accumulated for him. The stern windows and skylight were open in an attempt to pull in a little breeze. Hex had broken out Gabe's pistols, his long rifle, and swords; oiling and wiping them down.

Nesbit had brought a glass of lime juice for both Gabe and his cox'n. "That's the last of the limes, Sir Gabe."

"We'll be home soon and you can buy more," Gabe said, and then thought, *what I am saying. I may not even have a ship a week from now.*

***

THE DAWN ROSE WITH a fresh breeze. Always moody at this time of day, little more than a "Good morning, Captain," was said as Gabe mounted the quarterdeck.

Whereas Con Vallin loved the early morning and all its possibilities of what the horizon might bring, he'd learned his captain didn't, and he'd in fact found out that Captain Sir Gabriel Anthony was a hard riser. After he'd first been appointed as Gabe's first lieutenant, he'd made the mistake of saying, "Good morning, Captain, a wondrous day awaits." Gabe looked at Vallin and snarled, "That remains to be seen, Lieutenant." Dagan had been behind Gabe and made a motion for

Vallin to ignore his captain's remarks.

Gabe saw Dagan's gesture and spoke again, "My uncle apologizes for my bad behavior, Mr. Vallin, whereas it should be me. Please accept my apology. It was rude."

It was the first time Vallin had ever been apologized to by a captain. It also demonstrated that Dagan held more sway over the captain than anyone, including Lord Anthony.

As soon as the horizon was found to be clear, the master approached his captain and the first lieutenant. "I'm concerned about the weather, sir. I've been watching the weather glass. The mercury has been dropping some over the last few days. There's no longer the twice daily rise and fall, now it's just down. The same observation was noted by every master in the squadron."

George Jepson signaled and got permission to close within hailing distance of the flagship. He and Lord Anthony held a close relationship. His opinion was one Lord Anthony valued and trusted greatly. Not that he didn't trust *SeaHorse's* master.

The sky was now covered in a reddish haze, with the sun only breaking through at intervals. Taking up his speaking trumpet, Jepson shouted across the water. "I believe we're in for a real blow, my Lord. A hurricane is in the making, I believe."

Anthony waved to acknowledge he'd heard. He then turned and spoke to Captain Earl and the master, Waters. He picked up the trumpet and spoke to Jepson, "My master agrees with you, Captain Jepson. He says he's never seen the Caribbean sky thus."

They were now at a point the squadron would go more southerly, while *Leopard* and *Bulldog* would head in a nor-easterly direction to Antigua.

"I would come about and run before the wind," Jepson recommended. "I feel the storm will likely follow the trades through the Indies. It may even veer to the Bahamas."

"Understood," Lord Anthony replied and then turned to his captain. "I trust George to know the weather, Captain Earl."

"Aye sir, I do as well. I think it would behoove us to take his advice."

"Very well. Signal the squadron. We'll come about and run for it," Anthony said.

Overhead the sky looked like someone had taken a brush with red paint and made a swipe across it. The sea started to get up. At first, with gentle rollers that became heavy and slammed against the ship's hull, hurling spray on board soaking several seamen. The ships had finished coming about and were taking station on the flag when the wind died.

"Damn this perverse weather," Pittman, *Leopard's* master cursed.

The entire ship's crew could feel the master's frustration, his nervousness. Gabe, like his brother Lord Anthony, was concerned about the welfare of their family as were many of the others in the squadron. Captain Davy, who'd had little more than a quick honeymoon with Ariel before weighing anchor.

Where the ships had lain lifeless on the water when they'd been becalmed, they now moved as each swell, and each wave, slammed into the hull. As the waves increased, the bows of each ship were pushed around so that now the flagship was pointed amidships to *Leopard*. *Tomahawk* and *Bulldog* pitched bow to stern at times, and they'd roll violently.

"So much for running before the wind," Vallin swore.

"It'll come," the master returned, "and when it does you won't much like it."

"I don't like it now," Vallin replied. "Captain, permission to rig lifelines."

"Might be a good idea to send down the topgallant yards and mast," Pittman added.

"I was thinking the same," Gabe stated. "Call all hands, Mr. Vallin, let's be about securing the ship as well as we can. I'd not like hatch covers flying about, or worse, the cannons."

As the sky changed to a reddish orange, an almost coppery color, the men aboard Lord Anthony's flagship came alive in their efforts to make their ship as secure as possible. Thick, heavy ominous clouds were moving fast overhead. The wind was getting up and freshened steadily. The sails were double reefed. Throughout the squadron, it was the same. The captains had the crews making their ships as ready as humanly possible for what nature was about to throw at them.

On board *Leopard*, Gabe heard his stomach growl, he was hungry. He'd only eaten a pastry along with a cup of coffee. *The men must be hungry as well*, he thought. "Let's get the hands a quick meal and then put out the fires," Gabe ordered Vallin.

"Aye, Captain."

Mentally, Gabe clicked off the things that had been done in preparation. Relieving tackles had been hooked to the tiller in case the wheel lines parted. A portable compass had been installed with a lubber line laid out to indicate the ship's head. A lantern was rigged and hung so that the compass could be read. The big guns had been made fast using double lines on the breeching, tackles, and muzzles.

The anchor was catted and fished, secured with double rings and shank painters. A plug had been jammed into the hawsehole and caulked with greased oakum. Tarpaulins were placed in the weather riggings to give the watch-standers some shelter from the winds. *Long as they lasted*, Gabe thought. The last of the lifelines were being rigged on the upper deck as he watched.

A lifebuoy was made fast to the deep sea lead line with the reel secured aft. Should a man fall overboard, the life buoy was the only chance he had. Slim as it might be. A sea anchor was made ready. The carpenter had just checked the mast wedges to make sure they were not loose. Pumps had been made ready and the pump wells were sounded. Tarpaulins were stretched over hatches and they were battened down. Canvas covers had been put over the boats. Aloft, the royals and upper studdingsails were got out of the riggings. The tops were cleared of all extraneous gear. The topgallant yards and mast were sent down. Preventer braces were rigged. The fore topmast staysail sheets were doubled. Lastly, the mizzen gaff was struck and the boom securely lashed to its crutch amidships.

Damn, it made Gabe tired just thinking of all of it. The sense of danger had made the crew work feverishly with petty officers overseeing each task. Anything not done to their liking was done again until it was done to their satisfaction.

"It's yer life we're trying to save you fish lipped sod," a petty officer ripped a seaman who was battening down a hatch. "Ought to let your arse drown but you'd likely take one of me mates with your lubberly soul and I'd not like that."

Lieutenant Vallin approached his captain, "Would you like to make a walk through the ship, sir? I believe we have time."

"Yes," Gabe replied. "I'd like to speak to the men."

As the two men walked, with Dagan and Hex following, making their way through the ship,

Gabe was surprised at how many of the men's names he'd come to know. Each man was trying to hide his fear and felt better knowing the captain had taken the time to speak to them.

One of *Trident's* old hand spoke to Dagan, "What about it, mate? Will she swim?"

"Aye," Dagan replied. "She'll have to, because I can't." This made the whole mess break out in laughter. Dagan could swim and Gabe knew it, but it was the kind of exchange that gave the crew heart.

Well, everything had been done to make the ship secure, or had it? There was always doubt.

PART III

Oh Blow You Hurricane

Rain…Rain…it's a hurricane
Got no Jonah, we can blame
Will our timbers stand the strain?
Oh blow…you hurricane.

Different oceans call the doom
A cyclone or a typhoon
I just pray we got sea room
Oh blow…you hurricane.

See the waves how high they go
Lost the topsails now its bare poles
Will she poop nobody knows
Oh blow…you hurricane.

I feel the worst is yet to come
Before this mighty wind is done
Will I live to see the sun
Oh blow…you hurricane.

—Michael Aye

CHAPTER THIRTY THREE

OCTOBER THE NINTH, FAITH looked at the calendar. It had been seven months since Gabe had sailed away to Antigua. He was only to be gone a few weeks. That was before the Spaniards, the Dons, as the navy called them, had joined the war.

She had received letters from both Admiral Moffitt and Gabe. Admiral Moffitt had stated that he'd sent Gabe to warn Lord Anthony of Spain coming to the aid of the Americans. This was delivered personally by the dispatch vessel's captain. He'd also hand delivered a short, quickly written note from Gabe. *Damn this war,* she thought, *always taking her man, her child's father*. But for some reason, unlike in the past, she felt no anger toward Gabe. Could this be because she'd found herself supporting Ariel? She'd had no time with her new husband. Scarcely had the honeymoon sheets turned cold, when Lieutenant David Davy had had to sail away in his little sloop of war. *Damn the Navy and damn the sea*. They each, though entwined, seemed to have a greater pull on their men than she or Ariel did.

One of the differences this time, compared to Gabe's last departure, was she'd taken Lady

Deborah...Deborah's advice and found ways to keep her busy. Too busy to sit and brood over things she couldn't change...the war and her husband's call to the sea.

Today they were going on a picnic; a grand picnic and adventure. Everyone was talking of the new cave that had been discovered, Harrison's Cave. The islanders were all aghast at how big it was. Rumors had it the native islanders used to live in the cave. It was also said that runaway slaves hid there. Others told how it was a holding place for pirates' treasures, their booty.

Rupert Buck had dispelled those pirate rumors, saying it was too far inland to have been connected to pirates. He did not doubt the stories about the natives or slaves.

"Is you ready, girl?" Nanny asked as she walked in the room carrying little James. He was a happy baby. Watching him grow up was a joy. A joy, she thought with a sigh, that his father had missed much of.

"That rascal, Lum, has put our lunch basket in the wagon. It was all I could do to keep his hands out of the cookies I baked," Nanny said.

Faith couldn't help but smile. The smell of cookies baking had enticed her as well. Sam had even lifted his nose, sniffing the air. Always at her side, she wondered what she would do without the big brute of a dog.

Ariel bounced into the room. "Aren't you excited?" she asked.

She reminds me of me at that age, Faith thought. Not near as spoilt Nanny would say...and a cleaner mouth. How many times had Nanny fussed about her use of profanity?

"It's a good thang you married a sailor boy, don't know nary another man who'd put up with yo' nasty talk," Nanny would say.

"Humph," Faith would grunt. She rarely said any bad words except for damn, hell, shat, and arse.

It would cause Nanny to clap her hand over her mouth, roll her eyes, and rush from the room. Usually she would mutter something like, "I hope yo' mama is busy up there in heben. She'd swoon hearing her girl talk such." Sometimes Nanny would say, "I'm gonna get me a bar of soap foh yo' mouth."

Sam's ears rose up and he ran toward the door. A low growl came from him followed by his rear end wobbling and, as Lum called it, his grin...at times, a slobbering grin. Rupert Buck's carriage had arrived. In addition to Buck and his soon-to-be-bride, Livi, he'd picked up Deborah and Macayla as well. Crowe, the admiral's cox'n, was also along. Crowe and Jake Hex were childhood friends. Now they were both cox'ns. What had it been like being a smuggler, Faith wondered, knowing both had their sea roots in it.

A two-seated wagon had been rented for the picnic. In addition to the two seats, wooden benches had been put in the back of the wagon and fresh hay was on the floor. As the group got into the wagon, Buck looked at the sky. His seaman's instinct told him it would not be a good day to be at sea.

Before pulling himself onto the wagon's front seat with Crowe and Lum, he walked to the back of the wagon. "We have lanterns, oil, candles, water, and food. Lots of food," he said again, smiling at Nanny.

"Nuff to feed all yo' sailors, Mr. Admiral," Nanny replied. She followed with, "Yo' arm 'pears to be doing better. But I put a bottle of brandy in with the goods, in case you need it...medicinal, ain't that what they call it?"

"You are a love, Nanny. You ever get tired of Faith, you come on to our house. We'll give you a home," Buck said.

"That's nice to know, suh. But ain't nobody else would put up wid that girl. I best stay, somebody has to take care of the girl and watch over that lazy Lum."

Buck couldn't help but smile. Nanny might be spot on in regards to Faith, but nobody could call Lum lazy. Climbing onto the wagon, he said, "Let's be off, you lazy bugger."

Lum had heard Nanny's remarks. He grinned at Buck, "Yes suh," as he clicked to the mules. "Gid up, you worthless nags."

***

A FEW PEOPLE WERE leaving as Lum pulled the wagon to a stop. He put grain bags on the two mules and tied the harness to a leaded weight and dropped it to the ground. Ariel, as agile as anyone, hopped over the wagon side and onto the ground. She then caught Macayla, who jumped into her arms. As the ladies were helped down by Crowe, Lum was helping the less agile Nanny down.

As the group started up the rise, Nanny said, "We may have to eat in the cave. I believe it's starting to rain."

Crowe had felt the drops as well. His days as a smuggler had taught him how to recognize a storm in the offing. He looked at Buck, who met his gaze, "I think we'll get the rest of the things out of the wagon so that they don't get wet." Crowe nodded to Buck. *Or get blown away*, he thought.

Lum and Buck lugged the picnic basket, water, and candles on up and into the mouth of the cave while Crowe dashed back to the wagon for the lanterns and can of oil. The rain was coming down hard by the time he'd rushed along the rocky path to the cave.

"You are soaked!" Lady Deborah exclaimed as Crowe ducked into the cave.

"There is a bit of dead wood along the path," Crowe said. "It might be good to gather up a bit for a fire." What he didn't say was before this was over they might wish they had a fire.

Lady Deborah had taken off her shawl and was handing it to Crowe. "Not now, my Lady. It would just get soaked." He and Lum then went back out in the rain.

Over the next quarter of an hour, they made several trips. After the first trip, Ariel said, "Isn't that enough for a fire?"

"I think we may be here for a while," Buck said, as he was lighting a lantern.

Outside, the sky was darkening and the wind was picking up. Rain was now blowing into the cave entrance. When the lantern was lit, Buck called to the women, "Let's move back a bit, away from the wind and wet."

"We may be here for a while is what you're thinking, is it not?" Livi asked.

Buck nodded, but then added, "What more could we ask for? A roof to keep out the rain, and walls to keep out the wind."

Outside, Lum had approached Crowe, "You think we's in foh a storm, don't cha?"

"Aye, Lum, a bad one from the look of things." Lum nodded. "Let's get the benches out of the wagon and unhitch the mules. Maybe get them just inside the cave," Crowe said.

Thinking they were sure to need the animals later, Lum agreed. It would be better than leaving them out in the storm. Now the dark skies were lit up with ragged streaks of lightning and the sound of distant thunder. The mules, wild-eyed and nervous, seem to understand the men were there to help them. Unhitching the mules from the wagon, the men, each with a bench over one shoulder, led the mules to the cave.

As they entered the cave, Buck said, "Good thinking." They were sure to need the animals later.

"Should we light another lantern now?" Livi asked. Outside the sky was almost black as night and the single lantern didn't put out much light. "I think we need to get a fire going so that Lum and Crowe don't catch a chill, and that will add some more light," Buck replied.

Sam sidled up to Faith and whined. He did not like the weather and sensed the danger in the storm. Soon a fire was blazing, adding light, warming up Crowe and Lum and drying their clothes. Outside, the wind howled. The crack of lightning and the roll of thunder were almost constant. At the front of the cave, the mules stomped but did not attempt to go outside.

Buck looked at the women. All of them were looking at him. Honesty, Buck decided, was needed. "This storm is not just a passing squall, I fear. I think it's much worse than a simple squall. That's a high wind, a very high wind...probably a hurricane. We are better off here than we'd be at home. No roof to blow off or walls to cave in. We couldn't ask for a safer place. I don't know how long we'll be here, a day at least, I'd think. Crowe and I will search the cave to see what we might find. Those benches are about dry so sit on them or a rock." He had noticed a trickle of water running down on the cave floor where the wind had blown it inside. "Lum, if you will keep an eye on the mules and the women." Lum nodded his head.

At that time, Macayla said, "Mother, I'm hungry. I thought this was a picnic." Not understanding why, Macayla looked bewildered as everyone laughed.

CHAPTER THIRTY FOUR

ON BOARD THE SHIPS in Lord Anthony's squadron life was a watery hell, with each man filled with fear. Most were wondering if they'd live to see the sun. John Waters, master on *HMS SeaHorse,* stood in the chart room going over his charts and trying hard to remember past conversations about hurricanes in the Caribbean.

The lantern swung as the ship rolled and plunged through the angry sea. It was bad but Waters knew the worst was yet to come. Making up his mind, he reported to the captain, and then the two made their way to the admiral's cabin. Without any niceties, Waters spread his chart on the table.

"I've little to go on, Lord Anthony, other than conversations with locals and a few ship masters. They all agreed the hurricanes that formed in the Indian Ocean tend to pass through the Lesser Antilles, and then turn and approach Puerto Rico, Hispaniola, the Bahamas, and on toward Bermuda." Captain Earl and Lord Anthony listened without interruption. The master then continued, "With this in mind, sir, I would recommend we pass to the south of Grand Cayman and head toward the Gulf of Mexico."

"Not run up the coast of America?" Earl asked.

"No sir, on our present course, I fear we will be overtaken..." Both Lord Anthony and Captain Earl understood what the master meant.

"Very well," Anthony responded. "Make the necessary changes in our course. Signal the squadron, Captain. You might need to fire a flare for them to see the signals."

"That may help," Earl admitted. *But it may not*, he thought.

On deck, the wind howled and made a shrill whistling noise as it passed through the riggings, shrouds, and backstays. The signals midshipman was thunderstruck that the admiral would even try to send signals aloft. However, with the help of a master's mate, who was on deck, they put the signal together and amazingly it did not get torn loose as it was hoisted. The gunner and one of his mates fired off a flare. After an interval, they fired off a second flare and then a third.

***

ON BOARD *LEOPARD*, THE watch miserably counted down the minutes until they were relieved. Instead of the usual four hour watch, the captain had the men relieved every hour. Even that short time was a living hell. Rain fell like a deluge and it felt like hail or small shot slammed into the body and face. No one could see more than a few feet and to look straight ahead would render a person almost blind.

In addition to the wind and the rain, thunder and lightning were both tremendous and incessant. The helmsmen, two at a time, were attached to a lifeline. Any attempt to keep the ship on course was a nightmare, as it plunged into the waves, the ship rising and then slamming down. The deck would cant and footing was difficult.

Lieutenant Laqua had the watch. He'd seen the flares from the flagship. Trying to see the signal that the flares drew attention to was almost impossible. The flagship, like *Leopard*, was rising and falling and the ship disappeared at times. With the wind pulling at him so, Lieutenant Laqua took a step up the ratline trying to see the signal better. Wrapping his arm around the shroud and shielding his eyes, Laqua was finally able to read the signal. The watch was to be relieved at any minute. He'd pass on the change in course but also send a midshipman down to notify the captain.

Shouting into Midshipman Jarvis Jackson's ear, Laqua told him to advise the captain of the flag's signal and then he could go below to his mess. The other watch standers were coming on deck as Jackson stepped into the companionway. Water sluiced over the coaming and dripped down the ladder. As he approached the marine sentry, he wiped his eyes and tried to straighten his sodden uniform.

"Rough on deck, is it, young sir?" the sentry asked.

"Never seen the like," Jackson replied. The sentry announced him to the captain.

"Come in," Gabe called to the boy. "I believe, Dagan, we have a drowned rat in the cabin."

"Aye, looks malnourished as well," Dagan responded.

"Lieutenant Laqua's compliments, sir. A signal from the flag. A change in course, I believe."

While Jackson was making his report, Dagan poured two fingers of brandy into a glass. "This will warm your innards, young sir."

"Thank you, sir." Jackson took the glass and gulped it down. He felt the fiery liquid go down and said, "It warms the insides very quickly."

"Aye, especially when it's drunk thusly," Dagan said, a smile on his face.

"I will be on deck directly," Gabe said, as he found his foul weather cloak.

As Jackson left, he was thinking, *a drink of the captain's brandy. Wait until I get to the mess. I'll be the envy*, he thought.

"Too young to realize the danger," Dagan said as the boy left the cabin.

"He will learn," Gabe replied.

On deck, the watch had been relieved except for Lieutenant Laqua. He was not surprised. Lieutenant Daniel Bufford was never early and more often than not, he was late. The surgeon, Mr. Cornish, had hinted that if Laqua called him out, he'd be backed by not only the first lieutenant, but every other officer in the mess.

Finally appearing on deck, Bufford approached the quarterdeck. His legs were wobbly. Was it the ship's motion or drink, Laqua wondered, suddenly very concerned. He could not turn the watch over to Bufford if he was in his cups. It wasn't safe for the ship.

"Get below," Bufford snarled, "I have the watch." The smell of alcohol was strong on his breath.

"Sir, I don't think you are fit to stand the watch. Go below, I will stand it for you," Laqua said.

"No, you won't. I'll not hear you've been ill-treated by another soul," Bufford replied.

"Sir, you need to go below," Laqua said again to Bufford.

"You go below," Bufford shouted. "You are relieved."

"Mr. Glen," Laqua called to the new midshipman. "Go below and inform the first lieutenant that I do not feel Lieutenant Bufford is able to stand his watch."

As Glen made to leave, Bufford nearly screamed, "Stand as you were, Glen. Go below, Laqua, or I'll have you brought up on charges."

"No sir," Laqua said. "You are not fit to assume the duty. Mr. Glen, do as you were told. Lieutenant Bufford is ill and not fit to assume the watch."

"Aye, sir."

"No, you don't, you worthless snot. I'll throw you over the side," Bufford yelled at the midshipman.

Fear in his eyes, the midshipman didn't know what to do. Lieutenant Bufford was obviously drunk but he was senior to Lieutenant Laqua.

"Do as you were ordered, Mr. Glen," a new voice said. Turning, Glen saw the captain. "Have the first lieutenant send for the master-at-arms and then come back on deck. Mr. Bufford, consider yourself relieved of all duties. You are drunk on watch and not fit to run the ship."

Within a minute, Lieutenant Vallin was on deck. "Mr. Vallin, Lieutenant Bufford is to be confined to his quarters and he is not to have any wine or strong drink."

"Aye, Captain."

As Vallin reached for Bufford's arm, he jerked back taking another step backwards and he shouted, "He's the one not fit to stand the watch. He's not even fit to be an officer. He shames the ward..." Before he could finish his rant, *Leopard* plunged over a wave and slammed down into the trough.

No sooner had it plunged into the trough, the ship rolled to starboard, and then climbed another of the endless succession of angry waves until the bow seemed to be pointing skywards and then over, over until the bow plunged down and the stern up. Again and again the ship would rise up, up, up; and then plunge downward with so much force that a man's teeth would snap together. It felt like the ship would be torn apart, her keel broken. Again it rose and fell.

Everyone but Bufford was within grasp of the rail or a lifeline. Falling to the deck, Bufford slid forward when the bow plunged as the sea rushed inboard, swirling and knocking Bufford unconscious as his head bounced on the deck, the cascade of water hurling his body forward until his arm and leg dangled precariously at the entry port.

Laqua rushed forward, trying to catch the unconscious man before he was washed overboard. Holding on to the lifeline, Laqua fought the wind, rain, and the ship's movements trying to get to Bufford. He made it to Bufford and stretched to get the limp body but it was too far away. Turning loose the lifeline, he caught hold of Bufford as another huge wave crashed over the bow and slammed into the two men.

Laqua tugged on Bufford with all his might, trying to keep him from sliding overboard, while trying to reach the lifeline. Another wave and Laqua felt water rush over his body, his head and tearing his grip away. Spitting out saltwater and catching a breath, Laqua was able to grab Bufford's britches at the waist. With his feet against the rail, he pulled with all his might and gained some, and then more, but he was fully stretched out. He had no more leverage. He was weakened. He felt a slap to his face and shoulder and realized he'd been thrown a rope. Turning his head, he could see the captain and first lieutenant. They were both shouting but it was lost in the wind. He was in a daze. Somehow, he got the rope around Bufford's body, under his arms.

Another wave swamped Laqua, slamming his body into the bulwark, tearing Bufford's body from his grasp again. As the water rushed down the channels he tried to rise, choking, spitting, and trying to catch his breath. Another rope, a loop...someone had thrown him a rope. Somehow in his fog, he slipped the rope over his shoulders and felt himself being pulled across the deck. Hands seized his body and roughly he was pulled along the deck.

When he woke up, Doctor Cornish was looking down at him. "You're back with the living, I see." Laqua tried to smile but it hurt. His whole body ached. "You've been battered and bruised most awful," Cornish said. "You've also swallowed enough sea water to float a man o' war."

Rising, Laqua coughed and vomited what seemed like a gallon of foul tasting vomitus. A surgeon's mate was there with a pan to catch most of it.

"As I was saying," Cornish continued, "You will probably do that again. Hopefully, you didn't get much in your lungs. It could produce a pulmonary contagion. That would prove to be most distressing."

"How will I know?" Laqua asked.

"You'll know," Cornish said. "If you have no fevers in the next day or two, you will probably do well."

"I actually feel better now after vomiting," Laqua said.

"You should," Cornish replied. "Hopefully, you will continue to improve."

"How's our lieutenant?" Captain Anthony asked as he entered the room.

"He's awake and alert. Be careful to stand back though as he's prone to spew."

Gabe smiled and said, "Let her blow, Lieutenant, if that helps. We need you back to your duties."

"How is Lieutenant Bufford?" Laqua asked.

"He's not as well as you but thanks to you, he'll probably survive. His kind always do," Cornish said. Laqua nodded.

"I want you to know that you did the right thing refusing to turn over the watch to him. It would have endangered the ship and everyone aboard," Gabe said.

"I...I hope I'm not an embarrassment to the wardroom," Laqua said, recalling Bufford's words.

"No, I think you are a most welcomed member, Lieutenant, a well-rounded officer and experienced seaman. I think it's the other way around. Bufford is the embarrassment. Remember, Lieutenant, I recommended you for lieutenant. I sat on your board. You deserve your rank more than some. You can spend time with Doctor Cornish if you like. He will polish up your rough edges, as it were. But when it comes to trusting my ship to anyone, you'd be at the head of the line. You have proved your worth, Lieutenant. Now, get well so you can get back to you duties."

CHAPTER THIRTY FIVE

INSIDE HARRISON CAVE, BUCK admitted to the women that they might be there for a while. They would need to conserve the food as much as possible and try to catch water in the cups Nanny had packed. Back in the cave a few feet, water dripped down from the ceiling. It looked and smelled clean but was it safe? Buck wasn't sure.

"I've drank worse," Lum said. Being brave, he then pulled a cup full from a small pool. "It's good," he said. "Water ain't goint to be no problem."

The fire added warmth and some light. They continued to burn only the one lantern. Buck and Crowe had walked well back into the cave. The cavern grew larger but was damper. They might have to move the mules back there, but they would stay where they were since it was smaller and would take less firewood to stay warm. The stockpile of wood did not seem so big now, realizing it may have to last for some time.

"How long do you think?" Faith asked Buck.

"A day would not surprise me, maybe a day and a half," Buck admitted.

"Oh, my God," Faith suddenly spoke out. "If

it's this bad here, how bad is it for the ships in port and the ones at sea?"

Buck had whispered his same concerns to Crowe while they were exploring the back of the cave. However, so as not to alarm Faith or Deborah, he explained, "Lord Anthony and Gabe are experienced seamen. They would both turn away from the storm and if they couldn't outrun it, they would change their course."

"And the ships in port?" Lady Deborah asked quietly.

"I've little doubt Captain Markham hasn't ordered the ships to sea. Having no protective harbor he would not risk riding out even a small storm, much less something of this magnitude." Buck's confidence in Lord Anthony, Gabe, and Markham was comforting to Faith and Ariel.

Outside, there was no let up. The winds screamed past the cave entrance. The rain fell like Buck had never seen it fall and the sky was black. Occasionally, some object would fly past the cave entrance. The mules, while still nervous, seemed to realize they were better off inside the cave rather than outside so they didn't paw the ground or stomp their feet like they had done.

Buck looked at his watch, it was four thirty. They'd been there several hours already. It seemed longer than that. Well, he decided, I'm dry, fairly warm and not really hungry. I just wish I had a comfortable place to sit. Calling to Crowe and Lum, he said, "Let's see if we can put together a few rocks so we will have a place to sit."

"Aye," Lum replied. "I'm too old to sit on the wet ground."

There were very few rocks that could be moved but using some of the firewood and a large rock that Lum and Crowe rolled from the next cavern, they had suitable seating.

"Not like the chairs Livi's got at home," Buck japed, "but better than standing."

Talk had just about dried up. Macayla was sleepy and the women were deep in their own thoughts. Lum fished his pipe from his pocket and after the women said they didn't mind, he took a burning stick and lit his pipe.

"Smells like Gil's," Deborah volunteered.

"Yes ma'm, I 'spect it do as it was the admiral what gave it to me."

The cave grew quiet again, everybody with their own thoughts. Then Macayla broke the silence, "Mother, I need to go."

***

THE VIOLENT STORM STILL raged at six a.m. the next morning, October 10th. As Buck rose from where he sat on a rock and leaned on the cave wall, he felt pain in his wounded arm. His back and neck were stiff and every muscle in his body seemed to ache. Looking past the fire, he could see both Lum and Crowe were up and looking but not venturing too close to the cave entrance. Stretching, he made his way to the two men.

"No let up," Crowe volunteered. "If anything

it's worse." The sound towards the cave entrance was almost deafening.

"I've never heard the wind pitched so high," Buck said, "nor for so long."

"Like all the hounds of hell have busted loose," Lum added.

Looking at the women perched here and there, still asleep, Buck whispered, "I feel we will have to conserve the wood...and the food."

"We got food," Lum said, motioning toward the mules.

"I hope it'll not come to that," Buck answered. "I'm thinking that when this storm is over, those animals will be worth their weight."

"Aye," Crowe agreed. "Truth be known, Admiral, I don't see much surviving that." He emphasized that by motioning toward the cave entrance with his head.

"You're right. The governor's house is made of stone that's several feet thick but the roof is just an ordinary roof."

"They got a cellar," Lum said. "I been down to it. If they got down there, maybe they's will be safe."

A whining noise was heard and Lum felt Sam, Faith's dog, nudge his hand. "It's alright boy. We're safe."

"He's nervous by all this," Faith said as she walked up.

"All of us are," Buck admitted.

Seeing Faith's baby in her arms, Lum asked,

"Want me to hold the little man, Missy? You've had him the whole night."

"Thank you, Lum. If you can light a lantern for me, I have to go to the back of the cave."

"I'll light the lantern," Crowe volunteered as Lum took the baby. "Careful where you walk, there's a little river running toward the back from all the rain that's blown in."

"Might be a way to dam it up a little so the mules can drink," Lum said, thinking aloud. "All this rain and it ain't doing them poh mules a tad of good."

While the storm raged, Faith and Deborah sat together, worrying about the ships at sea. Nanny made a breakfast of leftovers she'd made yesterday morning.

"It's a good thing Nanny cooked as much as she did," Buck said as he munched on a cookie.

"Not the worst breakfast I've ever had," Crowe said in agreement.

"Only thing missing is a cup of coffee," Livi said. "Not hot tea like in England, but a good cup of morning coffee. Just smelling it wakes a person up."

"Yes ma'm, it sho' do and Nanny makes the best coffee you ever tasted," Lum said.

"I don't know about coffee but these cookies are sure good," little Macayla said, joining the conversation. "Mother, could we have cookies for breakfast every morning?"

Deborah smiled and hugged her daughter,

"Maybe on special mornings, we can."

"Like when daddy comes home?"

"Yes, when daddy comes home," Deborah said, tearing up.

CHAPTER THIRTY SIX

THE WINDS HAD CALMED down and the waves were just long gray rollers. Not the crashing white caps the squadron had fought for nearly a day. On board the flagship, Mr. Waters, the master, was in the admiral's cabin with Lord Anthony on one side and Captain Earl on the other.

"The weather has moderated and the glass has raised some. I think we've outrun the worst of the storm; of course, we came about in a timely manner. Another few hours and we may not have had the opportunity," the master said.

"Aye," Earl agreed, glad he and his lordship had decided to run when they did.

"I fear there are a lot of sailors who perished in that one," Waters said.

"Aye, ours and the enemies. We have trust in you, Mr. Waters," Anthony said to his old master. "A commander who ignores his master is a foolish man. Unless my back was against the wall I'd not risk my ship or crew when advised by a man as prudent as yourself. You are a credit to your occupation, sir, and I'm proud to have you as *SeaHorse's* master."

"Laying it on a bit thick," Bart would later say, but not really unhappy. "Not many admirals would thank the master for doing 'is job. We'll let the bloke shine for a bit. Maybe 'e'd be more up for a game later." *It's just possible*, Bart thought.

***

DAGAN STOOD LOOKING OUT the stern windows in Gabe's cabin. "I don't think we'll have to run all the way to the gulf," he said.

"I'm worried about Faith and James. They may have been in the path of the storm," Gabe said.

"Probably were," Dagan replied. "But don't worry, everybody is safe."

"Everybody?" Gabe inquired.

"Everybody in the family," Dagan responded.

Gabe felt a burden lift. He had been dreading going back to Barbados. Now, with Dagan's proclamation, he felt better.

"Think Gil will drop anchor at Jamaica?"

"Might be too crowded with the Jamaica squadron there. May pull in to Grand Cayman or just come about and head home," Dagan replied.

"Vallin wouldn't mind a few days there," Gabe said smiling.

"No, he wouldn't," Dagan replied. He closed the stern windows and as he walked past Gabe, he gave him a slight pop to the back of his head. "Think I'll go smoke my pipe. Were you any kind of a captain, you'd invite a few officers for dinner."

Gabe smiled at his uncle, "Might cocky for your age, I'd say."

"Humph..." Dagan snorted and then grew

serious. "Thought about what you'll do about Lieutenant Bufford?"

"He'll have to answer to Gil. I can't let him get by with being drunk on duty."

"I think he's a changed man. Near death experiences tend to make people mend their ways," Dagan said.

Gabe stared at Dagan, "I can't leave him on the ship."

"Aye," Dagan admitted. "But a little talk with Captain Earl and a transfer might be arranged; that and the knowledge that it's his only chance. Might be a way to salvage a good officer."

"Do you think he's a good officer," Gabe asked, sitting up in his chair.

"I've seen a lot worse. Could be he'd be grateful enough that he'd certainly mend his ways. He's already apologized to Laqua in front of most of the wardroom officers," Dagan said.

"I heard that from Vallin. Were it not for Laqua, he'd have been over the side for sure."

"He knows it," Dagan said.

"I'll talk to Stephen," Gabe decided, meaning Captain Earl.

"You put your boots on and you could come on deck and smoke a bowl. I don't think it would be amiss."

Grabbing his boots, Gabe said, "I'll be right up after I tell Nesbit that we'll have the officers not on watch for dinner."

***

GRAND CAYMAN, GEORGETOWN. THE arrival of Lord Anthony's squadron created much excitement. Everyone wanted to know the latest news. What was the latest word on the French, the Spaniards, and the American privateers? What was happening socially?

"I can only speak of Jamaica," Lord Anthony admitted to Mrs. Eden, William Eden's wife. Lord Anthony then explained that they'd departed Jamaica for Barbados when the storm started showing itself.

"Being a seaman, you changed your course," Mr. Eden said before Anthony could explain. "We have ships and men lost between here and Port Royal. Some I would have thought had better sense than to sail into a blow."

Not liking a landsman speaking ill of a sailor, Lord Anthony replied, "Sometimes the elements can change before you can prepare for them."

"I understand," Eden replied, sensing from Lord Anthony's tone that he had been offensive. Changing the subject, Eden said, "We continue to appreciate the protection that Captain Montgomery and his ship have provided. We had a ship from Jamaica come in. Lord Parker sent them over while Captain Montgomery stood down for a few days. Admiral Parker assured me he'd send a relief every month or so."

"I'm glad he remembered," Anthony said.

"It appears that the island women are smitten

with sailors, my Lord. First my niece with your Lieutenant Vallin, and now one of the free black women has set her cap for Captain Montgomery, I'm told. We have a weekly meeting of the island's militia and Captain Montgomery always attends."

"That's good," Anthony replied, but thought, *you haven't said anything about his attending any social functions. He's good enough to defend the island but not the right color for any social occasions.* "I'm glad to hear it," Anthony said, and then feeling devilish added, "I'd hate to think a man who'd risk his life and that of his ship and men to protect the island would not be welcomed and received in all circles. I believe it was you who said, 'things were different here in the islands, more accepted.' I believe that was the word you used."

"Hmmm...well, yes I do believe I may have mentioned that," Eden responded.

Lord Anthony could tell he'd made Eden uncomfortable. *Good*, he thought but let it drop.

***

CON VALLIN SAT ON the veranda with Hannah sitting next to him. Holding hands, the two were lost to all but the nearness of one another.

"Do they let wives on ships?" Hannah asked.

"There are a few, the wife of a captain mostly, but I know of a few others. Why?"

"Because I'm not going to sit on this island the whole time you are in the Navy," Hannah replied.

"Lord Anthony, Captain Anthony, and now

Captain Davy all have wives back on Barbados. That way being in the home port, they get to see them far more often," Vallin said.

"Humph...If my husband was an admiral, he damn well better have a place for me on his boat."

Vallin was shocked. He corrected her about the word boat. "It's a ship, sweetheart, a ship. A boat is something you row." He didn't correct her profanity. He'd heard from the captain that Faith could let loose when she was mad. Maybe it was the way it was now. Hannah was certainly an independent little wench.

"Do you want to get married while you are here?" Hannah asked, her hand lying on the inside of his leg.

"Of course, but I'd have to ask the admiral and you'd have to get permission from your parents."

"Backing water?" Hannah asked.

Vallin looked into Hannah's eyes and his heart melted. "Never, never, God as my witness."

"I wish we could, but you are right. We can't rush it in three days. If you could take Captain Montgomery's place we could," Hannah said.

"You forget I'm not a ship's captain," Vallin replied.

"You are both lieutenants."

"Yes, but he's a captain. I'm the ship's first officer."

"Well, you hurry up and get you a boa...ship, I mean. I'm ready to get married."

An island coaster pulled into Georgetown the

morning before Lord Anthony's squadron set sail. Word had come from Saint Lucia that the hurricane had wreaked havoc among the British Navy and many were lost, but no word had come from Barbados.

CHAPTER THIRTY SEVEN

THE STORM WAS OVER. The rain had lessened and the howl of the wind had diminished. The sky began to clear, and the wind and the rain was gone. Walking outside the cave for the first time since around noon of the ninth felt strange. It was now the morning of the eleventh. They had spent nearly two days in the damp but safe cave. Staring around, the group was in awe. Nothing was standing. Not a tree, hedge, or bush. Nothing.

With Deborah and Macayla astride one mule and Faith holding little James on the other, they set out. Admiral Buck leading with Livi holding on to him, Ariel and Nanny were walking slightly behind them, with Crowe and Lum leading the mules. They had not traveled far when they saw a man.

"The church," the man cried when the group approached him. "The church, it's been swept away. I can't find the rector."

"He may have been away," Buck said. "He may have been visiting. He may even be in Bridge-town."

"It's gone," the man cried as he turned to walk

away. "It's all gone, every house," he continued as he walked away.

"He's in shock," Buck said to the ladies. "He's ranting." *I hope*, Buck thought to himself.

Hours later when the group made it to Bridge-town, they discovered much to their horror, the half-crazed man was right. The buildings and houses in Barbados, as well as the forts, which were all built with strong, thick walls, had all given way to the fury of the hurricane. All were torn away to the very foundation. Many of the fort's heavy cannons were carried a hundred feet or so from the emplacements in the destroyed forts. The Government house was gone. Carefully, the group picked their way over the debris.

"Look," Livi whispered to Buck. A body, a dead lifeless body was lying in a heap. Mouth and eyes were open, one hand stretched out like he'd been pointing at something.

Deborah tried to shield Macayla, who quickly pulled her head away from her mother's hand. "Are all those people dead?" she said, pointing toward the right.

They were, and soon not only were they trying to step over debris, but bodies as well, thousands of bodies.

"Oh, my God," Deborah prayed.

Nanny looked about in terror. "The Lawd was wid us up yonder in dat cave."

"You're right," Faith said, "I hope that he was with our husbands."

"Amen," Ariel said, tears coming down her face.

"Hold James," Faith said, and as Lum took the baby, she slid off the mule and put her arms around Ariel. "Your sailor is fine, honey."

"That's right," Deborah added. "Gil would never risk the men and ships to a storm like this."

"I agree," Buck said.

"There's Governor Ragland," Crowe said, pointing to an approaching man.

"Thank God, you are all safe," Ragland exclaimed as he approached them. "We've, Linda and I, we were worried when we couldn't find no...ah, sign of you." *He means in the living or dead*, Faith thought.

"We went to the cave," Buck said. "Fortunately for us, Nanny packed a feast." Ragland nodded. "It's bad, worse than I imagined," Buck said, looking about at the total destruction. "Cataclysmic!"

"You're right and I fear it will get worse," Ragland replied. "There are very few houses left standing on the entire island. Not much food, less water, and no medicine for the sick and injured."

"Where were you?" Buck asked.

"In the house until the roof came off, and then we went into the cellar just before midnight."

"The ships, did they get away?" Buck asked.

"The Navy ships did. Some local coasters, island traders, fishing vessels and the like waited too long. Most are lying about in pieces," Ragland responded.

"Our houses, did any of them survive?" Lady Deborah asked Ragland.

"I'm sorry, Lady Deborah, they are all gone."

"Our house has gone where, Mother?" Macayla asked.

"With the wind, darling."

"Did it take our cat?"

"I'm not sure. We'll see," Deborah answered Macayla.

"We should have taken her, Aunt Faith took Sam."

"We'll look," Deborah promised.

"I'll help," Ariel promised.

Looking at the mules, Governor Ragland said, "I wouldn't let those animals out of your sight. They'll be gone if you do."

Catching Crowe's look, Buck asked, "Have you seen any more of our people?"

"I have not," Ragland admitted. "Let's go over to see if Linda has found anything we can eat," he suggested. "After that, I would think you and your men could go see what you can find that is useful or edible." Then as an afterthought, he added, "or drinkable. You might see if you can arm yourself. We already have had looting."

"Whenever there is disaster," Buck started, but didn't finish as in the distance a man could be seen going through the pockets of a body. "Go run him off," Buck said, but was countermanded by Ragland.

"No need, it might be a loved one he's found.

It's certainly not worth injury."

Buck could see the truth in the governor's words but didn't like his orders being challenged.

"I'm not hungry," Crowe said. "Mind if I go check on things?"

"No, go ahead," Buck replied, knowing that Crowe wanted to check on his friends.

"I'll go wid you, if you don't care none, Missy Faith," Lum said.

"No, it's probably safer if the two of you are together," Faith said.

"Better take the mules," Buck said. "You can carry more."

"Aye," Crowe replied and started off at a good pace.

"Ain't no need to kills the mules," Lum complained.

Even in his anguish, Crowe had to smile. *Aye*, he though solemnly. *No need to rush at this point*.

***

IT WAS AFTER DARK when Crowe and Lum returned to the site of the old Government House. Lanterns were being lit and a tent had been made of sailcloth. Both mules were carrying a heavy burden, including Chin Lee. He had been trapped in the cellar at Livi's house. When he heard Crowe and Lum shifting debris about, he started shouting.

Hearing the man, Crowe smiled, "I don't know what in the devils being said, but I know whose saying it. That's Chin Lee. Hush up that heathen chatter or I'll cut off your pigtail," Crowe called down to the little man.

"Me no fixy you sumthin eat, long, long time, you do," Chin Lee called back. Both men were happy to hear each other's voice.

"Where's Flem?" Crowe asked.

"Don't know. He go to ship, no come back."

Crowe only nodded, hoping his friend was in one of the squadron's ships.

"It looks like you found a lot," Buck said, happily surprised as he surveyed the mules.

"More than we could bring. We pulled boards back over the cellars of each house," Crowe said.

"Hopefully, it will keep the looters out," Buck said.

"If they have to work at it, they'll pass it by, I'm thinking," Crowe replied.

"At first anyway," Ragland agreed.

"We did come across some pistols, a couple of muskets with powder and shot," Crowe continued.

"I hope we don't need it, but I wanted to be prepared," Ragland said. "I remember how it was in London after a bad fire."

"Aye," Buck said. "I recall it as well. It never hurts to be prepared. Tomorrow, we will go back."

"Might be I could rig up a cart for the mules to pull," Lum said.

"Good idea, Lum. Tomorrow we'll all go."

"I stay. Me watchee the women," Chin Lee volunteered.

"Humph...heathen," Crowe growled.

"You think heathen, me go chop chop," Chin Lee replied, emphasizing his remarks by making a chopping motion, one hand chopping the other.

"Don't make him mad," Buck ordered. "Else we'll have indigestion for a week."

CHAPTER THIRTY EIGHT

LORD ANTHONY'S SQUADRON WAS sailing along under a fresh breeze. The sky was blue with puffy, white clouds overhead. Gabe's and Kirk's ships could just be seen on the horizon as they headed north-easterly toward Antigua. The rest of the squadron continued on a more souther-ly course to Barbados. Lord Anthony, like most every other man, was looking forward to getting home. They'd not thought much about the storm since dropping anchor at Grand Cayman.

The storm had continued a northerly direc-tion, hitting the southern tip of Puerto Rico and the eastern regions of Hispaniola. Reports had come in that the towns of Cabo Rojo and Lajas on Puerto Rico had been hit hard with extensive damage. There were also many reports of lost ships. Lord Anthony was sure by the time the toll was fully realized the numbers of lost ships and men would be staggering. He did not want to sound alarmed, but he was sure the island deaths would be just as severe on those islands the hurricane had passed over. Mr. Waters had been right in his recommendation to lay a west-erly course. His kind usually were right. What was it his father had said when he was a young mid. "Mind the master, and you'll live a long time." He'd made sure when Gabe was a young lieutenant with his first ship, that he'd had a seasoned master. Gabe...

Lord Anthony had been thinking of his brother. A good seaman, a good captain. Now he was about to give up his command, a temporary command it had been. But still a command. He had been tempted to put Frostbrier in the captured seventy-four, he still might. He hadn't openly discussed it with Frostbrier. He'd not really had the chance to.

It's always hard for a captain to admit his ship is unfit for duty. But Frostbrier had done so. "*Phoenix* has been abused most severely," Captain Frostbrier had said. "She'll swim, but I don't think she'll stand another battle. We man the pumps one hour in three." Therefore, he'd sent her to Jamaica, to the dockyard there to be overhauled. For some reason, he'd not mentioned the seventy-four after that.

"You couldn't," Bart said when the two were alone. "Wouldn't be fair."

Maybe that was true. Lieutenant Bufford was talking to a man on the forecastle. That had been a strange event. Gabe had met with Captain Earl, and soon after Lieutenant Bufford was transferred to *SeaHorse* and a young lieutenant had been sent to *Leopard*. He'd not questioned it. Earl was the ship's captain. If he and another ship's captain made a switch, that was between the two of them. Not any of the admiral's business. But Bart knew, he always seemed to know. Dagan had talked with Bart as Gabe knew he would, so it was not long before he had the true story. If Gabe felt the man might be worth salvaging, Earl would accommodate him. Another captain would likely have had the man shot or at the least, dismissed from the Navy. *What would I have done*, Anthony had asked himself.

Likely Dagan's influence, Bart had suggested in his own way, "Dagan's 'fluence, more like," Bart said.

Well, in three days, if the weather held out, they would be home, with all this behind them. David Davy could enjoy his new bride; Bart could tantalize the tavern wenches and the card players. Gabe would soon be home to Faith and little James and he'd be back to Deborah and Macayla. If everything went according to plan. For some reason, he was worried. Foreboding, but why? Time would tell.

***

"DECK THAR, TWO SHIPS off the starboard side." The lookout paused and then added, "Not carrying any canvas aloft."

"Mr. Glenn," *Leopard's* new lieutenant, Lieutenant Holton, called to the mid. "Notify the captain we have two ships sighted and they appear to be hove to."

"Aye, sir."

"What's that, Mr. Holton?"

"Morning, sir," Holton said, speaking to the first lieutenant. Handing his glass to Vallin, he pointed out the direction. "You can just see them."

Vallin looked and then climbed up a few feet in the shrouds. He had just jumped to the deck when Gabe came on deck, followed by his cox'n and Dagan. "Two ships hove to, Captain. Neither are under canvas. The larger ship appears to be a seventy-four and she is dismasted it appears. The other one appears to be a large frigate. I can just make out her furled sails."

"Storm damage, do you think, Mr. Vallin?" Gabe asked.

"Aye, sir." Vallin's further response was interrupted by the lookout.

"The smaller ship is making sail, sir." After a pause, the lookout shouted down again, excitement in his voice this time. "She be a Frenchie, a French frigate."

With everything that had happened since Gabe had sailed away from Barbados and Faith, the sighting of two French ships should not have been a surprise. Yet the frigate, big as she was, to act aggressive to a larger ship, with a second ship in company was puzzling.

"She'll get no help from the big lady," Vallin stated. His comment was unnecessary, but true.

It was very obvious that the French seventy-four had taken a beating from the hurricane.

Lieutenant Laqua who had joined the group commented, "Bet she's taken the crew off the big Frenchie."

"Aye, I think you are right, Lieutenant. Beat to quarters, if you will, Mr. Vallin. Grape on top of balls. If what Mr. Laqua thinks is true, she'll try to close and board us," Gabe said.

Dagan, who had been watching the enemy ship through his glass, spoke as he tucked the glass under his arm. "She's much heavier that the usual frigate. I'd not be surprised if she was not a razed sixty-four."

Hmm...Gabe thought. Stouter timbers, twenty-four pound balls would not be unreasonable. *Leopard* was a beehive of activity as men hurried to their battle stations. The thud of bare feet on wooden planks was echoed by the drummer as he sounded off.

"Reduce to fighting sail?" Pittman, the master, inquired.

"Not yet," Gabe responded, "but be ready." He wanted the enemy to see he was just as eager as they were to fight. "Signal *Bulldog* to fire at will." That would allow Captain Kirk to take advantage of any opportunity that presented itself, yet not endanger *Bulldog's* fragile timber.

"Three minutes, sir." Gabe looked at his first lieutenant. Vallin was holding his watch in his hand.

"That will get the crew an extra tot, Mr. Vallin." An extra tot and prize money.

"What say you men?" Vallin asked.

"Huzzah, huzzah."

Dagan touched his nephew's shoulder. "That was well said, 'Captain'."

Smiling, Gabe looked at his uncle. Seeing no look of concern in his eyes made Gabe fill better. "Hex."

"Aye, Captain."

"Be ready to call my boat crew together after we take the Frenchie."

"Aye, aye, Captain."

"Hear that?" One of the helmsmen said to the other man on the wheel. "We got nothing to worry about. Captain's already decided we'll take the Frenchie."

"Hmm," the other man said. "Wonder if they know that yet?"

"You'd spoil anything, mate. You ain't no Jonah, are ye?"

Before the man could reply, the French frigate fired. A wo wo wo sound was heard overhead and holes appeared in the sails.

"Firing to disable us," Vallin said.

"Aye," the master answered.

"Did you note," Gabe questioned his group, "the two forward and aft gun ports did not open? I don't think that she has a full broadside." The ships were now less than a mile apart. "Reduce to fighting sail, Mr. Pittman."

"Aye sir."

The bosun's pipes shrilled and the sail

handlers rushed to do their duty. Hex, who had disappeared for a few minutes now returned. He had Gabe's coat with the gilted buttons, lace, and gold swab. Dagan helped Gabe into his dress coat and then put on his sword belt. Hex handed Gabe a brace of pistols.

As Gabe tucked his weapons in his sash, Hex whispered, "I caution you, sir. Your pistols are primed and ready. I'd be careful to make sure they were clear of your sash before firing."

"You dog," Gabe threw back with a smile. He had heard where a captain pulled his pistol out but pulled the trigger before the weapon cleared the sash. Suddenly the captain had gone from a rooster to a hen. A little rhyme had been made up for the unlucky captain. 'Not like 'is dad, more like 'is sis, 'e 'as to sit to take a piss.'

CHAPTER THIRTY NINE

THE FRENCH HAD CONTINUED to fire their forward guns, doing little damage.

"Mr. Abraham, I think it's time to put our forward guns into action. Show yonder ship, we don't waste our powder and shot." The distance between the ships had closed to less than a quarter of a mile.

"Look at *Bulldog*," Vallin called. With the enemy seemingly focused on *Leopard*, Kirk had clamped on sail and drew away from *Leopard*.

"Look at her go!" Midshipman Glenn exclaimed. He was watching the sloop turn away, copper flashing in the sunlight, sails full and drawing.

"No doubt thinking of the day that he'll command a ship, like that un, Pittman," Vallin said.

Thinking back on his first ship, *HMS SeaWolf*, Gabe smiled. "Let the boy dream."

As the forward guns spoke, a shudder was felt in the planks. Alternating larboard and starboard bow guns, Abraham had set up a constant barrage. The larboard guns scored a hit and a cheer went up only to be silenced by a hit from the French frigate. Screams and cries of pain took the place of cheers. The gun seemed to have jumped backwards, crushing three crewmen. One man's hand flopped up and down as if hurrying help along, and then the hand dropped lifelessly as the man died.

The afternoon sun blazed down on *Leopard's* deck making hot work even hotter. Gabe shielded his eyes from the sun.

"Mr. Pittman."

"Aye Captain."

"Starboard a point if you please."

"Aye sir."

"This damn sun," Vallin cursed. "I can't see what's happening."

Gabe smiled. A week ago Vallin was cursing the storm. They were close now, almost broadside of one another. Shouts could be heard from the French frigate. Someone had worked the crew into a screaming frenzy. Nearer and nearer they came. The gunners squatted by their guns, all waiting for the word to fire.

"Now," Gabe shouted. "Fire, fire as you bear." He pounded the rail as he shouted, oblivious to musket balls that peppered the deck all around the well.

"Best move about, Captain," Hex said.

Lieutenant Tolbert, who was now the second lieutenant, having taken Bufford's place, ran from gun to gun making sure each shot went home. The French guns were not a beat behind *Leopard's*, as they crashed, slamming into

Leopard's stout timbers. Gabe couldn't help but wince as a ball passed close to him.

"At 'em, lads," a gun captain shouted as the quarterdeck guns roared, joining the melee.

Gabe shouted to Vallin, "Canister, use canister in the swivels."

"Look at *Bulldog*," someone shouted.

Unnoticed by the French, Kirk had brought his ship close to the French stern and fired at the rudder. The frigate slewed to larboard as the rudder was blasted away. The bow ground against *Leopard* amidships. A grapnel flew out as *Leopard* pushed the French bow. More and more grapnels flew through the air.

"Prepare for boarders," Vallin shouted. "Prepare for boarders."

Using the speaking trumpet, Gabe shouted at the men in the tops, "Cut them down. Cut them down."

Vallin was suddenly alongside Gabe. "Didn't figure on this shat, Captain."

The drag was slowing the ship considerably as French sailors climbed up on the bulwark to board *Leopard*. The men in *Leopard's* tops fired down on them with muskets and swivel guns. The French sailors caught in the hail of ball and canister fell back on to those behind them. Shouts and screams could be heard. Men started to back away but were pushed forward again by officers. The savage fire pushed most of the second group back but not all of them. A French officer, his sword in the air, was waving frantically, calling to his men.

The men followed their officer. Now the revived boarders swept over the bulwark. Into the deadly blaze of gunfire they came. Wild crazed faces, like demons, they poured onto *Leopard's* deck. The French officer, now hatless and blood oozing from a scalp wound was now on Gabe. His blade, red to the hilt and dripping with blood, lunged. Gabe parried it and saw the look of excitement upon the Frenchman's face as he now lunged with a small sword carried in his other hand. Trying to step back, Gabe's foot slipped in blood and he fell. The fall saved his life. The man's small sword would have impaled him, were it not for the fall.

The Frenchman was now off balance and Gabe thrust up. The man fell and but for the lanyard would have jerked Gabe's blade away from his grasp. A hand lifted Gabe as more Frenchmen pressed forward.

Vallin was in a struggle with two enemy sailors. Gabe pulled one of his pistols and, jamming it into the side of one of the men, pulled the trigger. The sound was muffled but blood spurted from the wound as the man went down.

Glancing about, Gabe could see Dagan cut down a man and Hex was just to his side. Still the Frenchmen continued to push. Were the men in the tops still firing, Gabe couldn't recall hearing one? The crack of muskets continued, and each ball was bringing a man down. Two men were fighting desperately to Gabe's left; one was Laqua. Taking his remaining pistol Gabe shot the large French sailor who was overpowering Laqua.

The melee was now so closely bunched together; it was hard to use one's sword. Feeling himself shoved to the side, a marine shot one attacker at point blank range. The ball taking not only the man the marine was shooting at, but also the man behind him as well. The marine then skewered another foe with his bayonet. More marines came forward, firing into the enemy and then lunging forward with their bayonets.

Above the din of battle, Gabe heard the marine sergeant yell, "Down in front." The marines went down as another group fired. This stopped the French advance.

Off to Gabe's right, one of the enemy officers shot an advancing marine. Falling, the marine fired, killing the officer and then he threw his weapon, the bayonet impaling another man in the face. Screaming, the French sailor fell forward, the tip of the bayonet protruding from the back of his skull.

Why aren't the swivels firing, Gabe wondered again. The thought was cut short when a British voice could be heard shouting, "Surrender! Strike, strike or die," it was Captain Kirk. At first, the calls were unheard.

Vallin was facing a French officer, who was trying to club him with a spent pistol. "It's over,"

Vallin shouted but the man was mad. The battle lust was upon him. Vallin backed away and shouted again for him to drop his weapon, but the man was beyond control.

Dagan, who was standing close by, hit the officer with the flat side of his blade. This knocked the wounded and enraged man to the deck. Before he could rise, the pistol was kicked away from his hands.

"Hold your fire," Gabe yelled.

A pistol went off and a man grunted and fell... an enemy sailor. "Cease fire," Gabe bellowed. This time all was still. "Throw down your weapons," he ordered. The French just stood and looked about. "Tell them to throw down their weapons," Gabe said to Laqua.

The lieutenant repeated his captain's command in French. Still the enemy stood. Laqua repeated the order but added, "Or die." First a solitary sword clanged as it hit the deck. After a pause, the French dropped their weapons in mass.

Sighing, Gabe looked about and saw Captain Kirk, "You saved us, Gregory."

"Aye, it was the least I could do after causing the Frenchie to ram you. I should have thought she'd slew when we blasted the rudder."

"How could you have known?" Gabe replied.

"Captain, it's the French captain. Dagan says that he's about gone."

Gabe, followed by Kirk, made his way over to

the French captain. "Would you please write a letter, M'sieur? The whole fleet, the storm took the entire fleet. It's gone. We alone survived. We tried to run."

"Run from where?" Gabe asked.

"Martinique, magnifique. All gone, four thousand soldiers drowned," the French captain said.

"Who was your commander?" Gabe asked. "Who was your commander?"

"It's no use, Captain, he's gone."

"Why did he fight if the entire fleet is gone?" The question came from Jackson, one of *Leopard's* midshipmen.

"For honor," Gabe answered. "For the honor of the fleet." Gabe stood from where he had knelt. "We shall bury this brave man wrapped in his country's flag, as soon as we put things to right."

"Congratulations on your victory, Captain," Kirk said. "You've another prize and maybe two," indicating the French seventy-four.

"We'll see, Captain Kirk, we'll see."

CHAPTER FORTY

GABE ROSE AND, FOLLOWED by Hex, stepped over the bodies torn by grape shot. Next to where a cannon was overturned, he saw the charred stumps and blackened bones. Once on board *Leopard*, he saw bodies of dead and wounded men. Men wounded and killed by sharp-edged weapons. The sight of it all sickened him. Sickened him until all he wanted to do was bury his head in disgust. *Why, why*, he kept saying to himself.

A whole fleet lost to a storm and then this. More lives thrown away to a man-made storm. The fury of cannons, small guns and blades, all in the name of the King. The politicians, men who had never stood the deck as the enemy fired its broadsides at you, facing sure death but counting on the odds that you would be one of the lucky ones to survive. Why!

"Captain."

"Yes, Mr. Vallin."

"I've a boat ready to go over to the big Frenchie."

Gabe looked at his first lieutenant. Multiple bandages, his uniform stained in blood and in tatters, but still functioning as a first lieutenant should.

"We'll go," Dagan said. Vallin nodded, he'd not contradict the man. If the captain allowed Dagan to speak for him, who was he to argue.

Turning to his uncle, Gabe saw his clothes smoke stained and a few blood stains, but no obvious wounds. "I see you are well, Uncle."

Dagan gave a slight nod, "As are you, Gabe."

Two boats were in the water. One filled with marines and his gig. As he went down the side, he saw a flash of fins. Sharks...the damnable fiends, devouring those who'd went over the side. *I hope that they were dead before they hit the water*, Gabe thought.

***

THE BIG FRENCH MAN-O'-WAR sat lifeless, still, barely rising with the swell of the ocean. "She sits low," Dagan volunteered. More bodies floated in the water. Drowned men with bloated bellies, which was caused by the gas in their bodies, it had caused them to rise. Some with torn or missing limbs, where the carrion eaters of the deep feasted upon them. They floated all about, the boats bumping into a few.

Another flash of fins caused a man in the boat to speak, "Don't worry you idjet. No shark is going to waste 'is time on ye sorry carcass." This brought a laugh before Hex at the tiller growled, "Silence."

Tying up at the entry port, the men gave way for Gabe to board the French ship. Hex laid his hand on Gabe's shoulder. "Let me go first, sir."

Without waiting for a reply, Hex, followed by Dagan, went up the battens and through the entry port. Hex's hand quickly covered his nose. The stench of death was overpowering. Once on board, Gabe tied his handkerchief over his nose. Dead bodies floated in the well.

"She's settling," Dagan said, "ready to take her men to their grave."

"Aye," Gabe and Hex both responded. "Go check the captain's cabin," Gabe ordered. As the men started off, he added, "See if there's an address. Someone we can write."

The boat with the marines bumped alongside. Before anyone could start up the side of the ship, Gabe ordered them to stay in the boat. After five minutes, Gabe was wondering what was keeping Hex and Dagan so long. Standing on the deck, alone except for the bodies of drowned men was eerie. A chill came over Gabe and he shivered involuntarily.

Damnation, where are they, he wondered again. *Settle down*, he told himself. Soon Dagan and Hex walked back on deck carrying a chest that was so heavy it took two to carry. In addition to the chest, they carried a sword with inlaid jewels and several papers

Seeing Gabe, Dagan spoke, "Captain's personal effects." Handing the sword to Gabe, he added, "May want to send the captain's sword to his family." Lowering the chest and other articles into the boat, Dagan and Hex headed back to the captain's cabin before Gabe could protest.

This time, they returned quickly, carrying two sacks each. The sacks held glass bottles that clanked. As they lowered the sacks, Dagan called down, "Break a bottle and I'll have your gizzards."

Hex ran back to the cabin and returned with one more bag that he carried down into the boat as he went. "A little something extra to go with our tot this evening with the captain's permission," he volunteered.

"That was thoughtful," Gabe said, but wondered what was in the bag. *More 'retirement'*, he wondered. Damn Dagan's, and now Hex's, larcenous ways.

***

BACK ABOARD *LEOPARD*, GABE saw his time aboard the sinking ship had not been wasted. Under the muskets of marines from *Bulldog*, Vallin had the captured French sailors putting *Sirene* back to rights while the carpenter, bosun, and *Leopard's* lieutenants were making repairs aboard their ship. By the time dusk settled the two ships were ready to get underway. *Sirene* was jury-rigged but with normal conditions should make it to Antigua.

Vallin approached Gabe just before they set sail. He had a French officer with him. "Frenchie has a request, sir," Vallin said.

"If M'sieur Capitan would allow it, sir, we'd like to place our capitan aboard our mother ship. We will need only a boat." Gabe was overwhelmed and agreed.

The French officer called his men together and gently lowered their captain into one of *Sirene's* surviving boats. They rowed over to the dying ship and carried their captain aboard. The ship's deck was now awash and it was listing badly.

"They've not headed back," Laqua said as the minutes passed.

"They're not coming back," Dagan said. "They'll be the final honor guard."

As the sun sank over the horizon, the once proud French seventy-four slipped beneath the waters.

"Damn," Vallin said. Tears had trickled down his face and Gabe was trying hard to hold back his emotions. With a cracked voice, Gabe ordered, "Take charge of the prize, Mr. Vallin, and let's be on our way."

"Aye, Captain, it's time."

CHAPTER FORTY ONE

"SAIL HO!" THE LOOKOUT'S voice could be heard in Lord Anthony's stateroom. By the time, he was on deck, the sighting had been recognized. Captain Earl saw the admiral and approached him.

"It's Captain Markham in *Dasher*, sir. It appears he's got the remainder of the squadron with him, sir."

In an hour's time, Captain Markham made his way aboard the flagship, followed by several women passengers. A bosun's chair had been quickly rigged and as the ladies were hoisted aboard, Markham reported.

"Barbados is gone, sir, destroyed by the hurricane. I took the ships and ran for it. Antigua is saved, only high winds, but Saint Lucia was hit hard as well. Admiral Rodney's fleet was there and he lost half of his ships. One ship was picked up by the winds and fell on the city's hospital, destroying all. We understand the French island of Martinique was hit hard and a whole French fleet is missing."

Before Markham could go further, Lady Deborah was settled on deck. Paying no heed to naval customs, she rushed over to her husband and embraced him, giving him a kiss that caused the crew to send up a cheer. "Huzza, huzza, for the admiral's lady."

Deborah released her husband, turned and bowed for the crew, which sent up another cheer. Next a seaman brought up Macayla, followed by Ariel, then Faith with little James, and Livi, Admiral Buck's lady, who was followed by Nanny. Shunning the bosun's chair, Lum climbed up the battens. He'd served with Gabe a few years ago and knew the proper way to board a ship.

Lastly, Linda, Lady Ragland, came aboard via the bosun's chair. Seeing her husband's gaze, Lady Deborah spoke, "Rupert stayed on Barbados with Lord Ragland to help put the island back to order. They will need lots of help, I'm afraid."

***

CALLING HIS CAPTAINS ABOARD ship, Lord Anthony discussed the needs of the people on Barbados. The first needs were the obvious, fresh water, food, and medicine.

"I'm making you acting commodore," Lord Anthony informed Markham. "We will load all the water and food we can spare on your ships. It's not much but will help. Take it back to Barbados. Those who need medicine more than can be handled by the ships doctors will be evacuated. I will leave that all to your judgment, Francis," Lord Anthony said, using Markham's given name. "I will head to Antigua and send you what supplies

I can. If the situation allows, I will return. Until then, you are the naval authority there. Do I make myself clear?"

"Aye, sir. Admiral Buck has no official standing at the present." Markham responded.

"Yes, but don't hesitate to listen to his recommendations, but in the end the decisions are yours. Now hoist your pendant and go help the people on Barbados, Commodore."

"Aye, my Lord. Thank you for your trust."

"Nonsense," Anthony responded. "You've earned it."

Once the ships had come about and headed back to Barbados, Lord Anthony spoke to his flag captain, "A bit of shifting about needs to be done, Stephen."

"Aye, my Lord. I've given my quarters to Faith and Livi. I've ordered Captain David to repair on board. It's likely he's spotted Ariel already."

"Yes," Lord Anthony smiled. "I'm sure our young captain will find space for his beautiful bride."

"Aye," Earl smiled. "I'd think something was amiss if he didn't."

EPILOGUE

ENTERING PORT WITH HIS prize, Gabe felt a bit melancholy. He was glad to be back, the only thing better would be setting foot on Barbados and seeing Faith and his son. Still, it was with a bit of sadness that he'd be giving up *Leopard*. Surely, Captain Price would have recovered enough to resume command of his ship. Probably far longer than he had expected to have to wait. *How had things gone with Trident*, he wondered. *Would she be ready for service again*? So many questions?

He was still deep in thought when he realized the harbor was nearly full of ships...both Navy and civilian vessels. The expected signal was hoisted for him to repair aboard the flagship. On deck, Dagan was waiting.

"Well, Uncle, we shall find out what our future holds before long."

Smiling, Dagan touched his nephew's shoulder. "I see clear skies, Gabe. Bright days ahead, my boy."

It always sent a thrill through Gabe to be piped aboard. But after today, he'd not be piped aboard as '*Leopard*' or would he? Thinking on Dagan's words, a glimmer of hope rose only to be shattered as he recognized the figure standing beside Admiral Moffit, with one sleeve pinned up.

***

"Gabe...Gabe, get up. You have to come see this." It had to be Dagan tugging on him. Nobody else would be at him so early. His head hurt and he was hung over. He had supped with the admiral and Captain Price the previous evening. Price had turned out to be a jovial sort.

After telling Gabe how much he appreciated what Cornish had done to save his life, he thanked him for making a name for his ship's reputation. "They'll not speak ill of the ship attacked by Don's and used so terribly. They'll talk about the *Leopard* who took revenge on the bastards who dishonored her. You've done my ship proud, Sir Gabe."

After the evening was over, Gabe had been taken back to *Leopard*. Captain Price would resume command today.

"Get moving," Dagan urged Gabe, and then swore. "Hurry now, and chew a bit of mint leaf. Your breath would stop a regiment."

Gabe quickly dressed and hurried on deck. Dropping anchor was *SeaHorse*. *Why*, he wondered? As he looked, he saw women...several women. Faith! Yes, by the Lord Almighty, it was Faith holding little James. *Why? Damnation*, he thought. *Why can wait.*

"Hex," Gabe called. "Clear away my boat." Yes,

until Price returned it was his ship and he was going to get his wife and son. "Hex, dammit man, hurry."

History

THE IDEA TO USE *HMS Leopard* as Gabe's next ship arose from a painting by the very talented Johannes Ewers. Mr. Ewers has allowed several of his paintings to grace the cover of Michael Aye books. In this book, Gabe's assignment was what is known as a job captain. I believe Richard Woodman had done the same in one of his books.

HMS Leopard is on the cover of Rif Winfield's book "The 50-Gun Ship". Dating back to the 1600's, many ships have been named *Leopard*. The ship in my book was not actually ordered until 1775 and construction began January, 1776. However, she was not completed until ten years later, long after my time period. But hey, it's fiction.

Spain's entry into the war was in 1779, mainly as an ally to France, but its goal was the recapture of Gibralter. Along the Colonial Gulf Coast, Count Bernardo de Gálvez, the Spanish Governor of Louisiana, removed British ships along the lower Mississippi River. In 1780, he captured Mobile, Alabama. In 1781, he took Pensacola, Florida. Spanish troops and supplies from Cuba, including Cuban cigars were used to entice Pensacola's commander to surrender. The attempt failed but he later surrendered to overwhelming odds.

The attack on Georgetown by the *Rattle-snake* is very much as I described it. About the only thing fictional with the events on Grand Cayman are my characters. My wife and I visited Grand Cayman and the description of Pedro Saint James, including the house and grounds, are from our visit. For anyone desiring to read more about the castle, I found a good review by Fodor that was spot on.

The events that took place on Cat's Island were staged in places we visited last year. An in-depth review of this trip was posted in Quarterdeck. The cavern where Gabe's men burned the privateer's plunder was the "Cave of the Shipwrecked Sailor." The attack on the privateer's ships at anchor was at the area known as New Bight. It is also where the Fish Fry is located.

Jamaica – I remember seeing the island of Jamaica rising up out of the sea as we approached the island as a young sailor on a Navy destroyer. The Blue Mountains seemed so high. The older sailors, my sea daddies, warned me about going ashore by my seventeen year old self. Much as it was in the days of Henry Morgan, Port Royal was a town where anything could be had. Rum was plentiful, food was expensive for a young sailor and I had no desire for other things. I found most of the things I wanted to see had vanished. Some by an earthquake, and some by years when the island hadn't realized its history could indeed be a huge tourist attraction. Today the island's main economy is the tourist trade. But instead of history, it is the island's beautiful beaches where all inclusive resorts bring in people by the thousands. Without the tourist and sugar industry, the island would be bankrupt.

Admiral Peter Parker was Jamaica's commander-in-chief during my time period. The admiral's house and comments about Lord Cornwallis, and his mistress, were all taken off the internet,

The battle between Lord Anthony's squadron and the French off of Jamaica, where the wind died and the ships lay in calm, was actually taken from a battle between Lord Cornwallis and the French.

The hurricane I described was actually the "Great Hurricane of 1780." It has been said it was the deadliest Atlantic hurricane on record. It struck Barbados with winds thought to exceed 320 mph. Every house on Barbados was lost, as were the forts. The wind even stripped the bark off the trees.

After Barbados, it moved to Martinique, Saint Lucia, Saint Eustatius and later passing Puerto Rico and Hispaniola. After passing Hispaniola, the hurricane struck Guadeloupe and then turned west-northwest. It hit the island of Mona in the Mona Passage. On Saint Vincent, 584 of 600 houses were destroyed in Kingstown. At Grenada, nineteen Dutch ships were lost. On Saint Lucia, one of Admiral Rodney's ships at Port Castries was lifted and fell on top of the hospital, destroying it. Many of the admiral's ships were lost at sea. Admiral Joshua Rowley lost *HMS Thunderer* with all hands.

HMS Stirling Castle was smashed on the coast with only fifty survivors. His other six ships were severely damaged.

A fleet of forty French ships, some carrying troops, capsized off Martinique. About four thousand soldiers drowned. The French warships *Palmier*, *Intrepede*, *Magnifique*, and *Junon* and all hands were also lost.

The hurricane produced a twenty-five foot storm surge on Martinique, destroying all the houses in Saint Pierre. The storm killed nine thousand on the island. While the winds were felt at Antigua, no ships or heavy damage was noted. At Saint Kitts, many ships were washed ashore.

Harrison's Cave, Barbados - The cave was named for Thomas Harrison who owned much of the land in the area in the 1700's. In 1733, he established Harrison's College. Harrison's Cave sits in a deep valley with high walls in the Barbados Parish of Saint Thomas. This is located in the center of the island. To get there in the allotted time given in my book may have been pushing it a bit but not overly so. The cave entrance was certainly large enough to fit all the occupants as described in my book. Had the men wandered a bit further in the cave, they'd have found streams, pools and even a lake of fresh water. There is even a thirty foot waterfall. In 1647, historian Richard Ligon wrote the cave was frequently used by runaway slaves.

About the Author

Michael Aye is a retired Naval Medical Officer. He has long been a student of early American and British Naval history. Since reading his first Kent novel, Mike has spent many hours reading the great authors of sea fiction, often while being "haze gray and underway" himself.

Lightning Source UK Ltd.
Milton Keynes UK
UKOW05f1812070517
300688UK00028B/553/P